Of Murder and Men

By Lynn Cahoon

Of Murder and Men

Fatality by Firelight

A Story to Kill

The Tourist Trap Mysteries:

Killer Party

Hospitality and Homicide

Tea Cups and Carnage

Murder on Wheels

Killer Run

Dressed to Kill

If the Shoe Kills

Mission to Murder

Guidebook to Murder

Of Murder and Men

**Lynn
Cahoon**

KENSINGTON BOOKS

http://www.kensingtonbooks.com

KENSINGTON BOOKS are published by

Kensington Publishing Corp.
119 West 40th Street
New York, NY 10018

All Kensington titles, imprints and distributed lines are available at special quantity discounts for bulk purchases for sales promotion, premiums, fund-raising, educational or institutional use. Special book excerpts or customized printings can also be created to fit specific needs. For details, write or phone the office of the Kensington Special Sales Manager: Kensington Publishing Corp., 119 West 40th Street, New York, NY, 10018. Attn. Special Sales Department. Phone: 1-800-221-2647.

Kensington and the K logo Reg. U.S. Pat. & TM Off.

ISBN-13: 978-1-4967-0439-9
ISBN-10: 1-4967-0439-8
First Kensington Mass Market Edition: December 2017

eISBN-13: 978-1-4967-0440-5
eISBN-10: 1-4967-0440-1
First Kensington Electronic Edition: December 2017

10 9 8 7 6 5 4 3 2 1

Printed in the United States of America

To my sister, Berta,
for always encouraging me
to step outside the box.

Acknowledgments

The process of turning an idea for a story into a finished book is long. Between the paragraph I gave my publisher when I sold the series and the final book you're now reading, a lot of decisions have been made. Some are author decisions, like what will the story be about, who will be visiting Aspen Hills, and who's going to wind up dead and why. But as I'm writing the book, others at Kensington are doing their jobs, like the magician who designs the covers, and the wordsmiths who craft the back-cover blurb. And my editor, who keeps all the balls in the air while we're mixing this stew together. This time, it's an Irish stew that is getting Shauna in deep trouble. The next book, the mixture will be a little different, but one thing remains the same: the love of story. And it's this love of story that binds us together—the writer (me), the publisher (Kensington), my editor (Esi Sogah), and you, the reader.

So thank you all for your parts in the release *Of Murder and Men*.

I hope you enjoy the ride.

Chapter 1

Trust. It was a hard word to put into practice. Especially when you applied it to humans, who—with the little thing called free will—didn't seem to worry about breaking promises.

Cat Latimer sank into the leather chair her ex-husband—well, now deceased ex-husband—Michael had purchased through an online estate sale. The soft leather chair had been advertised as part of Tom Clancy's writing office. She had a feeling that, at the price Michael had paid for the item, it probably was just an old chair. But it was lovely and comfortable, and still, after almost a year, smelled like Michael's aftershave.

The television was turned on to the Cooking Channel and a celebrity chef whom Cat didn't recognize was making cinnamon rolls. Normally, the house would smell like baked goods since they had a new group of writers coming in for the January retreat, but Shauna Mary Clodagh wasn't baking in the kitchen. Her best friend and partner in the retreat business wasn't even in the house. Shauna had promised to be here late tonight so there would be fresh baked goods available as soon as guests started arriving sometime around two. She'd talked Seth into doing the airport runs so all she had to do was cook and manage the lodging part of the retreat.

Cat wasn't holding her breath.

Shauna had moved to Aspen Hills, Colorado, with Cat last summer after Michael died. Because Michael had failed to change his will post-divorce, Cat had inherited the large Victorian she'd walked away from during the divorce. Since she was making okay money at this author gig, putting on a monthly writers' retreat had seemed like an easy way to supplement her cash flow.

The first couple of sessions had been rocky, to say the least, with one guest being stabbed in a second-floor bedroom and in the next, a guest accused of murder. Since then, they had gotten through the December retreat without anyone dying or going to jail. Cat thought they were getting the hang of this guest services business. Or people had been on their best behavior because of the holiday.

Seth Howard, Cat's high school sweetheart and current boyfriend, had become an almost full-time figure during retreat weeks. Which worked for him since his small self-employed business as a handyman often left him without enough jobs to fill a full month, especially in the winter. Seth had always been there. A friend she could trust, even when they weren't a couple.

Cat pulled the crocheted throw closer to ward off a chill as the wind whipped the snow outside the window. Colorado winter weather was completely trustworthy. Snow had covered the ground for months. Spring would be a welcome sight when it finally arrived.

Glancing at the half-emptied desk drawer open to her left, she pushed away her rambling thoughts and returned to the task at hand: cleaning out Michael's study. She'd found out more about the man in the last six months than she'd known in their entire marriage. She had one last drawer to go through and the desk would finally be cleared out. Michael had been an economics professor at the same college where she'd gotten a master's in English and had her first teaching job. Michael had been tops in his field, at least locally. Knowing his potential legacy, Cat didn't want to trash his papers before she'd had a chance to go through them.

And then there was the matter of the side project he'd been working on when he died. A project that could have been the reason for his death. No, it was better all around for Cat to box everything up and take it to her office, where she could go through stuff at her leisure.

"Working hard, I see." Her Uncle Pete stood in the doorway. He walked over and sat in what she always thought of as her chair. "I thought you were getting this room ready for your guests, not learning how to bake."

"I may have to learn if Shauna doesn't stop playing house with Kevin Shield and get back here for the retreat." That had come out harsher than she'd wanted it to. She really needed to learn to hide her feelings, just a bit. "Anyway, I'm almost done boxing things up. The shelves have been cleared of the books I'll be donating to the library, and in a few hours, this room will be a writer's dream."

Cat had moved her craft books down from her personal library for the retreat guests to use while they were there. The one thing this house wasn't shy on was bookcases. Her office upstairs had ceiling-to-floor built-in bookcases across the one wall that didn't have windows. Michael's office—the study, she corrected herself—had a wall of bookcases. Now, with the economics tomes all boxed up and ready to deliver to the library, there was more room for writing books, as well as fiction.

Even with the memories of their brief marriage still floating in the air here and there, the house was room by room becoming her own. She stood and stretched, laying the throw over the leather chair. "What are you doing here anyway?"

"You're always so welcoming." He laughed at the look that must have filled Cat's face. "No response needed—I was kidding. Anyway, I got a call from an Alaskan detective who wanted to let me know she was coming into town. Doing some research on a cold case apparently."

He leaned forward on the chair. "She's one of your writer guests. I was just checking in to see if she'd arrived yet."

"No one's coming in until tomorrow." Shauna had left Cat a schedule of Seth's airport runs and when the guests would be arriving.

Uncle Pete checked his phone. "That's not what I have in my notes. She said her plane was arriving this morning. I guess she was planning on taking a cab out here."

"That's going to cost her a fortune." Cat grabbed

her phone. "What time does her flight arrive? I can see if Seth can run into Denver really quick."

"Ten this morning." They both looked at the large clock on the wall. It was three. Even with the possibility of bad roads, the woman should be here any minute.

"Look, she said she had cleared this early arrival with someone here. I guess it was Shauna?" They both looked at the television, where a smiling home chef was explaining how to make muffins. Uncle Pete shook his head. "Maybe you could take her to The Diner for breakfast tomorrow? I'll take her somewhere for dinner tonight, professional courtesy and all."

"Are you sure? I mean, if you're busy, I don't want you to have to babysit our guests because of a mix-up." Cat was going to have a long heart-to-heart with Shauna about at least letting Cat know what was going on. True love or not, she was depending on Shauna to help run this place.

"I wouldn't have offered if I didn't want to. Besides, I'd love to hear what she's working on and if it's connected to Aspen Hills." He let the subject hang in the air as they both knew that the writer's cold case being connected to the small college community wasn't totally unlikely. With the history Cat had just recently discovered about the town where she'd grown up, she knew that "connected" probably had multiple meanings here. It could mean that the victim had a connection here or the suspect had committed the crime here or, more likely, that the incident or the players had Mob connections.

"I believe I was happier before I knew Covington

College's little secret." She walked around the desk. "Do you want to stay around to greet her?"

"If you don't mind." He looked around the room. "If you have things to do, I can hang out here. I'm sure I'll find something to read while I wait."

"I'll just run upstairs and make sure at least one of the rooms is ready. What did you say her name was?" Cat frowned. She really needed to be more on top of the guest list, especially with Shauna's new interests.

"Shirley. Shirley Mann." He stood and crossed the room, pausing to give her a hard stare as he did. "Don't tell me you didn't have Harry Bowman run a background check this session. I thought it was going to be a standard practice?"

"Don't lecture me. Besides, I did get the checks." She flushed, envisioning the envelope on her desk upstairs, unopened. "I just didn't read the report yet."

Her uncle sighed. "One of these days, you're going to regret not being more careful. You realize you had a murderer masquerade as a writer just a few months ago, right? You could have hindered his access if you'd at least read the report before letting him into the house."

"I'll read it this evening. I suppose I can trust the woman who used to be a cop, right? The others, I'll read their background checks before Seth puts them in the shuttle tomorrow." She followed him to the doorway. "Besides, my uncle is the police chief. What kind of trouble can I get into?"

"Seriously?" He gave her a quick hug. "You are kidding me, right?"

Cat shut the door to the study behind them. "You'd think. Go get some coffee and hang out in the living room. Let me know when Shirley arrives."

She grabbed a welcome kit out of the hall closet and took the stairs to the second floor two at a time. Shauna had cleaned the rooms last week, but typically they did a quick run-through together before the guests arrived. The welcome kit held a map of the town, one of the college, a notebook with the retreat's name on the front, pens, and an assortment of local treats including teas and hot cocoa. Shauna had put a plate of fresh cookies in everyone's room during the last retreat, but Shirley was going to have to deal with the Colorado delicacies in the basket if she wanted any snacks. At least until tomorrow, when the chef-in-residence would actually be back *in* residence. Cat checked the towels and bath items and fluffed the pillows. Walking over to the window, she opened the drapes to let the sunshine in. She glanced around. The room looked lovely. She hoped Shirley would arrive before the sun disappeared for the day.

The writers' retreat was the one way she could continue to pay the utilities and the remodeling loan on the Victorian. She'd sunk most of her savings into the furniture and other amenities that the retreat needed. If she had to hire someone to take over Shauna's role, she didn't know how she could afford to pay for all the things that her friend took care of now.

"No use worrying about something that hasn't happened yet," she told the reflection of herself in the mirror. She pushed her brown hair back behind her ears and peered at her image. A quick shower, some makeup, and some clean clothes might make her look a little more like a professional author. An image she didn't feel totally comfortable with, at least not yet. If they really wanted to meet the author persona, she should wear yoga pants, a cami, and her old sweat jacket. That's what she typically wore, especially when she was on deadline, like she had been a few weeks ago. Now, she had a few weeks before she had to start up a new story. Time to let it percolate in her head.

She headed upstairs to her room and quickly got ready for her new guest. On the way back downstairs, she heard laughter coming from the living room. Cat put on a smile and took a deep breath. Time to be perky and cheerful for another week.

Or at least friendly.

Uncle Pete sat on the couch. Shauna sat next to him and waved Cat over. "There you are."

"I've been here. You're the one that's been MIA." Cat bit her tongue, hoping the words wouldn't come out as a complaint. "Did you know we had a guest showing up today?"

Shauna's eyes widened. "Oh, no. Shirley's coming in early. I totally forgot. Did Seth pick her up at the airport yet?" She glanced at her watch, then back up at their faces. "Did I forget to ask Seth to go get her too?"

"Apparently, she's getting her own transportation." Uncle Pete patted Shauna's knee. "I chatted with her last night on the phone and the woman seems to have a solid head on her shoulders. I think she'll be fine."

"That's not the point." Shauna stood. "I need to set up her room."

Cat sat down. "I already did. I could use some help with the food for tomorrow morning though. Uncle Pete says he's taking her out to dinner, so we just have to have a breakfast ready for her."

"No problem. I can whip up something before I head back to the ranch." Shauna sank back onto the couch. "All you'll have to do is heat it up in the oven."

"You're going back to the ranch tonight?" Cat rubbed her eyes, feeling the stress build.

"I have to. I told Kevin I'd be there for dinner so we can celebrate." Shauna smiled and held out her hand. A large diamond twinkled on her ring finger. "He asked me to marry him. Can you believe it? I thought we were breaking up over Christmas— I didn't see him at all. And then out of the blue, he asks me to marry him."

Cat's breath caught. She didn't want to burst Shauna's bubble, but Kevin had been a total jerk to her friend the entire time they'd dated. And now, he wanted to marry her? "But you've only known each other a few months."

"Six months, exactly." Shauna stared at the ring. "I didn't quite say yes, not yet. But he told me to wear the ring anyway. I think he wants me to get attached so I have to say yes to keep it."

"Do you want to marry him?" Cat was still in shock. All the things she'd worried about were happening. She was losing her friend and her partner in the retreat.

Shauna didn't look up. "I'm not sure."

"Well, I'm happy for you, no matter what you decide. It's about time Kevin manned up and did something right. Although, you know, if he hurts you, I'll be there to put him in his place." Uncle Pete pulled Shauna into a hug. "We're very happy for you, dear. Aren't we, Cat?"

Cat met her uncle's gaze and saw his warning not to be a jerk to her best friend about the proposal. "If you're happy, I'm happy."

Shauna turned toward her and hugged Cat. "I'm so glad to hear that. I was so worried you'd be upset."

"How can I be upset when you're getting married? We'll figure things out with the retreat. And I can deal with breakfast tomorrow as long as you can do the rest of the time." She patted Shauna's back and rolled her eyes in her uncle's direction.

Shauna pulled away and wiped her eyes. "I better get in the kitchen and get the muffins started. I'll do a breakfast casserole and start some soup for your dinner tonight."

"I can feed myself, you know." Cat smiled as Shauna stood and focused on her ring, again. "The ring is pretty."

"I know, right? For once, Kevin did good." Shauna smiled and disappeared into the hallway.

Uncle Pete and Cat sat on the couch, not talking for a few seconds. Then he shook his head. "That boy's going to break her heart, you know that, right?"

Cat nodded. "I'd lay money on it. But if he does, I'm going to make him pay."

Chapter 2

Before Uncle Pete could lecture her about leaving things, especially relationships, alone, Cat heard the front door open. A strong female voice called out, "Hello? Is anyone here?"

"Sounds like our guest is here." Cat popped up and started walking to the front lobby.

Uncle Pete caught up with her and put a hand on her arm, stopping her. "Cat, you need to let Shauna deal with this engagement. Good or bad, it's her life."

Cat pressed her lips together and nodded. She didn't like it, but her uncle was right. Nothing good would come of her trying to keep Shauna away from Kevin. She would just have to pick up the pieces once he blew up Shauna's life and walked out the door. "I'll be nice."

"I'll believe that when I see it." Uncle Pete released her arm. "Let's go meet our new friend. I have a feeling she's going to be very interesting."

Shirley Mann stood at the counter, her bags at her feet. She had steel-grey hair, cut shorter than

Cat's, and deep blue eyes that watched as Cat and Uncle Pete walked toward her. Cop's eyes.

"Looks like I'm in the right place. The cab driver didn't realize there was even a bed-and-breakfast here in town."

"We're not really a bed-and-breakfast—we're only open for the writers' retreat. I don't know if I could deal with a house full of people all the time. I'd never get anything done." Cat held out a hand. "Shirley? I'm Cat Latimer, and this is my uncle, Pete Edward."

They shook, and Shirley turned toward Uncle Pete. "I enjoyed talking with you last night. Thank you, again, for letting me visit your lovely town. I never want to just walk in without permission from the local law enforcement department. I would have expected the same courtesy when I was on the job."

"We do have a set of codes, don't we? Anyway, I'd love to come visit Alaska someday. I never seem to take a vacation from the job though. You know how it is." He leaned against the registration desk. "I'd like to take you to dinner tonight, if you're feeling up to it. The place isn't fancy, but it has good beer and an excellent steak dinner and we can talk about that cold case you're looking into."

"That sounds perfect. I ate something at the airport in Salt Lake, but you know airport food. It all tastes the same." Shirley focused back on Cat. "Do I need to do anything to check in?"

Cat went through the registration process, ran Shirley's card, and handed her a room key. Seth had brought someone in from Denver to set up the card key system when they'd opened the retreat. "The doors are locked at nine, but your key will open the front door at any hour."

"I don't think we'll be out that late, Cat." Uncle Pete chuckled and pointed to Shirley's luggage. "Can I help you with your bags?"

"I can get them." Shirley reached down and grabbed the two bags. "I'll just freshen up and be back down here in ten minutes. Will that work?"

"I'll grab a cup of coffee and be in the living room. Don't hurry on my account. My niece has some interesting books about the local area I've been meaning to peruse." He waited for Shirley to disappear up the staircase to the guest rooms. "Well, at least you have one guest that's not a flake."

"Most of my guests aren't flakes. Writers are just an unusual bunch." Cat put the registration stuff in a drawer for Shauna to deal with later. "Thanks for babysitting tonight. I wanted to get those boxes of books finished to have Seth deliver them to the library on Monday. It feels good to be moving on with this."

"Even if you don't really know what happened to Michael?" Uncle Pete didn't look at her as he walked with her to the kitchen.

"Maybe I'll never know. No matter what, I need to put that part of my life to bed. I'll clean out his office, go through his papers, and see if there's anything there. If not, at least I tried." Cat pushed the kitchen door open. And if she was honest with herself, she felt good about finally setting the past aside. She'd loved Michael, then she'd hated him, and now, her emotional state was somewhere in between. "Besides, I have a whole two weeks before I have to start another book. It will give me something to do."

Shauna was just putting a batch of muffins in the oven. Cat noticed she'd put her ring on the nose of an elephant statue she had at the kitchen sink. Shauna always took her rings off while she was cooking. A habit she'd gotten from her mother after the woman had lost her wedding ring down the sink drain one too many times.

"Hey, Cat, I'm heating up some clam chowder. What kind of sandwich do you want to go with it?" She stirred the pot on the stove. "And what about you, Pete? I can whip up something for you and the guest so you don't have to go out."

"No, we're good. I'm going to enjoy spending some time with a woman who understands my job for once." He poured a cup of coffee and then started to leave the kitchen. He paused at the door, apparently amused at the two women's expressions. "What? You both are great, but I can't really talk about my job, now, can I?"

After he left, Cat poured herself a cup of coffee and sat down with a pad and pen at the table. "You have Seth set up for the rest of the airport runs? When will the first—I mean, second—guest arrive?"

"I just called him and left a message. The first run should be here tomorrow at two. So besides setting out breakfast, that should be all you need to do. I'll be back bright and early. Kevin's not really happy with me leaving without Sunday brunch, but he'll get over it. He has a job—he's going to have to realize that I do too." Shauna wiped her hands on a kitchen towel. "I'll get the breakfast casserole ready, and all you have to do is pop it in the oven at seven. She can get coffee from the kitchen if she's an early bird. Which I assume she is."

"I'll hold down the fort, but don't stay away too long. People come to the retreat for your mad cooking skills as well as time to write." Cat tapped her pen on the paper. "Can we go over the schedule for the rest of the week while you get that ready?"

By the time Shauna put on her coat and left for her dinner with Kevin, Cat felt like they had everything under control. She ate her soup and sandwich at the kitchen table while she read a mystery novel she'd been holding off starting until she finished writing her latest novel. Then, glancing at the clock, she rinsed her dishes and put them into the dishwasher. It was nine, and Uncle Pete and Shirley were still out. How long was dinner going to take?

She turned off the kitchen lights and left the entry area lights on so Shirley could find her way when they did decide to return. Cat pocketed her cell phone, just in case someone needed her, and went upstairs to get ready for bed. Shauna typically was downstairs at five, getting breakfast ready for the group. Cat thought with just one guest, she might get away with going down at six. But even that meant less sleep than she was used to getting.

Not for the first time, she wondered if opening the retreat had been that great of an idea. Especially if she was now going to be handling it on her own. Shauna said she wanted to keep working, but who knew what would really happen if she and Kevin got married. Especially if they started having kids. Shauna would be too busy with her brood to come cook for a group of writers for a week.

"Not today's problem," Cat reminded herself as she climbed the stairs to her room. Today, all she needed was some sleep. She'd deal with tomorrow at 06:00. And she'd deal with someday when it arrived.

Her alarm woke her and she, bleary-eyed, peered at the clock on her night side table. Five-thirty. Why on earth had she set her alarm so early? Then she remembered. She had a casserole to get into the oven and coffee to be made. She pulled herself out of bed and then stood in the shower under the warm water until her eyes started to open. When she'd finished drying off, she had only a few minutes to get dressed and get downstairs.

The first thing she did was put the casserole in the oven and set the timer. Then she poured herself a cup of coffee from the waiting pot and poured the rest into the dining room carafe. It took her only twenty minutes to set up the breakfast room with muffins, coffee, hot water for tea, and a plate of cookies, just in case.

"I *can* handle the retreat by myself," she announced to the shiny carafe as she admired her work. Then she grabbed the book she'd started reading last night and took it and her coffee to the living room. The only thing she needed to do was take the casserole out of the oven in an hour. She had plenty of time to relax and read.

At seven-thirty, she pulled herself out of the book. Looking at her phone, she cursed. The alarm she'd tried to set hadn't taken or she'd just ignored the noise. As she rushed into the kitchen, she realized she'd changed the cell phone a few days ago to vibrate only when she'd gone to the library to discuss the final details for the donation of Michael's books with Miss Applebome, the head librarian. Hope filled her as soon as she walked into the kitchen. She didn't smell burning casserole. Then she sniffed again. She didn't smell the spicy sausage or the warm bread odors either. She opened the oven door, and the casserole sat, unbaked, on the rack.

She froze, trying to remember her steps from earlier that morning. She'd put the casserole into the oven, shut the door, set the alarm, and then gone to make coffee. She slapped her hand on her head. She'd missed one crucial step. She hadn't turned the oven on.

The kitchen door opened behind her. "Hate to bother you, but I'm out of coffee out there." Shirley walked in with the carafe Cat had filled earlier. "And will there be anything to eat besides the muffins? I'm on a low-sugar diet."

Cat grabbed the second casserole Shauna had made for tomorrow, turned the oven on, and then reset the alarm. This time, she was going to stay in the kitchen and wait for the casserole to finish. She turned to greet Shirley and take the carafe out of her hands. "I've just put the casserole in—we should be good in about an hour, maybe less." Cat hoped the second, slightly smaller pan would cook faster. She could have just cooked the first one, but the thought of giving her guest food poisoning made her pause. Thank God Shauna had made two, or Cat would have been calling her to pick something up for Shirley at the diner on her way back to the house. "Let me fill this up for you."

She turned toward the coffeepot and realized it had turned itself off. She touched the pot—the coffee was cold. Cat spun back around and smiled at Shirley. "Where are you working? I'll make a new pot and bring it to you."

Shirley flushed. "I saw you were in the living room, so I went looking for rooms and found a study on the first floor. I'm sure you're doing some remodeling since there are boxes of books stacked in the room. If you want me to move, I will. . . ."

Cat shook her head. "No worries if you don't mind working in the middle of the chaos. Monday, the boxes will be taken to the library. It was my ex-husband's study." Cat frowned as she thought about how she'd left the desk. "I probably should come in and finish clearing out the desk sometime today."

"I'll move to the living room." Shirley put a hand up to stop Cat's next words. "I was wrong by assuming I could just go looking for a place to write."

Cat wiped the frown off her face with a smile. She shook her head. "No, you were fine. The room will be available for use by everyone Monday There's no reason you can't use it now. I'll clean out the desk later."

"If you're sure?" Shirley glanced around the room. "Pete told me about your husband. I'm sorry for your loss."

Her loss had happened during the divorce, not when Michael had passed away. "Thank you, but we were divorced before he passed."

"Doesn't mean that you didn't care for him at one point in your life. My ex got killed by a bear a couple years ago. Totally messed me up, even though we'd been divorced for close to ten years." Shirley rolled her shoulders. "I need to clear my head and run sometime today. Do you have a treadmill available for guests?"

One of the amenities that Seth had been bugging her about providing, but she couldn't see setting up a home gym in the basement. "Sorry. There's a gym at the college you can use. I'll show you how to get there on the map if you'd like."

"Works for me. And I get to burn more calories by walking there." Shirley turned toward the door. "Let me know when the coffee's ready. I'll be in the study until after breakfast, then you can get whatever you need to get done without me hanging around."

Shirley was nice. Cat would have to ask her more about what she was working on. The woman was determined—that showed. She was here a day early and up before nine on a Sunday. Cat walked back to the living room and picked up the novel she was reading. Taking it back to the kitchen, she made coffee and read until the pot finished.

True to her word, Shauna showed up just as the casserole was ready to come out of the oven. Cat hadn't called her, but as she pulled the pan out of the oven, she snuck a peek at her friend. "So if I had let this set out, uncooked, for over an hour, would that be a problem?"

Shauna hurried over and stared at the casserole. "You're kidding me, right?"

"I forgot to turn on the oven."

Shauna took a deep breath. "The only thing raw in the dish is the eggs, so I think we'll be okay since you can leave them out for up to two hours, but seriously, Cat—you didn't turn on the oven?"

"Cooking's not my strong point. Besides, I had to make coffee too. Don't worry, I threw the first one out and cooked the second one you had in the fridge." Cat's gaze dropped to the novel. "I was a little distracted."

Shauna laughed and the sound filled the kitchen. Gentle and chirpy, like some bluebirds had escaped from a storybook and were hanging out in the warm room. "I promise I'll be here for all the breakfasts this week. I can't have you giving our guests food poisoning. "

She went and washed her hands before inspecting the casserole. Cat laid the book on the table. "Shirley's working in the study. She's on a low-sugar diet."

"Well, it would have been nice for her to mention that ahead of time. Maybe we should add it to our application. Dietary needs?" Shauna had her hair up in a clip and was pulling out ingredients, bowls, spoons, and butter.

"How was dinner?" Cat felt like something was different. "Wait—you aren't wearing the ring. What happened?"

"Oh, I still have it. Kevin just thought it might be prudent for me to hold off wearing it for a while." Shauna didn't turn to look at Cat when she spoke, her head bent toward the bowl and cookbook on the counter.

"What? Is he insane?" Cat rushed over to her friend and put a hand on her back. "Are you okay with that?"

Shauna turned, her eyes angry and red from

crying. "Of course I'm not. He asked, I told him yes last night, now he's all, 'well, maybe we should slow down.' We're engaged, we're not engaged. Why can't the man make up his damn mind?"

The kitchen went still as the door to the hallway opened slowly. Shirley peeked around the door, looking worried. "Sorry, but I'm starving. Is that casserole ready? And maybe some coffee?"

Cat patted Shauna's back one more time, then rushed to the stove. "I'm so sorry, Shirley. I should have brought this to you as soon as it finished."

"I didn't mean to interrupt."

Cat smiled, hoping the gesture covered the anger she felt toward Kevin. That man was playing with Shauna's emotions. And it wasn't fair. She took a plate out of the cabinet. "You didn't interrupt. If you need something, just come on in and one of us will get it for you."

Shauna turned, her eyes still wet from tears. "I'm sorry. This is my fault. I'm having man issues."

"I can't understand that. You're so beautiful, any man would be lucky to have you." Shirley didn't come farther into the kitchen, shifting her weight from foot to foot.

Shauna laughed. "I've learned one thing in my life—everyone can have the same issues. And everyone is carrying something that they probably should have set down years ago."

"Well said." Shirley reached for the plate and filled cup Cat handed her. "I'll go into the breakfast room with this."

"You can eat in here with us." Cat motioned toward the table. "We're a little cluttered, but there's always another spot."

"I'm working on a project and I'd like to keep going, if you don't mind." Shirley held up the coffee cup in a good-bye wave. "I'm sure we'll find time to talk during the retreat. I'm very interested in the history of your house. Maybe we could slot in some time before the rest of the guests arrive today?"

"Of course." Cat considered her day. Seth wouldn't get back from Denver until after three, maybe three-thirty. "What if we do lunch in town? That way we'll be out of Shauna's hair as she gets everything ready."

"I can make you a better lunch here than what you'll get at The Diner, you know." Shauna threw a towel over her shoulders.

"But you've got things to do." Cat shook her head. "We can even bring you back something. That way, you don't have to cook lunch at all."

Shauna went to the table and looked at her list. "I am a bit behind."

"Then it's settled. Shirley and I will walk into town and have lunch at the Sandwich Stop. You just let me know what you want and I'll get a to-go order for the walk back." Cat smiled at her friend. "Unless you want to go with us?"

"The only reason I'm agreeing to this is I have too much to do to make lunch too." Shauna waved them away. "Go on, be gone with you. Can't you see I'm busy here?"

Cat grabbed the book she'd been reading and a muffin. "I'm going to work on Michael's papers." She paused next to Shirley as they both headed toward the door. "I'll meet you in the foyer at noon? It's only about a ten-minute walk."

"Works for me." Shirley paused. "Can you show me where the gym is on our way back? That way, I can head over there after lunch and work out."

"Of course. See you at noon." Cat hummed as she walked up the stairs to her office to start going through another one of Michael's boxes. The retreat had started early, but even with the few hiccups this morning, she had a strong feeling that this week was going to be stress free.

Chapter 3

Cat had finished reading and reviewing the stuff in one box by the time her phone alarm went off, notifying her that it was fifteen minutes until the time she'd agreed to meet Shirley. She looked at the three piles she'd made: keep, give to college, and trash. The good news was the college and trash piles were bigger than the keep one. The bad news was she had twenty more of these boxes to get through.

"One step at a time." If the retreat stayed quiet, she could get through most of them this week and start the process of figuring out what Michael had really been up to in the years after the divorce. She bagged up the trash pile, put the college pile into the now empty box, and then set the few "keep" items on her desk. Three blue notebooks were in that pile. Michael had loved blue so she'd stocked up on the cheap spiral notebooks one fall when the back-to-school sales hit Denver.

When Cat arrived downstairs, Shirley already sat waiting on the bench in the front of the foyer, her green puffer coat on and a matching green beanie on her head that had the initials FAPD embroidered on the front. She noticed Cat looking. "From the job. I loved these caps. They kept me warm on many cold days of search or stakeout."

Shirley's hair poked out from the sides, and even though it was grey and matched the wrinkles around her eyes, somehow, the cap made Shirley appear young, ready to take on the world. Cat wished she felt that way. All she had to do was get through the retreat, finish going through the boxes in her office, and solve her ex-husband's murder. Easy peasy. She should be done by Saturday at the latest.

As they walked down the street, Cat heard her name being called. Well, "Catherine!" was blaring out of Mrs. Rice's front door. Mrs. Rice and Cat's mother had been friends. Well, at least they'd been bridge partners for years before Cat's parents had moved to Florida and the land of the retired. When her mother had heard Cat was moving back to the Warm Springs house, she'd made Cat promise to be nice to the woman. Cat was finding keeping the promise exhausting.

Mrs. Rice hurried out to meet them at the sidewalk wearing house slippers and an oversized sweater. Her neighbor leaned on the gate so hard, Cat worried that her weight might bend the metal. "I'm so glad I caught you. I wanted to talk to you before you hired someone."

"I'm sorry? Hired someone for what?" Cat was confused, but most every conversation with her neighbor started out with Cat feeling that way.

Mrs. Rice just started talking like you knew the backstory before she even opened her mouth.

"To help you run the retreats, of course." Mrs. Rice smiled, but the wide grin didn't feel warm or welcoming. "I've heard about Shauna's engagement, and, although I'm not very happy with her choice of men, I'm sure they'll work out all their problems. I want you to know I helped run a B and B in Vermont one year when I was a college student. I have experience."

Shirley chuckled, probably thinking there weren't bed-and-breakfasts around during the time Mrs. Rice was a college student. Cat shot her a warning glance. No need to get Mrs. Rice upset— Cat would put an end to this now. "I'm not sure what you heard, but even if Shauna marries Kevin, she'll still be my partner in the retreat business."

"You modern women just don't understand family. As soon as she sees that little baby, she's going to want to stay home and cuddle. It's a maternal thing." Mrs. Rice sniffed. "I suppose you think it's going to be like this forever? Friends are fine when you don't have family, but once you do, life changes."

"Look." Cat made a show of looking at her watch. "We've got to be going. Shirley has an appointment in town. Before we leave, let me be clear. I'm not hiring anyone to help with the retreat."

Mrs. Rice peered for a long moment at Shirley like she had just appeared on the spot as Cat's excuse. "Yet."

"I'm sorry?" Cat narrowed her eyes.

"I said yet. You're not hiring someone, yet." Mrs. Rice turned away from the gate and made her way back to her front door. When she reached it, she called out to Cat, "Just remember I came to you first. I get first dibs."

Cat turned away. "Like I would hire you anyway," she muttered under her breath.

"Your neighbor is interesting," Shirley said. "I think they were called rooming houses back when she was in college."

"I'm not sure she even went to college. She's never talked about it before." Of course, that wasn't really fair. Cat didn't hang out with Mrs. Rice. She could call and ask her mother, but really, she didn't want to know. In fact, she mostly just ignored the woman. "I shouldn't say things like that. I don't know enough about Mrs. Rice to make a judgment. Although I'm betting on the fact I won't need to hire her."

When Cat turned to look at her companion, Shirley laughed. "You all keep it interesting around here. I can see why Pete likes it so much."

"You and my uncle were out pretty late last night. Is there something going on I should know about?" Cat teased.

"You're pretty good at changing the subject when it fits you." Shirley brushed snow off the edge of a wooden fence as they walked by. She ignored Cat's question and held up a hand full of snow. "I love winter. I guess I'd have to after living in Alaska all my life. I don't get why people talk about moving to Florida or someplace warm when they retire. I like my four seasons. It makes you appreciate summer so much more."

"My folks are in Florida and I loved my time in California, but, I have to admit, Colorado is home.

Always has been." Cat decided to set her question about Uncle Pete aside. She pointed to the trees, their branches iced over and sparkling in the sun. "Winter's lovely, but I'm partial to fall as far as seasons go. It's warm enough to get outside and play, yet there's always a hint of a chill, reminding you that winter is on its way."

They chatted about everything and nothing all the way to the sandwich shop. Shirley was the type you could talk to about anything. No wonder Uncle Pete had kept her late after dinner. As Cat had hoped, the dining room was almost empty. The college students typically chose to eat at the cafeteria, and the professors and administration staff either brought their lunches after a long holiday season, or wound up eating with the students. People were creatures of habit. She'd come here every Wednesday when she'd taught at Covington. And she'd gotten to know the town's patterns. After ordering, she sank back into the bench and focused on Shirley. "So what are your writing goals for the week?"

"Done with the chitchat and back to work, are we?" Shirley waved away Cat's protests. "Don't get me wrong, I do have goals for the week. I'm hoping to finish my book while I'm here. It's a police procedural, set in a college town, so your uncle is going to be an excellent source of knowledge and inspiration."

Cat smiled. "He'll like that. Of course, he'll grumble and gripe, but he likes talking about his job. I think he sanitizes it for Shauna and me when we're having our Sunday dinner together. He doesn't want to scare us, I guess."

"Well, I hope he doesn't get tired of me before I take off on Sunday." Shirley smiled. "I can be a little determined when I'm researching."

"If he does, one of the other guests is writing a mystery too. Maybe you two can talk craft and structure." Cat sipped her hot chocolate. Good, but not as good as Shauna's. What if Mrs. Rice was right? What would Cat do if Shauna decided to become a Stepford wife?

"Tell me about the rest. How many others will be here?"

"Five, counting you. I don't like making the sessions too big. It loses the homey feeling." Cat thought about the four additions coming today. "There's Jordon Hart. He's the mystery author I mentioned. Then there's a paranormal romance author, Melissa Lowe. She writes vamps if I remember right. Her friend is coming with her, Pamela Harrison. I think she writes American historical romance."

"That's quite a mixture. Do you limit retreat guests to fiction writers?" The food was delivered, and the conversation paused for a minute.

Cat focused her gaze on the sandwich, hoping she could make her answer as casual as the question had been. "Actually, no, we don't screen. Have pen, you can get a spot. We've had non-fiction writers and a poet. Our fifth guest at this upcoming retreat, Collin Adams, writes nonfiction."

"History?" Shirley glanced around the dining room, which was filled with rustic mementos of the Colorado gold rush.

Cat shook her head. "He's writing some kind of

dummy's book on the college experience. Write what you know, I guess."

"He's a professor at the college?" Shirley took a bite of her French dip sandwich, the au jus dripping from the crusty roll.

"No, Collin's taking our Covington student spot. Each retreat, we hold one spot for a graduate student chosen by the college. So far, the students have all been from the English department. The college only pays room and board costs for the session. In exchange, the college provides us with library privileges and a one-hour lecture from one of the English professors. Typically, it's on Hemingway since Covington has his papers." Cat dipped her own sandwich and took a bite. It was her favorite sandwich and tasted the same since the first time she'd stopped here for lunch more than five years ago.

"I used to adore reading Hemingway. It's one of the reasons I chose your retreat." Shirley waved a French fry at Cat. "No matter what you think of his works, the man knew how to live."

Cat had never gotten into the author's works. She'd been more interested in reading and collecting Stephen King, and then, of course, Harry Potter. Michael always teased her about her affection for genre work. He'd warned her that if her colleagues found out she read popular fiction for pleasure, she'd be kicked out of the English department. He wasn't far from the truth. Even though she was a published author with a middling to good following, at least in the teen set, the college professors looked at her writing as less worthy than the more literary tomes. It didn't matter—Cat had all the accolades she needed in her semi-annual royalty checks. She dipped a fry into the house-made special sauce. "I'm more of a genre reader these days. I guess getting a graduate degree in English will do that to you."

"Don't tell me you're downplaying the excellent education you received here at Covington." A man stood at the table. Cat looked up into the gaze of Christopher Ngu, dean of the economics department and Michael's former boss.

"Dean Ngu, so nice to see you." She held out her hand. The dean and she had never been on a first-name basis, even once she'd married Michael. Maybe it was her need to prove herself as a fellow faculty member. Or more likely, the guy didn't really consider them friends. After they shook hands, she turned her attention to Shirley. "This is Shirley Mann. She's part of this month's retreat group. The rest of the guests should be arriving later this afternoon."

"Oh, I didn't realize that was still going on." He pulled out his phone and read a text message, ignoring Shirley's outstretched hand. He shoved the phone back into his coat pocket. "Sorry, work. I was hoping we could get together soon about Michael's papers. I know you're busy, but it's a task better done before the documents are accidentally destroyed."

Cat felt a niggle of frustration at the man's lack of tact. "As I've told you before, I'm going through Michael's things and as soon as I can, I'll donate his papers to the department. You'll just have to give me some time."

"None of us know what kind of time we have. It's

best not to put off things better done today. Think of what happened to poor Michael." He leaned closer. "Maybe I'll just come over next week with a few of the boys and we can box up what he left?"

"No!" Cat's firm response made him jerk back away. "I told you, I'll let you know when I'm ready. As you know, I am the executor of his estate and I control the timetable."

He straightened, narrowing his eyes at her. "I'm only trying to help. Friends try to help."

"I don't need your help. And we're not friends." Cat could see Shirley shift in her chair. If Ngu didn't step back, he was going to be on his butt. A question niggled in her mind. "So what's the rush? Why do you want his papers so bad?"

The question made him step back, holding up his hands as if he were warding off an attack. "Seriously, all I want to do is help. Look, I'll talk to you when you're not so emotional about the whole thing. Sorry to have bothered you."

Cat and Shirley watched Dean Ngu walking away. They both turned back to their food once he left the restaurant. "He's kind of intense."

"The man has a bug up his butt about those papers." Shirley held up a fry but paused before putting it in her mouth. "Are you sure there's not something incriminating in your ex-husband's possessions? I don't mean to pry, but Pete and I talked a bit about your husband's situation."

"It's okay. I haven't found much in his papers. I have a few dozen boxes to go through though." Cat dunked the last bite of her sandwich in the au jus. Uncle Pete must really trust Shirley to be talking about Michael's death. "Maybe Uncle Pete thought you'd be able to help find Michael's killer while you're here at the retreat."

"Maybe I can." Shirley finished off her fries.

Cat felt a twinge of regret that she'd spoken so quickly. "I really was teasing about you helping me with the Michael thing. I don't want to release anything until I'm sure there's not a clue in the paperwork about what he was doing."

Shirley finished off her sandwich and then took a sip of her coffee. Cat felt Shirley's gaze on her as she finished her own lunch. Finally, after they'd paid the waitress for their meal, Shirley leaned forward. "I wasn't kidding. I'm good at what I used to do, and I think I was led here to help you figure this mystery out."

Cat pulled her coat on. "I don't want you spending your time investigating Michael. You came here to write."

"I'll write. And I'll help you find your ex's murderer." Shirley's eyes twinkled as she held the door open for Cat. "I'm pretty good at multitasking. Now where's that gym? After listening to that guy, I feel like I need to burn off some energy before I hit someone."

Cat showed Shirley the way to the gym. Cat left her there and then went back to the house. The grandfather clock chimed two. Cat hadn't realized they'd taken so long. She hung up her coat and went to the kitchen to help Shauna. "What can I do?"

"Nothing. I've got tomorrow's muffins in the oven. A new breakfast casserole is ready in the fridge. The rooms are clean and prepped. Afternoon treats are already set up in the dining room. All we need are four more guests. I've got Kevin's favorite dinner, Irish stew, on the stove and I made myself a salad for tonight. I'm never hungry during retreat weeks. Must be all the baking." Shauna looked up from her phone and sighed. "There is one more thing I forgot to tell you."

"What's that?" Cat pushed away the vision of Mrs. Rice standing by the gate in her slippers. *Please don't quit, please don't quit,* she repeated wordlessly as a charm mantra.

"Don't hate me, but Sasha Smith is coming on Monday and staying for a couple of days." Shauna set her phone down. "I know you like more notice than this, but we needed to get her here before school starts up again."

"Wait, who's Sasha Smith?"

"You know. The bookseller from California? She's from South Cove, that cute little tourist town you stopped at for the last release?" Shauna pushed back her red hair and pulled it into a bun in the back of her head, where she clipped it. "Actually, she called to tell us she wasn't working at the bookstore anymore and wouldn't be able to come to talk."

"I don't understand, she's no longer working at Coffee, Books, and More?" Cat did remember the girl. She'd been almost speechless prior to the talk, but afterward, she'd been chatty. "What happened?"

"Something about an internship in marketing and school. But I told her we still wanted her to come and talk at our retreat, so she's coming Monday. I'll have Seth run to Denver and pick her up at the airport."

Cat thought about the young woman who had spoken so eloquently about her love of books and why she wanted to pass it on to others. "She has a daughter, right? Is she coming too?"

"Apparently, the grandmother is babysitting. She'll only be here until Thursday, so you need to schedule her sessions with the group before she leaves." Shauna pushed a copy of the retreat schedule toward Cat. "I know I should have asked you first. But you were at the library, then I kind of forgot with all the Kevin crap. I really wanted to get her out here before she goes on to bigger things."

"No, that's fine. I wanted to start adding a new workshop each session anyway. Maybe next month we can have the local bookstore owner come and talk. She was very energetic about the retreat the last time we talked." Cat made a note in her schedule. "If we limit the people we have to fly in and cover room and board for to no more than four per year, we should still be under budget."

"I'm glad you're thinking about money because I didn't even consider our budget." Shauna shook her head. "Maybe I'm not the best partner you could have. You should ask Seth to step up and handle the finances."

"Why, because he runs his own business?' Cat shook her head. "Nope, this was our thing from the beginning and I'm keeping it that way. Besides, we're keeping him busy enough with the remodeling and upkeep."

"Not to mention driving during retreat week." Shauna closed her planning book.

"When is Seth expected back from the airport?" Cat stood to grab a cup of coffee and rejoined Shauna at the table.

"Any minute now. And then, if it's okay, I've

asked him to stay over this week. Kevin is being clingy and wants me to sleep at the ranch. I've told him that even if we do move in together, I have to be here for the retreat." She tossed her phone down on the table. "I don't know about this whole thing. I've been my own boss for a long time. I'm not sure I'm the kind of girl who just hands over her life."

"I don't think you have to hand over your life just to get married." Cat put a hand on Shauna's arm. "Let's just get through this week. Maybe it's the engagement that has him so crazy. I hear guys freak out a bit once they make the decision."

Shauna took a tissue out of the box on the table. "I can't believe you're being so nice about this. You don't even like Kevin."

"That's not true." Well, it *was* true, but Cat had never told her friend that. "I don't know him well enough to not like him. But sometimes I don't like the way he treats you."

She blew her nose. "That's true. It seems like we're always tucked away at the ranch. We rarely go out, and when we do, it's in Denver, not Aspen Hills. If I didn't know better, I'd think he was hiding me from some wife."

"Are you sure you know better?" Cat asked, but before Shauna could answer, they heard the front door open, followed by the sound of the little silver bell Shauna had set up on the reception desk.

"Sounds like the retreat has begun." Shauna stood and wiped her eyes. "We'll talk about this after they're all gone next Sunday. From now until then, it's all about the retreat."

"I can do that." Cat paused before she stood. "If

you need to talk though, we can hole up in my room for an hour or so. They won't miss us. Especially if you leave out a pan of those cheesecake brownies you made last week."

She left the kitchen and was surprised to see two men in the lobby area. One was clearly her Covington guest, Collin, as he sported a backpack along with a computer bag. His blond hair looked like he was about two weeks late for a haircut, being just a little too long to be short and too short to be considered long. He had deep brown eyes covered by round wire-rimmed glasses. When he saw her, he grinned. "I'm Collin and I'm checking in."

She handed him the guest card they had everyone fill out and then turned to the delivery guy holding a vase with two dozen roses. "Hi, Frank."

"Someone's trying to get your attention. What has Seth done now?" He set the vase on the counter.

"They're not from Seth." Cat held up a five-dollar bill she'd tucked in the desk drawer. Starting with the second retreat, she'd received two dozen red roses from Linda Cook on opening day. It had become an inside joke between Cat and the widow who called at least once a week. Linda was becoming a friend after spending time at Warm Springs Retreat while Uncle Pete tried to figure out why her husband had been killed. The woman had a sleuthing gene, just like Cat. She handed the bill to Frank, but held tight when he reached for the money. "And if I start hearing rumors about who's sending me flowers circulating around town, your tip will be cut in half next month."

"My lips are sealed. Besides, I'll get to deliver an order to Mrs. Rice as soon as I get back. She always calls one in as soon as she sees my van here. She's sneaky at trying to get the gossip, but I keep telling her I don't read the cards. That way, I get two tips out of the deal." He did a one-finger salute and headed out the door.

"Here's my registration card. I didn't fill out the credit card section. You don't need any money, right? The school is paying my way, correct?" Collin held out his completed card.

"You're fine. I probably should make up some new cards for our Covington guests, but right now, this works just fine." She grabbed a key and coded it. "There's treats and drinks available in the dining room during the day, and breakfast will be served at nine every morning. Other than that, and the Saturday night dinner, you're on your own for food."

"I'll go eat at the campus cafeteria. I've got a room and board plan." He paused, looking around the lobby. "Where's your chef? I hear she's really amazing in the kitchen."

Somehow, his tone made Cat feel tense. Like he didn't really mean his words. "Where did you hear that?"

"The last student who got the spot told me all about her crazy desserts." He swung his backpack over his shoulder. "Do we have any group meetings tonight?"

"Just a get-together in the living room about seven." Cat paused, wondering if she should have run a background check on Collin as well. She'd saved the money on one less report since she had to accept the college's selection no matter what. "You have a complete schedule in your room in the welcome packet. You don't have to go with us to the library orientation tomorrow if you don't want to go."

"We'll see." He took the stairs two at a time, and Cat hurried to show him the room.

Cat headed downstairs after getting Collin settled to tell Shauna about what he'd said. She'd just started down the stairs when she heard the next wave of guests arrive in the lobby. When she got there, Shauna was talking to a woman with spiky dark hair and, according to her outfit, a fondness for leather. Cat hurried over to help. A younger woman in a grey sweater set and matching grey pants stood waiting.

"Can you fill this out for me?" Cat grabbed a registration card and handed it to the woman along with a pen. "You must be Pamela. I'm Cat Latimer."

She shook her head and pointed to the other woman talking to Shauna. "That's Pamela. I'm Melissa Lowe."

Cat glanced between the two women. She must have read their files wrong. "Sorry, Melissa. We're so happy to have you two here. I love it when people share the retreat experience with friends."

Pamela Harrison handed over the complete card and took her room key from Shauna. "I'm so excited to be here. I'm dying to dig into the library and get researching Colorado history."

Cat looked at the cards again. "You write American historicals?"

"Yeah. I guess I was born in the wrong era. I love all the cowboys and saloon girls." She grinned. "You thought Melissa was the historical writer, huh?"

Melissa giggled and handed Cat her completed card. "I'm into the paranormal scene."

"You look like a librarian." A man dropped his suitcases and Seth followed him in the house with a couple more. "You really need to think about your 'author' persona, right, Ms. Latimer?"

"Call me Cat. And that's a great question for one of our discussion times. You're Jordon Hart?" Cat handed Melissa her room key and then gave Jordon a pen and a guest card.

"Guilty as charged." He took the pen and took over a corner of the registration desk next to the roses.

Seth walked over to her and gave her a quick kiss. "Everyone here?"

"Except for our surprise expert coming tomorrow. Make sure you get the details from Shauna before she leaves tonight." She grabbed the key to the extra room that was quickly becoming Seth's second home. "I hear you need a room key too."

He took the key, pocketed it, and then leaned in. "I don't *really* need a room."

"Oh, you're *not* staying?" Cat stepped toward the staircase. "Melissa, Pamela, can I help you with your suitcases?"

Seth grabbed Melissa's larger case, and Pamela handed Cat her computer bag.

"You two are such a cute couple. My folks fight like this all the time." Pamela followed Cat toward the stairs. "I just love this house. You live here all year long?"

Chapter 4

"You're all set up. I'll be back no later than five, five-thirty depending on the roads." Shauna glanced around the breakfast room. The breakfast table had plates, silverware, cups, and glasses. The all-day treat table overflowed with cookies, muffins, and an assortment of drinks, including a large tub filled with ice and sodas. "Just keep an eye on the coffee and hot water levels tonight. I doubt that you'll be up before I get back, but if you are, make coffee. Just don't try to cook anything."

"I'm not that bad of cook." Cat set down the pile of napkins she'd taken out of the sideboard and then looked at her friend's shocked face. "What? So I forgot to turn on the oven. Once. It could happen to anyone."

Shauna glanced at her watch. The engagement ring sparkled on her hand. Apparently she'd decided to keep wearing it, no matter what Kevin had said last night. "I'm late." She kissed Cat on her cheeks. "You and Seth have a casserole in the oven for dinner. There's a salad to go along with it in the fridge. But if you decide to eat out, just turn off the oven and put the casserole away when it cools."

"We'll be here." Cat had set up a reservation for the group at the local pizza place, complete with walking directions. Of course, that was the one good thing about having a Covington student as a guest. He could serve as the town's information guru for the new arrivals. "I want to talk to Seth about the plans for finishing the attic."

"Pillow talk. You two are so sweet." Shauna gave the room one more glance. Then, apparently satisfied, she moved toward the kitchen.

"So are you going to tell Kevin that he can't just take back his offer that way?" Cat followed and grabbed a soda out of the fridge. "I see you're wearing the ring."

"I don't know what I'm going to say, except that I can't keep leaving you during retreat week. He's going to have to deal with the fact I have responsibilities too." Shauna shrugged on her coat and pulled her red hair free as she talked. She grabbed a box that Cat guessed must be filled with their dinner supplies. "I may not be doing million-dollar housing projects in Denver, but my job is important. Especially to those five people upstairs."

"Good luck." Cat didn't think Kevin thought anyone else's job was as important as what he did, including the head trauma surgeon at a hospital or the President of the United States. The guy was full of himself and liked to flaunt his money as well as the success his company had obtained. At least he was getting one of his favorite meals to eat while Shauna laid down the law. Cat didn't understand what Shauna saw in him. Maybe he had a good heart. Way, way down inside.

After Shauna left, Cat worked on email and marketing stuff in the kitchen. She didn't want to leave the room while dinner was still baking. Not after this morning's incident. She heard footsteps on the stairs and checked the time. Five-thirty. The group must be banding together for their walk to dinner. She made her way to the lobby to send them off.

"There you are." Shirley frowned as she took in Cat's still slippered feet. "Aren't you and that lovely man of yours coming to dinner with us?"

"Not tonight." Cat took a quick inventory of the group, making sure no one was missing. "We host a group dinner on Saturday to talk about how the retreat worked for you. Tonight is time for you all to get to know each other. Tomorrow, we'll head over to the library to get your passes."

"The pizza's really good," Collin said, glancing around the lobby. "Deep dish, Chicago style in the middle of Colorado. Who would have thought?"

Cat's mouth watered a little at the thought of Reno's Pizza. The place had been a local hangout for as long as she could remember. And the pizza was great.

Seth came down the stairs. "Sorry, guys. You can't steal her away tonight. We've got business to talk about."

Pamela smirked. "Business? Is that what they call it in Colorado?"

Cat flushed at the innuendo but shook her head. "Romance writers. You all see things in a different light."

"Love, passion, heat, and a happily ever after.

Not a bad way to see the world, even if it isn't always true." Melissa pulled a stocking cap over her brown curls. She looked like an Ivy League college student, not someone who wrote vampire novels. "Let's go, guys. I'm starving."

"Call me if you get lost or have a problem," Cat called after the group.

Seth walked to the front door with her, and they watched the guests make their way down the walkway to the sidewalk. Pamela threw a snowball at Melissa, who was talking to Shirley. She just brushed off the snow and kept walking. When they turned right, toward town, Seth let out a breath. "At least they're heading in the right direction."

Cat put her arm around his waist. "It's like watching your kids go off to school alone."

"You know what?" He kissed the top of her head. She lifted her head to meet his gaze.

"What?"

An evil grin curved Seth's lips. "We have the house all to ourselves for at least an hour. Let's say we skip dinner and go make out on the couch."

Before she could answer, her stomach growled.

He turned toward the kitchen. "Never mind. Let's eat."

"I didn't say no," Cat protested as she followed him.

He held the door open for her, and the smell of Shauna's beef stroganoff hit her as she walked into the room. This time, her stomach growled louder. "Your stomach answered for you."

"Are you mad?" Cat went to the cupboard to grab two plates and silverware.

Seth took the casserole out of the oven. "Why would I be mad? You have a business to run. We rarely have alone time during the retreats. Besides, I'm hungry too. Is it just me, or is Shauna being weird this week?"

"If you take into account all the pull and tug she's getting from Kevin about this marriage thing, I think she's holding up well." Cat narrowed her eyes at him. "Why? What happened?"

"Nothing. I mean, it was just weird. Forget I even mentioned it." They worked together getting the dinner ready and on the table, and then Seth grabbed two beers out of the fridge and held them out. "You're off the clock, right?"

"I'm never off the clock once the retreat starts. At least not if Shauna isn't here to be the adult." She waved away the beer. "Grab me a soda. I'd hate to have to tell one of my guests I couldn't drive them to the hospital because I'd been drinking."

Seth returned the beers to the fridge and grabbed two sodas. He set one in front of her and then sat down to eat. "This smells wonderful."

"You could have a beer." She dished salad onto her plate and passed the bowl to Seth. "I wouldn't mind."

He put salad on his plate and set the bowl down before he answered. "I know. But the thought of you driving anywhere on these roads makes me nervous. I'll adult with you."

His response made her feel warm and connected. They were a team. Her, Shauna, and now Seth. She just hoped the team would stay together for a long, long time.

* * *

Her alarm went off at five, and Cat pulled herself out of her warm bed and toward the bathroom for a shower. The first day of the retreat was always the busiest. It took people a while to get comfortable in a new situation. As she turned on the water, she smiled at the way the group had acted when they'd returned from dinner. They had been bonding. Laughing, joking, and even a little teasing as they'd removed their coats and then gathered in the living room to continue their conversation. Cat had stayed until ten, but then excused herself. She wondered what time they'd finally given up and gone to bed. It had been like an adult slumber party, with stories and chatter.

As she let the water warm her body, she realized this was why she'd wanted to start the writers' retreat in the first place. A getaway where writers could focus on the craft of writing and support each other in their development.

Humming, she headed downstairs to greet Shauna. When she pushed the kitchen door open, she realized it was still dark. She flipped on the light and then checked the clock on the stove. Five-fifteen. The roads must be bad this morning. Cat poured herself a cup of coffee from the pot Shauna had set on a delayed timer and then went to the breakfast room to get both the coffee and hot water carafes. She'd help get things set up so Shauna didn't have to do everything. They were a team. And she could set up the coffee.

By six, Cat was beginning to get nervous. She

picked up her phone and dialed Shauna's number. No answer.

Staring at the phone, she poured her third cup of coffee waiting for her to call back. Five minutes passed, then ten. No call.

Looking in her contacts, she found a number and punched it in.

"Hey," Kevin said into her ear. Cat started to ask if Shauna was there, but then he went on with his recorded message. She'd reached his voice mail. If they were just sleeping in, she was going to kill Shauna.

She was just about to call the police station and see if there had been any accidents reported on the road when she saw the lights of a car pulling into her driveway. Relief filled her body and she curled her shaking hands around her coffee cup. Shauna was home.

Shauna burst into the kitchen and ran for Cat. Her coat was still on, and snow fell off her boots in clumps. "Oh, Cat, it was awful."

Cat didn't want to be the one who told her friend I told you so, but she could have warned Shauna that driving on the roads before the sanding trucks got out to do their magic wasn't the safest thing to do. She patted Shauna's back and realized her friend was shaking. "Are you okay? Did the car skid? Did you hit a guardrail? Tell me what happened."

Shauna stepped away and went to the coffeepot, pouring a cup and drinking it half gone. She didn't take off her coat or boots, just came back and sat at the table. She didn't look at Cat, instead stared at her hands wrapped around the cup, mirroring Cat's movements a few minutes ago.

"Shauna?" Now Cat was scared. Something had happened. Something bad.

Letting out a breath, Shauna lifted her head and met Cat's gaze. "Kevin's gone."

Chapter 5

Shauna focused on the kitchen, seeming to realize that the snow from her boots was melting on the floor. She shrugged out of her coat and went to the coat rack. Sitting back on the bench, she seemed to be lost in her thoughts.

"What do you mean, he's gone?" Cat went to the coffeepot and poured a cup. Kevin had probably taken off on one of his business trips without telling Shauna he was leaving. After insisting she spend the time with him, he'd rabbited. What a jerk. Handing Shauna the warm mug, she sat down next to Shauna and wrapped her friend's fingers around it. "Drink this and then tell me what he's done."

"I'm not sure. He wasn't feeling good after dinner. He said he had a headache, but I thought maybe he was getting the flu. His stomach was upset and he just looked so pale. We went to bed last night, and I heard him get up several times during the night. He got up early, but he typically does. He has a home office a few rooms down from the bedroom. When he wasn't in bed when I woke up, that's where I thought he'd gone." Shauna sipped the coffee. "I slept until my alarm went off, then got up to make coffee. When I took him a cup, he wasn't in the office. Or in the house. I went to the other side of the house and woke up Paul, but he said he didn't know where he'd gone."

"What about his car? Did you check the garage?" The fact that Paul Addison, Kevin's live in assistant and royal pain in the butt was unaware of Kevin's plans didn't make sense. She was beginning to worry herself. Kevin never went anywhere without Paul knowing where he was going. Even when he went on dates with Shauna. It had been a bone of contention between the couple.

"All the cars are there." Shauna finished her coffee and looked at the clock. "I really have to get busy. We have a house full of guests. I called Pete and he's out there now, talking to Paul. I didn't know what else to do. Kevin's going to be ticked off if he's just out for a walk, but honestly, Cat, I'm scared."

"You should have just called. I could have handled breakfast." Cat patted Shauna's hand.

Shauna laughed and stood. "I'm happy you're concerned about me, but we both know if you were in charge of breakfast, the guests would be eating store-bought muffins and those frozen breakfast sandwiches."

"But what about Kevin?" Cat didn't want Shauna to have to deal with her missing boyfriend—no, fiancé—*and* have to feed the guests.

"I can worry while I cook. It will give me something to do." She headed to the sink to wash her hands. "Besides, your uncle's looking for him. There's nothing more I could do there anyway."

"As long as you're okay. If you need something, you make sure to tell me." Cat refilled her coffee cup. "Is there anything I can do now?"

"You work on setting up the dining room." Shauna glanced at the clock. "I'm pretty sure we'll be seeing a few of the guests up and about in a couple of minutes. Shirley doesn't seem like someone who sleeps in. Ever."

As if Shauna had summoned the woman, Shirley stepped into the kitchen. "Any chance there's some coffee ready?"

Before Cat could move, Shauna stepped away from the sink, wiping her hands on a tea towel. "Of course. By the way, I have some fruit cups in the fridge if you want something naturally sweet. I could put it together with an assortment of cheese or nuts."

"Sure, that would be great." Shirley took the cup from Shauna, sitting down at the table, next to Cat. "I've been thinking about your situation. I want to talk to you this afternoon about your ex-husband. I'd like to run through some scenarios with you and see if anything clicks."

"You really don't have to . . ." Cat began, but Shirley held up her hand, stopping her words.

"This is what I do. Besides, I like solving puzzles, and from what you said, this one is a doozy." She looked at the paper calendar she held. "Can I have an hour of your time around three?"

Cat looked down at her own notebook. "I'll be taking everyone over to the library around ten. Then I'm free for the rest of the day. Three should work. If . . . you're sure you want to spend your time on this rather than writing."

"By the time we go to the library, I'll have already hit a word count that is way over my normal production day. I'm thinking I might need the distraction so my brain will reset and be ready for more words tomorrow." She took the cup Shauna handed her and stood. "I'll be in the first-floor study again today if that's okay. I tried working in the attic room, but man, that place is cold."

Cat looked upward, as if she could see the offending room. "It's not supposed to be."

"I'll have Seth look at the system before he goes to pick up Sasha at the airport." Shauna scribbled something in her own notebook. Apparently, everyone in the room knew the value of a well-used to-do list.

"I thought all the guests were here?" Shirley paused, her cup hovering above the table.

"Sasha isn't a guest. She's a bookseller coming in to talk about what makes a book sell once it's on the shelf. She worked mostly with the teen demographics, but I'm sure we'll all be able to glean some valuable knowledge from her talk," Cat explained.

"Well, that's nice." Shirley turned away toward the door. "I'm sure we'll all learn so much from her."

Cat wasn't sure if Shirley was being sarcastic or if she really did want to meet Sasha. She'd have to watch her cop-in-residence so she didn't ruffle feathers with the rest of the group. Maybe Cat was overanalyzing the simple statement. When she turned to look at Shauna, she saw the same concern in her friend's eyes.

When they were alone, Shauna let out a long breath. "Wow, she's focused. I don't think she understands the word no. Or cooperation."

"Must be the ex-cop in her. I think she's used to getting her own way. Hopefully she won't try to steamroll the others." Cat felt the stress of making the retreat a success fall on her shoulders. And she'd had such high hopes for the week to be a breeze.

When it was time for the group to go to the library, Cat only had to look in two places. The study and the living room. No one was braving the newly remodeled—and currently frigid—attic. She'd sunk a lot of money into the remodel, including a new heating/cooling system, since Seth's friend had insisted the old system couldn't keep up. Now, the new system wasn't working at all. Seth had called the guy, but he was tied up until Wednesday, which meant they'd be without the new space for half the retreat. It didn't seem fair. Cat had been counting on the new space, especially for the winter months, when going to the campus to work would be harder.

They reached the library ten minutes late, and Miss Applebome was standing by the door of the conference room. She narrowed her eyes as Cat waved the group inside. "You know I have a busy schedule, Miss Latimer."

"I know—I'm sorry. It's been kind of a crazy day already." Cat thought about Shauna and the still missing Kevin. Before Cat had left the house, Shauna had called Uncle Pete about three times before he'd told her to just stay put and he'd come see her as soon as he could. So, Shauna did what she always did while she worried: she cooked. Cat was sure they'd probably have enough food prepared for two retreats by the time Shauna was done.

"There is no excuse for tardiness. As a former professor here at Covington, you, of all people, should know that." She followed Shirley into the room and then moved to shut the door on Cat. "They will be done at ten after two. You may want to be on time so they know their way back to the retreat house."

Cat looked at the now closed door. The way Miss Applebome had said retreat house, it may as well have been frat house. At least now she knew where she stood with the grumpy librarian. Maybe she'd bring back a pan of Shauna's brownies to try to sweeten the woman's disposition.

She turned around to leave and ran straight into Collin. "Oh, I didn't realize you came with us."

"I didn't." He grinned and hoisted his backpack higher up on his shoulder. "I've been here all morning working on my book. I'm going back to my dorm room to chill for a bit before lunch. I heard what Miss Applebome said. Do you want me to meet up with the group at two so you don't have to come back?"

"That would be great." Cat paused, thinking about her schedule. "Are you sure you have time? I know research can keep you busy, especially at the beginning of a project."

"No worries. By then, I'll be sick of working on the networking chapter. How many times can you tell people they need to be nice?" Collin pushed back his blond hair. "Everything okay at the house? Your friend seems a little distracted."

"Shauna's fine." Cat paused and looked at Collin. "What are you writing again? A business book?"

"No, it's called *How to Rock Your First Year at College.* I've already landed a contract, but my advance didn't even cover a semester of tuition. They said if this one does awesome, they'll give me a second, more lucrative contract. Besides, either way, I could start getting royalties in a couple of years. That should help limit the amount of student loans I have to take." Collin glanced at his watch. "I've got to scoot. I'm meeting up with my roommate before lunch."

"But you'll walk the group back at two?" Cat wanted to confirm before she let him disappear. Collin seemed to have a good head on his shoulders, but she had just met the kid. She glanced at her watch. If she hurried, she could visit Dean Ngu and see what he knew about Michael's second job. It had occurred to her last night that someone at the college must have set him up with the connection. Maybe it had been the boss he'd trusted.

"I'll be here as soon as that door opens. Miss Applebome is nothing if not true to her word." Collin waved and headed toward the back door in the direction of the dorms.

Cat headed toward the front. She wanted to get back to the house to be there for Shauna, but this side trip shouldn't take long. Her friend was holding up well, but Cat could see the strain as the hours passed without Uncle Pete calling with good news. Where could Kevin have gone? It wasn't like there were a lot of places open in Aspen Hills in the middle of the night. And his ranch was at least ten miles out of town. Someone had to have come and got him.

But why would he leave his bed to get into a car in the middle of the night? Unless he expected to be back before Shauna woke the next morning. If Cat was right and Kevin was already cheating on her friend, Cat was going to kill him.

Or at least make him sorry.

The business school had its own building. A shrine to corporate America, it was even called The Colorado Investment Group Building after the company who had donated a chunk of money during construction. Now, Cat wondered who was really involved in the financial company. Maybe that was who Dante Cornelio pretended to work for. She'd learned a lot about the man, who apparently was part of a New Jersey mob family since she literally ran into him in front of the coffee shop a few months ago. One of the many families who had sent their offspring to Covington College for years. Another fact she hadn't known until she moved back home.

Cat took the elevator to the top floor, where the business departments had their professor offices. Dean Ngu had a nice window office with a view of the mountains. Michael's had been the office next door. When she walked by, she saw the new professor's name on the door and for a second, she paused. Reaching out to touch the dark oak, she remembered the last day she'd been here.

She and Michael had always eaten together in his

office before his Wednesday night class. That last night, instead of cooking, she'd stopped at Reno's Pizza and picked up dinner to celebrate her finishing a first draft. She had been a few minutes early, but she'd brought a book to read, in case he was busy. She had called before ordering the pizza, but had had to leave a message on his machine. When she'd opened the door, a coed had been on the desk and Cat's husband had been kissing her.

Even now, when she realized he'd set up the scene, the pain of the moment came back and emotions flowed through her quickly. Anger, pain, concern, and now just sadness. He hadn't trusted her to be strong enough to deal with whatever he'd gotten into, so he'd sent her away.

She pushed the memory away and focused on the next door. Dean Ngu's office had two rooms, one for a secretary/receptionist and the larger, more swank office for his personal use. No one sat at the first desk so she went right to his inner office door. She knocked and heard the "Come in" response before she pushed the door open.

"Catherine." Dean Ngu sat at his desk and closed a file. "I was expecting one of my staff. We have a performance evaluation meeting in a few minutes."

"This won't take long." Cat breezed into the office and sat at one of the visitor chairs before he could send her away.

"I suppose you're here to make arrangements for the transfer of Michael's papers? Great. I'll just check my schedule and see when I can get some boys out there to box everything up." He reached for his mouse and opened a calendar program on his desktop.

"Sorry, no."

His hand froze and he turned to look at her. "What do you mean, no?"

"I mean I'm not here to turn over Michael's papers. I'm here to ask you a question."

Dean Ngu sighed and leaned back in his chair. He formed a temple with his fingers, as if he were trying to find some patience with an unruly child. "What can I help you with, Catherine?"

"Cat. My name is Cat." She was done letting people push her around. This might be a dumb place to fight a battle, but she had to start somewhere.

"Sorry. What can I help you with, Cat?" The sarcasm in his voice was obvious, but at least he was calling her by her name.

"I want you to tell me who Michael was working with before he died." She held up a hand, stopping the easy lie she saw forming on his lips. "And I don't mean the college. I mean the second job you set him up with."

Cat could see the answer on his face, even before he formed the new lie. "I don't know what you're talking about. I didn't know Michael had a second job. Of course, I know sometimes living on a professor's salary is challenging. Many of our staff take on additional jobs, especially when they're trying to support a family and a house."

"You didn't refer him to anyone about a project?" Cat pushed. She knew he had, but how could she get him to admit it?

"I assure you, I have no idea where he was working. I would have assumed that as his spouse, you would know more about his personal life than I did as his boss." Now the guy had a smirk on his face.

Before Cat could press further, a knock came on the door and a small, mousy woman stuck her head inside. She frowned when she saw Cat in the office. "Did I get our appointment time wrong?"

"Come on in, Rachel. Mrs. Latimer was just leaving." Dean Ngu stood and stared at Cat.

The woman stepped into the room, approaching Cat and holding out her hand. "Oh, I'm glad to finally meet you. Your husband and I co-taught Intro to Economics. He was a lovely man. I'm sorry for your loss."

Cat rose from her chair, accepting the handshake. She'd learned what she'd come to find out. Dean Ngu had known who Michael was working with and he didn't want to tell her.

"Thank you."

On the way home, she thought about Kevin and Shauna. When she got to the house, she saw Seth's truck in the lot. She hurried inside to talk to him about the attic. Maybe he could fix it somehow. At least get it up and running until Wednesday when the expert could come and do his magic.

She went around the side of the house to the kitchen door. Flinging it open, she called out, "Seth? Are you here?"

The kitchen was empty.

She took off her snow boots and hung her coat up on the rack. Then she put on her house slippers and poured herself a cup of coffee to help her warm up. The cabinets were filled with cooling cookies, pies, and cookie bars. From the smell, at least one batch of brownies was still cooking. On the stove, a pot of potato soup bubbled. Cat went over and stirred the soup, letting the warm, comforting smell of the creamy dish calm her nerves. Shauna knew the magic of getting her thoughts together: food.

The kitchen door swung open, and her friend came in with a basket full of towels needing to be folded. She dumped the laundry onto the table. "Hey, you're back."

"You've been busy." She grabbed a cookie and her coffee and took them to the table. "Want me to help?"

"No. I want to do it myself. I'm trying to keep my hands busy—then my mind doesn't go off to places that make me crazy." She nodded to the cookie. "That's a new snickerdoodle recipe I got from Mrs. Rice last week. You just missed her. She came over to see how the retreat was going. She's being really nice lately."

Cat snorted and took a bite of the cookie. "She wants your job."

Shauna paused mid-fold. "What did you say?"

"She's convinced that you're going to want to be a kept woman as soon as you and Kevin get married. Especially once the babies start to arrive. She thinks you won't have time for the retreat." The cookie was actually pretty good. Cat guessed Mrs. Rice would be at least a passable replacement in the baking department if Shauna took off. "The cookie's good."

"Well, she can just keep her family recipes. I'm not leaving the best job I ever had. Besides, as a partner in the retreat, it's not just about the work. It's an investment of my time in our future."

"I thought you might see it that way." Or at least Cat had been hoping that was what was going through

Shauna's mind. "I've told her I'm not hiring, so then she did something very adult. She called dibs."

"So now if something happens to me, you have to hire her." Shauna laughed as she shook out the final towel. "Smart way to interview."

"All I know is you better not ever leave. I think I'd have to close the retreat if I worked with Mrs. Rice day in and day out." Cat finished the cookies, watching while her friend smoothed the stack of the clean laundry. She'd loved hearing her laugh, even if it was just for a minute. "Nothing from Uncle Pete yet?"

"No. And after the lecture I got the last time I called, I don't think I'll be dialing his number any time soon." Shauna worried the fabric from the top towel with her fingers. "Good news is all the guest rooms are made up and cleaned. And we have lunch ready anytime you want to eat."

"Where's Seth? I saw his truck still in the drive-way." Cat's stomach growled. She wanted to eat, but she could wait if Seth was busy for a few minutes.

"He took the SUV to Denver to pick up Sasha." She set the basket of towels on the floor. "They'll eat when they get back. I'm really happy she's taking the time to visit. I'm looking forward to hearing about her new life in the city."

"Well, her talk is scheduled for Wednesday, so you'll have a lot of time to talk before she flies back to California on Thursday." Cat hoped that having Sasha here as a distraction could help Shauna get through whatever this was. "Let's eat. I'm sure you haven't eaten anything all morning."

"You'd be right on that. I didn't even taste test

the cookie dough. And you know I love cookie dough."

Cat went to the cupboard and grabbed two soup bowls. Shauna went to the built-in oven and took out a foil-wrapped packet. She set it on the table, then went to the fridge to get butter and grabbed silverware, two small plates, and a couple of napkins. Cat brought the filled bowls to the table and watched while Shauna opened the foil. The scent of fresh bread filled the room.

"This is heaven." Cat sighed. As they ate, she watched her friend to make sure she was eating, knowing she was still worried. The soup did its magic. After a slow start, Shauna finished her bowl and two slices of the bread. The color in her face seemed to perk up as she ate. The body needed fuel, but during times of stress, many people tended to forget that.

They cleaned up the dinner dishes, and Shauna left the kitchen to return the now freshly laundered towels to the guest rooms upstairs. Cat saw her uncle's Jeep pull into the driveway and her heart sank. If it had been good news, he would have called so that Shauna wouldn't have to worry unnecessarily.

Even from this distance, Cat could tell her uncle's face was set in stone, and he made his way slowly up the driveway.

Cat met him at the door, helping him out of his coat. He slipped off his boots and put on the house slippers that Cat kept for his frequent visits. Finally, when he was done, she looked him in the face and sighed. "What happened?"

"Where is she? I think she deserves to hear this

first." He started toward the kitchen door, but when he had only made it halfway across the floor, the door flew open. Shauna stood in the opening. "Shauna . . ."

She crossed the room before he could finish and fell sobbing into his arms. "No, please, no."

Chapter 6

After he'd gotten Shauna into a chair, he joined her at the table and Cat put a hot mug of tea in her hands. She turned to her uncle. "Coffee?"

"Please." He waited until they were all sitting with hot drinks in front of them. Cat had put a box of tissues on the table. Pete put his hand over Shauna's. "We found him out in the horse barn. Before I go on, I need to ask you a question. How much do you want to know?"

"As much as you can tell me." Shauna sat taller, squaring her shoulders for the blow. "Did he freeze to death?"

"No." Uncle Pete looked at Cat, who nodded. As bad as it might be, Shauna needed to know the whole story. He sighed. "We think someone lured him out there about three this morning. There was a text on his phone just before that time. There appears to have been a scuffle."

"He couldn't make it back to the house or even the barn phone to call for help?" Shauna shook her head. "Kevin knew better than that. He'd been in one of the Gulf Wars. He'd been shot and lived through it. He would have lived through a simple altercation."

"I need to ask you a question, Shauna." He looked at Cat again, but when she didn't stop him, he sighed. "The coroner thinks maybe Kevin was poisoned. Was he feeling ill during the evening?"

She looked at him, any color in her face gone. A hand flew to her mouth. "I'm going to be sick."

Shauna ran out of the room and Uncle Pete leaned back into his chair. "I thought about how I was going to tell her the entire drive over here. She was so worried about him."

"Apparently for good reason." Cat sipped on her coffee. "She told me he wasn't feeling well, but they thought it was the flu. Who would poison him?"

"That's for me to find out. Thanks—that helps with the time frame. I don't want to bother her any more today. Once I get a final ruling on time and cause of death, I'll be back to ask her more about last night." Uncle Pete drained his coffee and then stood. "Tell Shauna I'm so sorry for her loss. I need to get to the station and start working this investigation."

Cat watched him leave. Then, as Shauna hadn't returned to the kitchen, Cat went looking for her. She found her in the downstairs bathroom, sitting on the floor, her head in her arms. "Hey, let's get you upstairs to your room. I'll bring up some videos and some drinks and you can take the day."

"I'm not sick." The muffled answer came from under her hair.

Cat kneeled next to her. "I know. But you might

be in shock. You need to rest somewhere besides this hard bathroom floor."

"I want to argue, but I think you're right. I need some time." She held her hand out. "Help me up. I'm taking a day to mourn Kevin, then I'm back on the clock until this retreat is over. Are you going to be okay setting up the treat room?"

"With all the food you made? I think I'd be fine for most of the week, if not the next retreat after this as well." Cat pulled Shauna up and then grabbed her for a hug. "I'm so sorry for your loss."

"I loved him. As big a jerk as he could be, I loved him." Shauna squeezed her. "I'm going upstairs. I'll see you tomorrow morning for breakfast."

"Do you want me to bring you up dinner?" Cat followed her out of the bathroom.

Shauna didn't look up. "Right now, I don't know if I'll ever eat again."

At one-thirty, the SUV pulled into the driveway, and Seth and Sasha poured into the kitchen. They were laughing about something, but the laughter died when Seth saw Cat's face. "What happened?"

She ran to him and fell into his outstretched arms. "They found Kevin. He's dead."

A gasp came from Sasha and Cat lifted her head. "I'm so sorry, I should have been more sensitive with that announcement."

"I'm just surprised. I mean, it's not like we don't have people die in South Cove. I don't know why I should be surprised that the same thing happens here." Sasha shook her head, her tight black curls shimmering in the kitchen lights. "Maybe I should go home?"

"No, we still have a retreat to get through. And

those people did pay for a writer's experience. Having you here will help make it feel more normal." Cat went over and gave Sasha a hug. "I'm so happy to see you. Let's get you settled in your room, then you can come down and have some lunch. I'm anxious to hear about what's been going on with you."

Seth followed them upstairs to the third floor. They'd just finished remodeling this guest bedroom so invited speakers didn't have to be on the same floor as the retreat guests. Cat liked the distinction between guest and staff, even if it was only in their sleeping arrangements. Everyone needed a little down time and privacy.

When Cat swung open the door, Sasha's quick intake of breath made Cat turn in concern. "Are you all right?"

Sasha walked into the room and sat on the bed, running a hand up the wrought-iron bedpost. Cat had decorated the bedroom in early medieval, kind of an homage to her *Game of Thrones* addiction. "Are you sure this is my room? I don't need something this fancy."

"It's your room until Thursday." Cat smiled as she looked around the room with its dark oak and marble furniture. "I guess I went a little crazy with the decorating."

"It's perfect." Sasha bounced on the bed and let out a squeal. "I'm FaceTiming Olivia tonight and showing her this. She's going to be so jealous. She loves playing princess."

Seth took the luggage rack out of the closet and set Sasha's case on it. "I'll see you downstairs."

He left the room, leaving the two women alone.

Sasha stood and put her hand on Cat's shoulder. "I'm sorry for your friend's pain. Losing someone you love is hard."

Cat nodded, not trusting her voice, but seeing the pain in Sasha's eyes too. There was something more the young woman wasn't saying, but it really wasn't Cat's place to ask. "Thank you. The desk is filled with pen and paper, including a few note-books. There's fresh towels in the bath, and the television has a good selection of channels. You get all settled and come down when you're ready. Shauna made soup for lunch, but if you want something else . . ."

"Soup will be lovely." Sasha sat back down on the bed. "Although I really don't want to leave this room ever."

"Your talk is scheduled for Wednesday. The rest of the time is yours to do with as you wish." Cat moved to the hallway. She started closing the door, then paused. "We really are glad to see you, Sasha."

As she walked past Shauna's room, she considered stopping, but as she paused, she heard the music flowing through the door. Carole King. Shauna liked her music sad and soulful. She decided to let her friend mourn in private. At least for a while. Besides, she'd told Shauna she would set up the dining room and the guests were due back from the library soon.

Cat brushed her hand on the door and said a quiet prayer for Shauna before heading downstairs to work. One more retreat that would be marred by murder. Cat shook her head at the coincidence. Maybe the house—or, more likely, either she or Shauna—was cursed. Even Uncle Pete said Aspen

Hills had been quieter, and probably safer, before she'd moved back. The stress must have shown on her face because, when she entered the kitchen, Seth stopped setting places at the table and walked over to her.

"Are you okay?" He pulled her into his arms and she laid her head on his chest.

Trying to match his breathing helped her keep away the tears she'd been building up to all the way down the stairs. She mumbled into his flannel shirt, "I don't want to be cursed."

He pushed her away so he could see her face. Wiping away the tears that had fallen, he shook his head. "Stop talking nonsense. Neither you nor Shauna, or even this house, is cursed. You've just had a run of bad luck, that's all. Nothing supernatural about that, not at all."

She shook her head, and, honestly, she almost agreed with him. "Even if we are, I don't have time for a pity party. I need to fill Shauna's shoes for at least today. Can you help me set up the dining room for afternoon treats?"

"Of course. We're a team, right?" He turned back to the countertops filled with baked goods. "What do you want to serve?"

They carried out several plates of treats, refilled the hot water and the coffee carafes, and restocked the fridge with the sodas and juices. After they were done, Cat stood back, nodding at the room. "Looks almost as good as if Shauna had done it herself."

"High praise. Now, can I eat?" He held the door open for her and they went into the kitchen, trying to keep the conversation light.

Sasha joined them a few minutes later. As she got settled, Cat put the focus on the new arrival. "I hope I'm not prying, but Shauna said you left Coffee, Books, and More. Tell me why you're not at the bookstore anymore. I thought you loved working there. What was your boss's name again? Jill?"

"Jill Gardner. And, I did love it. But even Jill will tell you that I did the right thing by accepting the marketing internship last summer. They are paying for all costs at school this year, and the money Jill gave me as a grant covers Olivia's preschool and daycare. And in June, when I graduate, I have a full-time position with the company. It's a win-win."

"It sounds like it. I'm still paying off my student loans," Cat said.

"I should be debt free in two years with what they're paying me including my housing. It's a great job." She spun her spoon around in her soup. "It's just not as fun as running the youth book clubs and dealing with the bookstore. I guess if I have to work for a living, I might as well make good money. Besides, Jill still lets me read and review for their newsletter and the staff picks column on their website."

"Best of both worlds, then." Seth smiled. "Sometimes you don't get to do exactly what you want in life, at least not at the beginning. We all have starter jobs. Mine was in the army. I like working for myself much better."

"I know I'm lucky, and believe me, I'm not complaining. Coffee, Books, and More was just a sweet spot to learn the ropes of working an adult job."

After the meal, Sasha excused herself to go call her daughter. Seth and Cat cleaned up the dishes from lunch. Cat didn't look at him as she washed the dishes to go into the dishwasher. "So I always expected you to go career in the military. That's what you talked about when you joined."

"I changed my mind." He put the leftover soup from the pot into a storage container. "Look, I need to tell you something."

"About us?" Cat turned off the water, busying herself so she didn't have to look at him. Standing next to him in the kitchen was powerful enough. She didn't think she could deal with the emotions that would swamp her if she had to look at him.

"No, not about us." He moved closer. "I don't know why you always go there first."

"Sorry. So what do you want to tell me?" She turned toward him, folding the dishtowel over the sink.

"Shauna had a bottle of cyanide in her stuff when she left to go to the ranch yesterday."

The implication hung in the air. Cat felt like someone had hit her in the gut. "What are you saying? You think Shauna poisoned Kevin? Why would she do such a thing? She'd said yes. They were going to get married."

"I didn't say she poisoned him." He shook his head. "Look, let's just forget I mentioned it. Maybe there was a good reason she had poison in her basket next to the Irish stew she fed him for dinner and avoided eating herself."

"That's cold." Cat was furious. "There is no way she'd do something like that."

Seth shrugged. "You know her better than I do. I mean, people do stupid things sometimes in the name of love."

"Let's just change the subject. Shauna couldn't have done something cruel like that." Cat sank into a kitchen chair. No matter what Seth said, she trusted Shauna. But the question rolled around in her brain, haunting her. Why did she have cyanide in her box? "What were we talking about?"

"Why I chose not to continue a career in the military."

Cat nodded. At least this subject didn't have any land mines. Not like Shauna and who had killed Kevin. "Why did you leave the service?"

"I was done." He shrugged. "It didn't make sense in my life plan anymore."

"Just like that?" She snuck a look in his direction. He was staring right at her. This conversation was almost as weird as the Shauna one had been.

"You really don't know why I didn't reenlist?" He leaned against the stove, waiting for an answer.

"No." Cat didn't know if she wanted to know. Not now. Her breath caught in her throat as she waited.

He closed the lid on the soup and took it over to the fridge, setting it inside before he answered. "I went into the service to build a life for us. When you married Michael, I didn't want that life anymore."

"Seth, I'm sorry." Memories of him standing in the back of the church as she'd taken her vows with another man seared her heart. She'd been so in love with Michael, she'd thought the choice she'd made had been the right one. Now, she didn't know.

"Water under the bridge." He nodded to the window. "I better get out there and scrape the ice off the sidewalk. Your guests should be getting back anytime."

He didn't say another word, just shrugged into his coat and left through the kitchen door. A cold wind whipped through the room as he left. Cat felt the chill all the way to her bones.

The group arrived back at the house promptly at two-thirty. Milling around the dining room, they all filled plates with sweets and sat at the table with warm drinks. "You guys are on your own for dinner. But before you leave, I'd like to introduce you to Sasha Smith. She'll be doing a bookstore relations discussion on Wednesday. I'm sure she'd love to tag along."

"We were going to The Diner. Collin says it's a must-do in Aspen Hills." Shirley spoke for the group. "We'll be glad to add one more to our group. Are you sure you and your crew don't want to join us?"

Cat shook her head as she debated how much to tell the guests about Kevin's murder. They'd find out sooner or later. Aspen Hills was too small not to talk about one of its wealthiest citizens being killed. "Actually, one of Shauna's close friends just died, so I think I should stay close to the house."

"I'm so sorry." Shirley's eyes gleamed in that cop way that said she wasn't as sorry as she was curious. "Anything I—I mean, we—can do?"

"No, I just didn't want you to be surprised if you hear any gossip around town. Shauna's pretty torn up about it so giving her some space would be appreciated." Cat checked her watch. "I'll be in the kitchen if anyone needs anything. And tomorrow, Professor Turner will be here around ten for his lecture on Hemingway. He's a nationally known scholar on the subject and curates the library's Hemingway collection."

Cat didn't mention that Professor Turner had also for a short time been Dean Turner, but when the college had picked the candidate to fill the permanent position last month, he'd lost it to a professor out of Boston. Cat wondered if Covington politics had more to do with the selection than either professor's resume, but she'd hold that thought to herself.

At least until tomorrow, when she could try to find out more from Professor Turner.

When she got back to the kitchen, Seth was there, watching the sports channel on the small television that Shauna kept on the sideboard. He turned the volume down when he saw her enter. "Sidewalks are all cleared. Anything else you need me to do? I'm not used to just sitting around on a work day."

"You're on call. It's not really a nine-to-five job. You just need to be available anytime we need you." She poured a cup of coffee and opened up the laptop. "You can watch the game. I'm going to work on the accounting review."

"You're paying me like it's a real job. I should be doing something." He slapped his head. "I was going to take the books over to the library today."

Cat waved him down as he started to stand. "Hold off and do that tomorrow. It's late afternoon and you know Miss Applebome likes to leave promptly at three. She won't like it if you try to donate these when she's not there."

"You mean she won't like you. Miss Applebome loves me. At least she does ever since I built her a front porch on that little house of hers." He walked over to the fridge and grabbed a Coke. "And I know, no alcohol during the week either."

"I need you available." Cat grinned. "Honestly, it's not that bad."

"Sure, you get to drink at the dinner Saturday. I'm the designated driver." He cracked open the soda and took a long drink. "I was going to pick up a pizza and watch the game in my room. Want to join me?"

"You can pick me up a veggie pie and I'll try to entice Shauna with some. Sasha is going to The Diner with the group." Cat opened the file on her desktop. "But otherwise, I think I'll read in the living room and pretend to be an author for our guests."

"You don't have to pretend. You are an author, even if you have a weakness for college basketball." He kissed her on the head and sat back down. "This is kind of nice, you know."

She looked up from the computer, distracted. "This?"

"Playing house. I'm liking playing house with you, even if we don't share a room." Seth's phone rang. He glanced at the display. "And that's my cue to leave. Hank must have found some time in his schedule."

Cat watched as Seth walked out of the room. He was having no problem picking up their relationship from the spot they'd left it so many years ago. So why was she? She went back to the accounting and was just finishing up when Shirley popped her head into the kitchen.

"There you are. I guess we missed our three-o'clock date." Shirley pulled on her coat as she walked, looking around the empty room as she approached.

"Sorry about that. Things got a little hectic around here." Cat hadn't wanted to tell everyone that Shauna's fiancé was dead, but Shirley would have already heard from Uncle Pete.

"No worries, we can do it later." She glanced around the empty kitchen. "You sure you don't want to come to dinner with us? It looks like your cook's MIA." And Seth's pizza-run offer had vanished once he had received the call from Hank.

"She's upstairs." Cat closed out the program, releasing a sigh to have the job completed. Numbers weren't her thing. It must be the fact she was so word driven. Words made sense. Seeing patterns in numbers, that didn't. "We'll be fine. In fact, I was just going to take out a casserole and pop it into the oven. I'd rather not leave her, just in case she needs something."

"Okay then. I just thought I'd offer. Your friend Sasha is coming with us. She's very unusual." Shirley pulled on her green beanie.

"Why do you say that?" Cat stood, but she didn't move away from the table. If the woman was going to bash Sasha for her race, she'd rather it happen here in the kitchen, where Cat could put her straight.

"She's such a strong woman, for someone so young. She told us the story of how she had her daughter young, then found the internship at the coffee house. Now, she's on the path to make almost six figures when she graduates." Shirley patted her heart over the puffy ski jacket. "It does a feminist good to see the next generation stepping up and taking care of what they need to do in order to succeed."

Feeling slightly embarrassed at what she had thought the older woman was going to say, Cat detoured toward the fridge to take the beef stroganoff from the freezer. "She is pretty amazing. That's one of the reasons I wanted her to come and talk to your group. She's the proof there's more than one road to Oz."

Shirley headed to the door. "Don't wait up for us. I believe at least a few of us are going out to Bernie's for drinks after dinner. I'm going to try to get the entire gang to go. I'd love to talk to them about their writing journeys."

The house grew quiet after the front door closed. Cat knew Shauna and Seth were still inside, but it felt empty. She put the casserole in the oven, checked that she'd turned it on to the correct temperature. Then checked again. One ruined dish a week was all she was having on her watch.

She went into the dining room, cleaned up the empty dishes, and refilled the drinks. Then she brought out new treats, carefully leaving the plastic on to keep them fresh. It took her longer than she'd wanted, but she didn't want Shauna's absence to be noticed by the guests. Nor did she want her friend to feel like she needed to work if she didn't want to. Finding out about Kevin had been a shock, even to Cat. She could only imagine what Shauna was going through.

Glancing around the gleaming dining room, she called the refresh done and took her empty trays back into the kitchen. A knock at the door made her jump as she washed the trays off in the sink.

Crossing over to the door, she realized Kevin's assistant stood there in the gathering darkness. In the winter, night fell early in Colorado. She'd missed that when she'd been in California. The darkening sky, the chill gave her an excuse to cuddle up with a good book. In California, she'd felt like she was wasting the light if she didn't stay active and about. She opened the door.

"Paul, I'm so sorry about Kevin. Do you have news?" She stepped aside to let him in and realized he held a large box.

He came in and dumped the box on the floor, then returned to the porch, where he'd left a large suitcase.

Since he hadn't spoken, Cat had a bad feeling she wasn't going to like the answer, but asked the question anyway. "What's all this?"

"I don't mean to be rude, but the family is coming in tomorrow morning and, well, I thought it better if Shauna's things weren't all over the house." Paul adjusted his leather gloves and rocked back and forth from one foot to the other. "How is she?"

"She's in her room." She didn't want to give him any details of how wrecked Shauna really was, especially since, when she found out he'd cleaned her presence out of the house, well, Cat believed the Irish temper would explode. "What family? His parents?"

"Kevin's parents are dead." He gnawed at his bottom lip. "Jade and the boys are coming. They might not have been married, but Kevin was important to her. And of course, he was the father to her children. They should be here to mourn."

"Wait, Kevin had kids? Who's Jade?" Cat thought about the few conversations she'd had with Shauna about the reclusive rancher. Had she even known?

"If it's any of your business, yes. He actually has three sons, two with Jade and one with his high school sweetheart. Although he broke ties with that boy as soon as he turned eighteen." Paul glanced at his watch. "I don't see how this is any of your business. Besides, I really need to be going. I just wanted to . . ."

"I know, dump all her stuff here so that this Jade woman wouldn't know Shauna existed. You know she's going to be at the funeral, right? And people in town knew they were dating." Cat narrowed her eyes, hoping her distaste for the man and his actions showed. "She's grieving too. They might not have been married, but she loved him."

Paul dropped the suitcase next to the box. "Look, I've got to go. You can tell Shauna she can keep the suitcase. No one's going to miss it."

Cat watched the man skulk toward the kitchen door, too shocked at his attitude to stop him. She was still standing watching out the window at the darkening evening when Seth came up behind her. He put his arms around her and pulled her back into him. He leaned down and whispered into her ear, "Are you okay?"

"Better than Paul's going to be when Shauna finds out what he just did."

Chapter 7

Cat sat trying to read in the living room. She'd had Seth put the box and suitcase upstairs in her office, hoping to figure out a way to tell Shauna about Paul's actions—and about Kevin's secret kids. Of course, maybe they weren't secret to Shauna. Maybe she already knew about his family? Apparently, with Kevin gone, Paul made the decisions about what happened at the ranch and, probably, in Kevin's business dealings. The man was perfect for running a business. He had no heart.

She closed the book and set it aside on the coffee table. She wasn't going to be able to lose herself in the high fantasy story, not tonight. She couldn't follow the names, and she was sure she'd read the same page at least ten times.

Cat paced through the first floor, stopping here and there to straighten a rug or a pillow, or, worse, grab a cookie from the dining room. When the clock on the wall struck nine, she gave up waiting for the guests. They could find their way to their rooms when they finally came in from their night at

Bernie's. She turned down the lights, leaving some on so that when the group did come in, they could see their way. Besides, they might stay up and use the living room as a gathering spot to keep the discussion going. Book people didn't like to stop talking once they'd found others who loved talking about story structure as much as they did.

She made her way to her room and collapsed on the bed, fully clothed, and fell right asleep.

The next morning, she was halfway down the stairs, showered and dressed, when the smells from the kitchen hit her. She glanced at her watch. She'd gotten up early, and yet, apparently, Shauna had gotten up earlier than she had.

A plate of muffins was already on the table and the coffeepot looked full. Shauna stood at the counter, feeding sugar into her mixer as she started yet another batch of desserts. "Are you sure we need all these?"

Shauna didn't turn before she answered. "Baking makes me feel better. I want to punch someone, but instead, I'm making muffins. Aren't there stages of grief? Maybe I'm in the 'keeping myself busy' stage. Anything happen last night that I should know about?"

Cat poured herself a cup of coffee, then went over and sat at the table. No time like the present. "Come sit with me. I have something we need to talk about."

Shauna turned off the mixer and refilled her own cup before sitting down. "I don't like that look.

Which one of our guests wound up dead last night?
Or are they just in jail?"

Trying to keep the smile off her face, Cat shook
her head. "Neither." She went on to tell Shauna
about Paul's visit and what he'd brought, and about
the kids and baby mama coming into town today.
"Did you know he had kids?"

Shauna nodded. "He'd told me about Kerry and
Todd. They're twins. Apparently, Jade was visiting
Paul one summer, and, well, things got out of hand
one night."

"Jade was Paul's girlfriend?" Cat set her cup
down. She knew her eyes must be as wide as saucers.
She hadn't liked Kevin, but this seemed low, even
for him.

Shauna took a sip of coffee before she answered.
"No, Jade is Paul's sister. So his nephews are now
the heirs to the ranch, the business, and all of
Kevin's land holdings. Paul just became trustee to
a very large estate until those boys turn eighteen."

Cat sat back, stunned. She met Shauna's gaze.
"That's interesting, don't you think?"

"What's more interesting is, had we been married, I would have been inheriting." Shauna rubbed
her shoulder. "I don't want to think badly about the
man, but Paul was the reason Kevin asked me not
to wear my ring. He said Paul would come around
eventually. But now he doesn't have to, does he?"

The kitchen was quiet for a few minutes as they
each thought about Paul's position. Finally, Cat
stood to refresh her coffee. "Have you mentioned
this to Uncle Pete?"

"No. And I don't want you to either. Just because

Paul didn't like me doesn't mean he didn't love Kevin. There is no way he could have hurt him. None. The man worshiped Kevin." Shauna laid her head on the table, and her red hair made a circle around her. "I just want to wake up and have this be a bad dream."

"There's one more thing I need to ask." Cat felt like a heel bringing this up. She would have ignored the idea if the source hadn't been Seth. "Shauna, why did you have cyanide when you went to the ranch?"

"What are you talking about? I didn't have . . ." She ran her hand through her hair. "The rat poison I picked up at the hardware store for Kevin. It's cyanide. Is that what killed him?"

Cat shrugged. "I don't know. I don't even know if Uncle Pete knows yet. Why did you have rat poison?"

"How did you know about that . . . ? Never mind. Whatever I say, it's going to look bad, isn't it?" Shauna stood up to pace. "Kevin's been having problems with mice out in the barns. I told him I'd pick up something and bring it out so he didn't have to make a special trip. When I got there, he gave the bottle to his ranch manager and I didn't see it again."

"You need to tell Uncle Pete this."

Shauna glanced at the clock. "I'm surprised he hasn't come by yet. I guess he wants his ducks in order before he talks to the main suspect."

"I'm sure you aren't the main suspect." But even as she said it, Cat knew she and Shauna were probably fooling themselves if they thought any different.

This was bad. Cat needed to find out who had killed Kevin and fast.

The room was quiet until Shauna came back to sit. She put her head in her hands. "This is a complete nightmare. And I just miss him."

Cat knew how her friend felt. She'd felt exactly the same way many times after the divorce. She'd roll over in bed, reaching out her hand to Michael, but the other side of the bed would be empty. And had been for months before she stopped automatically reaching out in the early morning hours.

"Let's get through today. One day at a time. Do you know when the funeral is?" Cat hated seeing her hurt this much.

"No. I guess it might be a while, since your uncle is still investigating. Isn't that what happens in cop shows? The body can't be released to the family?" She lifted her head and ran her hands over her face. "I just called Kevin 'the body.' And I'm going to be shut out of all the discussions and decisions because I'm not family. This is awful."

"We'll get through this. I'm so sorry." Cat watched as Shauna took a deep breath and shook off the grief.

"Well, I may not be Charming Charlie the next few days, but I won't be a Sobbing Sally, not while we have guests in the house." Shauna put on a small smile. "Besides, the way these things go, I'm guessing Kevin's funeral should be delayed at least for a few days. And by then the guests will be gone. Then I'm locking myself up in my room with a bottle of whisky and drinking that guy out of my mind."

"If you need time . . ." Cat started, but Shauna stood and pulled her hair back into a tight bun.

"No need to wallow now—there's work to be done. And where did you put the stuff that weasel brought last night? I'll put it away in my room and save the unpacking for the crying day." She wiped the back of her hand under her eyes. "I probably just smeared my mascara, didn't I?"

"You look fine." As Cat watched her friend, she was amazed at the strength and determination she saw in Shauna's face. The girl would be all right. There would be some bad nights to come, but Shauna was strong. And losing Kevin had just made her stronger. "The box and the suitcase are in my office."

"Well, then, time to get breakfast going. Those guests of ours are enjoying the food offerings. Or else you didn't put out treats last night for their after-dinner snack." The timer went off on the oven, and Shauna walked over and pulled out a pan of brownies.

"I filled up all the trays." Cat felt offended by her friend's lack of trust. "I refreshed the drinks, put out cookies and brownies, and even set up some fruit. There were tons when I went to bed."

"Like I said, our group likes to eat. The fresh fruit was still there, but the baked goods were down to crumbs." Shauna broke off a crumb from the brownies and popped it into her mouth. "I guess it's good we aren't claiming to be a healthy retreat. I bet some of our friends leave here with a few extra pounds on them."

As Shauna laughed at the idea, the sound made

Cat smile. She was happy to have cheered Shauna for a little while. "Before I head upstairs to work, I'm walking through the downstairs to get ready for the day. Professor Turner is coming at ten-ish. The group should be through with breakfast by then."

"I've already cleaned up the mess they left in the living room, but I didn't check the study. Since Seth's friend hasn't been here to fix the nonexistent attic heat, would you check in there and make sure it's at least clean of leftover food?"

Cat filled up a travel mug with coffee. She grabbed a muffin off the table and started eating it as she left the hallway. Shauna was an amazing baker. A few months ago, she'd talked about making a cookbook for the retreat. Maybe Cat should help her get started with that so she'd have something to do besides grieve her loss this month.

She walked into the study and almost dropped her coffee.

"I really don't mean to scare you. I was waiting for you to awaken. Your friend Ms. Clodagh is an early riser, isn't she?"

Dante Cornelio sat at Michael's desk, his long wool coat draped over the top. He was drinking coffee from a mug advertising the coffee shop downtown, The Morning Bean.

"I would like it if you actually knocked on the door at least once before breaking and entering. What is this, a family tradition?" Cat felt furious. How could she get on with her life with the past sneaking in at all times of the day? She could see that she'd scored a point when Dante winced. He'd told her a few months ago that Martin, his nephew, had been the one who'd been causing all the strange noises in her house along with a series of prank telephone calls. The kid had been trying to scare her. Dante just liked surprising her.

"Martin has apologized for his misdoings. And he still raves about Ms. Clodagh's beef stew. Apparently, it's better than his mom's." A sad smile creased his lips, causing a dimple to form on one cheek. "I'm sorry for her loss."

Darn, the man was handsome. Short blond hair, sea-green eyes, chiseled chin—he could pose for a romance cover. Cat sat down in her reading chair, using the small table to free her hands of the muffin and coffee. She rubbed her hands on her jeans. "I'm really not in the mood for small talk. What do you want, Dante?"

He looked at her, a mix of pity and amusement bouncing in his gaze. "Very well, I will get to the point. You have to realize, though, I am interested in you, Catherine. Very interested."

"Well, if that's why you're here, we can end this now. I'm dating someone and not on the market for another relationship." She paused, waiting for a reaction. When none came, she cocked an eyebrow. "Are we done?"

"Actually, there was something I needed to speak with you about. I'm afraid the Michael problem hasn't completely gone away. I'd hoped that by leaving the issue alone that, well, some people would also leave you alone."

A cold chill ran down Cat's back. She knew the

answer to her question before she asked it. "What Michael issue?"

"You trying to figure out why he's dead. That issue, or had you truly forgotten about your husband and his untimely death?" Dante stood, and picked up his coat. "I will do all I can do to keep you safe, but you need to be careful."

"Keep me safe from who?" Cat couldn't move. "Was Michael working for you?"

Dante slipped on his coat and then paused next to her. He brushed her hair out of her eyes with one finger. "You are quite remarkable. Just stay safe, please."

He stroked her hair, then left the room. When Cat got her breath back, she jerked upright and ran to the lobby. It was empty. She looked up the stairs and then burst into the kitchen.

Shauna jumped at the movement. She put her hand over her heart. "You scared me. Did you get the study cleaned?"

"Did he leave?" Cat ran to the door and peered out the window.

"What are you talking about? Did who leave?"

Cat turned around and faced her friend. "Dante Cornelio."

Shauna's eyes widened. "He was here?"

"He just left the study. I didn't see him in the lobby so I thought he came through here." She walked over to her friend. "So he didn't come through the kitchen."

"No. Believe me, if I'd seen Dante stroll through my kitchen, I would have stopped him and made him tell me why he was here in the first place."

Shauna went to refill her coffee cup. "Do you need more?"

"Let me go get my cup, and I'll tell you why he was here." Cat headed to the study to retrieve her coffee and treat. She glanced around the empty space. How had Dante left so quickly? Through the front door? Or had he popped into the dining room to refill his coffee and left after Cat had run into the kitchen? The guy was human, not a spectral image. Or at least she thought so.

She went back into the kitchen and told Shauna about her conversation with Dante. As she finished up, Shauna summarized her feelings about what Cat had relayed in one word. "Crap."

"I know, right?" Cat took a second muffin. "So what do you think he meant by keeping me safe? Am I on some Mob guy's hit list now? For wondering what happened to Michael? It doesn't seem fair."

"Or you were getting too close to the truth." Shauna tapped a fingernail painted a glossy black on the table. "I'm glad I asked Seth to stay over this week. Things are getting strange around here."

"No more than usual. And I was thinking we might have a quiet retreat this month." Cat rolled her shoulders. "Anyway, I have things I need to get done. I can't be worried about who and when someone's going to whack me."

"You should call your uncle." Shauna nodded to add emphasis to her words, more to herself than anyone else. She did that when she was stressed. Cat liked to call it "convincing yourself."

"I don't know. It's not like he said anything Uncle

Pete could follow up on. And he's already told me to stay away from Dante." Of course, with him showing up all the time at the house, unannounced, it wasn't really her fault. It wasn't like she was going looking for him. Besides, it was her house. If she called Uncle Pete about anything, it would be to have him tell Dante to stop showing up. "Like that would do any good," she muttered

Seth strolled into the kitchen dressed in jeans and a John Denver T-shirt. He poured himself a cup of coffee, sat at the table, and opened the paper. Then he asked, "What?"

"Nothing you need to worry about." Cat shot Shauna a look, and her friend shrugged and gave a look that said, *It's your life.* "What's on your schedule today?"

"Hank is coming by around noon and hopefully, we'll get your attic up to a reasonable temperature. Do you need me for something?"

"The books?" Cat pulled out her own calendar and looked at the to-do list. "Maybe we should put that off until next week once the retreat's over?"

"I can take them over this morning if I can use the SUV. I don't want the boxes to get wet." He pulled out the sports section and passed the local over to Shauna. "You know I'm not buying the 'nothing I need to worry about,' right?"

Shauna paused, her hand on the front page. "I was going to take it this morning. My compact doesn't do well with icy roads."

"Do we need groceries?" Cat glanced at the fridge. She'd thought it had looked full, but then again, Shauna had been on a baking tear the last couple days.

"No . . ." Shauna rubbed the back of her neck.

Now Cat was curious. "Then where are you going?"

Shauna stood and walked to the oven to check on her strata. "If you have to know, I'm going out to the ranch to give Paul a piece of my mind."

Chapter 8

Cat looked at the clock. Shauna had left over an hour ago. On good days, it took thirty minutes to get to the ranch. The roads were clear. She should already be on her way back.

Professor Turner was telling his one and only Hemingway joke to start up the lecture. The joke Cat had heard at least a dozen times. Each time, he got a few titters, but even Cat with an English degree didn't understand the literary reference. She sat in the corner, her notebook in her lap, but instead of working on the plot outline for her next book, she was writing down everything she knew about Kevin.

She had no plans to try to solve Kevin's murder, but she really needed Uncle Pete to figure it out so Shauna could move on with her life. Of course, if information just happened to fall into her lap, she wouldn't look the other way. Who was she kidding? She'd become addicted to the rush of adrenaline solving a murder gave her.

So far, Cat had Paul at the top of the list with two stars. No matter what Shauna thought, the guy had

monetary reasons to want Kevin gone. And how did
he really feel about Shauna and Kevin's engagement? Cat also wrote down Paul's sister. It wasn't a
big stretch that a woman who was raising Kevin's
sons wouldn't be excited to hear that her baby
daddy was getting married. And what about this
high school sweetheart whose son had been cut off
when the kid hit eighteen? That had to sting. She'd
been thinking about this for less than an hour and
had three good suspects. And that was only a list of
possible killers based on Kevin's love life. There
had to be a bunch of suspects from his business
dealings. The man was known as a hard-driving
businessman. He'd bought most of his land holdings at rock-bottom prices when the prior owners
were unable to pull out of debt.

She needed to stop thinking about Kevin and
who, besides her friend, would want to kill him.
Sometimes her best ideas came when she was thinking about something else. And Cat had plenty to
think about. She turned the page and stared at the
white, blank space. She needed a new story. In
Tori's world, it was the summer before junior year.
Before Cat knew it, her main character would
graduate and move on to college. Should the series
follow her, or should she start with a new fish-out-
of-water character and keep the high school setting?
Maybe Tori has a cousin? Cat had a lot of questions,
but not very many answers. Yet.

She made notes about a new main character and
spinning the series off into eight new books. She
could take this series and follow Tori to college.
She made a note to email her agent about the idea,

then started working on Tori's summer plans. By the time the lecture was over, she had a good start on the new book. Where it would start, what the main conflict would be, and where it would end. Everything in between was up to Tori and the other characters. Or at least, that's how the process had worked for the last three books. She didn't want to look too hard at the muse or change things up while they were working.

Professor Turner was already packing his suitcase, and the room was empty besides the two of them. Her guests would be making their way to town for lunch soon. Maybe she should schedule his talk for later in the day, to keep people talking longer, but Cat knew some groups just didn't love Hemingway. A fact she couldn't tell the professor since he didn't understand the concept.

"Thank you for coming. It was a lovely lecture." Cat tucked her notebook under her arm. Professor Turner didn't need to know she hadn't been furiously taking notes during his session.

"I'm afraid I'm a little flat this month. What with losing the dean position, and the theft of a prized piece of the Hemingway collection, personally it's been a bad winter." He looked up from his packing and gave Cat a small smile. "I'm awaiting the arrival of spring to set my mood to happier things."

"I was sorry to hear they brought in someone from another school for the position." Cat handed him the coat he'd laid on the desk when he walked in. "It's not fair, especially since you were doing such a great job as acting dean."

"You are too kind, but I believe I was just surviving.

And the board knew that." He slipped on his wool coat. "I've come to accept that administration isn't one of my strengths. I'm better in the classroom, enriching young minds."

"Well, I'm just glad you have time for my retreat guests. Having the Hemingway papers here at Covington adds to the draw of my retreat." Cat walked with him to the front door. "Thanks again. I know they all enjoyed the discussion."

"Hemingway is a fascinating fellow. Who wouldn't enjoy an hour listening to stories about one of the masters of the craft?" Professor Turner wrapped his scarf around his neck and opened the front door. "See you next month, Catherine."

Cat closed the door behind him and turned and leaned into it. Another man who insisted on calling her Catherine. What was it with teachers? She'd never gotten any of her elementary, junior high, or high school teachers to call her Cat. Just Cat. Three little letters. When she'd gone to Covington, she'd registered that way, and, therefore, no one had had her first name. Until she'd started teaching and Dean Vargas had insisted she use her full name as it sounded more professional.

She closed her eyes and thought about the argument they'd had on the subject just after he'd hired her. Looking back, she knew if Michael hadn't intervened in her getting the job, her inability to keep her mouth shut with the dean would have blackballed her from teaching not only at Covington, but at a lot of the local colleges. But the school hadn't wanted to lose one of their best economic professors. Cat heard footsteps and looked up to find Shirley watching her.

"The man could put a meth head to sleep." Shirley held up her travel mug. "I should have stocked up on coffee before going into that seminar. I thought I'd liked the stories, but after that lecture, I started to wonder who even reads Hemingway anymore?"

"College kids." Cat pushed herself away from the door. "Are you on your way into town for lunch?"

"In a few. I wanted to find out where I could look through your ex-husband's papers. I suppose you've already gotten rid of a lot of them, but a good detective never assumes anything." Shirley took a sip of coffee as she waited.

"You really don't need to work on this. You're here for your writing, not to find out who killed Michael." Cat felt uncomfortable even talking about this. She'd tried to dissuade Shirley earlier, but apparently, the hint had fallen on deaf ears.

"I don't need to, I want to. Besides, you and your uncle have been so gracious, I'd like to return the favor. Just let me do my thing, and if I haven't found anything by week's end, I'll go back to Alaska and forget about it. Honestly, once I get home, I'll be too busy to worry much about some cold case." She held out one hand, palm up. "What can it hurt?"

Cat thought about Dante's warning. If she allowed Shirley to dig into Michael's past, would that rile up anyone who was still watching the house? She made a quick decision: no man was going to sneak into her house, scare her, then dictate what she could and couldn't do about her history. "You're right." She pointed toward the stairs. "There are a bunch of boxes in my office on the third floor. I've been going through them and trying to determine what, if anything, I'm going to keep."

"I'll also need a new spiral notebook. Got any of those up there?"

"Third drawer in my file cabinet. There should be a stack from last year's back-to-school sales." *In for a penny, in for a pound*, she thought.

As she watched Shirley go up the stairs, she saw Sasha come down. Cat met her at the bottom of the stairs. "How are things going? Are you enjoying your time?"

Sasha broke into a big grin. "It's been lovely. I spent the morning cuddled up on my window seat reading, attended the Hemingway session, and now, Pamela and Melissa want me to go to lunch with them to talk about the whole bookstore business."

"I'm glad you're having fun." Cat was also glad Sasha had lunch plans since Shauna still wasn't back from the ranch and there was nothing cooking in the kitchen. "I'd love to take you to dinner tonight. It would be just you, me, Shauna, and Seth, if he's not busy. We need to catch up on your life. You've had some big changes."

A brief look of pain crossed Sasha's face, and for a second, Cat wondered if she'd said something wrong. Then the look was gone and a smile replaced it.

"I'd love to." She looked around the lobby. "This really is a lovely home. I can't quite believe you're opening it up to share it with people like me."

"Smart, intelligent book lovers like you?"

Sasha laughed. "You know, sometimes I still feel like that scared teenager who didn't know what she was going to do with no job, no education, and a little baby who was depending on her. I didn't always make the best choices in life."

"And yet, look at you now. You're on a great path and you've given your little girl the best gift ever." Cat appraised the pretty young woman standing in front of her. Sasha had gone through some hard years and made it out, if not unscarred, stronger. "You're teaching her to follow her dreams."

Sasha gave Cat a quick hug. "And you're opening up another whole world for me. I just might go home with more dreams for the future."

"That's not a bad place to be in your life." Cat glanced at the clock. "Meet me down here at six and we'll head over to the new farm-to-table restaurant out near the highway. Shauna's been dying to eat there."

As Melissa and Pamela came chatting down the stairs, Cat watched the twenty-something women get ready to leave. They weren't much younger than Cat, but they all had their lives ahead of them. She'd been married, divorced, and kind of widowed, and had worked as a professor and now a writer and hostess for a retreat. That was more than some people had happen to them in a lifetime. And yet, she knew there was more ahead for her. A family maybe? She hoped Shauna could bounce back from losing Kevin and this didn't derail her from her own future. Kicking Paul's butt this morning was probably a good sign she was working through the grief steps.

Cat went into the kitchen to work on her book outline while she waited for Shauna to come back. She made a note on tomorrow's list for Seth to drop off Michael's books at the library. As she pondered the Michael thing, she wondered what, if anything, Shirley would find in the papers. She'd still have to go through the boxes just to make sure there wasn't anything personal or embarrassing to Michael's memory before she handed them over to Professor Ngu. After the brief encounter she'd had yesterday, she still felt there was something he wasn't telling her. He hadn't even blinked when she walked in, demanding information, even after she'd told him to back off at the restaurant. Of course, the guy did have a job besides annoying Cat.

Frustrated, she closed her notebook and grabbed a soda out of the fridge. She wasn't getting anything done on the new book anyway. She looked one more time out the window at the completely empty street and then headed into the study. She could finish cleaning out the desk while she waited and most of the guests were out of the house.

She paused before opening the door. Then, hating herself for the hesitation, she pushed through the doorway. If Dante was sitting in Michael's chair, this time she'd call Uncle Pete. She was done feeling uncertain in her own home. And whatever this place used to be for her and Michael, now it was her home. And she wouldn't be intimidated by a room or a man who really shouldn't be in her life in the first place.

No one sat at Michael's desk. *The desk*, she corrected herself. She scanned the room. Nothing else out of place. The box she'd been filling with Michael's personal items sat next to the desk, half full. Boxes of books lined one wall, waiting for Seth to take them to the library. And the bookshelf was more than half empty. She'd have to start changing that. She could bring down a set of her own books for guests to read. A subtle marketing idea, but she didn't like the whole *Look at me, I'm an author* thing her publicist insisted on every time a new book was released. And as the books started gaining traction, she'd been asked to do more and more events.

Next month, she was attending a conference to give a talk about "Why a Writers' Retreat" and had a couple of weeks of signings scheduled all over the country for book three's release. Maybe she could talk Shauna into going with her. She'd hate to leave her alone in the house, especially after what had happened.

She sat down in the big chair and pulled out all the files and notebooks in the last drawer. She'd refill this with notebooks for the guests to use. Maybe colored pencils or Sharpie pens so they could brainstorm. She glanced at the wall where the boxes were. She'd have Seth put up a whiteboard and then guests could use the space for group brainstorming. She'd heard about authors who came together to plot. She could find someone experienced and have them come in for a session. She grabbed a notebook and found an empty slip of paper, writing down all the thoughts about changing up the room and the new workshop session idea. Then she returned to the desk. Before closing the drawer, she saw a slip of paper stuck in the bottom ridge. She leaned closer and took the tiny bit by her fingers and pulled. She heard the rip. When she looked at the paper, it had part of a word written on the edge in Michael's handwriting.

What had it ripped from? She ran her hand across

the bottom of the drawer—nothing. But she'd heard the ripping sound. The rest of the page should be there somewhere in the drawer. She sat back and studied the drawer. Something was off.

Then she sighed. Michael had built another secret spot. This time inside the desk. She looked around the drawer, under the desk, in the drawer on top of the bigger one, and came up empty. Wherever the spring for the hidden compartment was, she couldn't find it. She needed a flashlight.

She left the study and made a beeline to the kitchen. When she stepped inside, she stopped short.

A very quiet Shauna sat at the table, a cup of coffee in front of her. Cat's entrance made her look up, and Cat could see her friend's eyes were red rimmed, like she'd been crying. She'd looked better this morning, so apparently the visit to Paul hadn't helped with Shauna's mood.

"You're back." Cat cringed at her Captain Obvious statement. She crossed the room and sat at the table, putting the thought of finding the flashlight on a back burner. "What happened?"

Shauna shook her head. "Nothing. He wasn't there. At least that's what Bobbie, the guard, said at the gate. I know Bobbie. He knows who I am, and yet he wouldn't let me into the compound. I'm not welcome there anymore."

"Honey," Cat started, but wasn't sure what to say. "Maybe Paul just asked for no visitors while they figure out this whole thing. It could have been Uncle Pete who told them to keep everyone out."

Shauna looked up at her. "Do you really think so?"

Cat didn't, but if it kept her friend from feeling

worse, she'd agree. "Of course. You know how he is about crime scenes. He probably just wants to keep it as secluded as possible until they find out who did this to Kevin."

She considered Cat's words, then nodded. "I guess I shouldn't have gotten so upset, but it just hit me all at once. I loved spending time at the ranch. I know it wasn't mine, but if we'd gotten married . . ." She let the thought trail off. "I'm being silly now. Thinking about myself and what I'll be missing out on instead of focusing on Kevin. I am going to miss the guy. As much as he drove me crazy sometimes, he could always make me laugh. And he got me. You know? He knew what I was thinking without me telling him."

Kevin had been good at dealing with people. Cat had to give him that. "You go ahead and grieve for him and what might have been. I know it's hard now, but you need to let it all out." Cat paused. "Hey, I invited Sasha to dinner tonight."

Shauna's eyes widened and she started to stand. "I haven't even thought about lunch yet. You must be starving."

Putting a hand on her arm, Cat brought her back to a sitting position. "I didn't mean you needed to cook. I thought we'd go out to the FarmHouse. You've been wanting to try it."

Shauna narrowed her eyes. "You're kind of sneaky, you know that? You know I wanted to check out that place."

"Just because I want you to enjoy a nice dinner with friends?" Cat leaned back in her chair. "Sue me, I'm considerate."

Shauna considered the thought. "Dinner would

be nice. And I feel bad that I haven't spent any time with Sasha yet. This is a great idea, Cat."

"What are you two hatching up now?' Seth walked through the kitchen, brushing dust off his shirt. He grabbed a soda, then plopped down in a chair, looking at them.

Cat picked a cobweb out of his hair. "We're doing dinner tonight at the FarmHouse with Sasha. Want to come?"

"You picking up the tab?" He opened his soda and chugged what looked like half of the can.

"No, I thought you would. That's why I invited you." Cat shot a glance at Shauna, whose lips were curved in a smile. At least she was enjoying the banter.

"Then I'll have to pass. Winter's tough on a guy. Besides working for you this week, I'm mostly just doing parking lot snow removals until the weather turns." He finished the last of the soda and took the can to throw it away. Then he went to the sink and filled up a water glass, bringing that back to the table.

"I was kidding. This is a work event. I'll even pay you to be our designated driver."

"Actually, so was I, but I really can't go. Hank's staying in town so we can get that furnace finished in the morning. He just left to order the part from the hardware store. It should arrive by ten tomorrow. We've got a game and pizza planned for the evening." Seth grinned. "You ladies are welcome to join us."

"No thanks. Do I need to set up a room for him?"

Seth shook his head. "No need. Since I'm staying here for the week, I'm letting him crash at my place. I'll be back tonight, but it will be late. You okay with that?"

"Since the only reason you were staying over was that . . ." Cat paused, looking at Shauna. "Sorry, I didn't mean to bring it all up again."

Shauna stood and went to the fridge, pulling out vegetables and the makings for a salad. "Life goes on. Since the only reason that Seth was staying here was I would have been with Kevin, it's okay he's late tonight. Look, I said it. The world didn't end." She narrowed her eyes at Seth. "I take it you were the one to tell Cat about the rat poison?"

"She had a right to know." Seth froze in place, and Cat could feel the tension between the two.

"Maybe you should just keep your nose out of things that don't concern you." Shauna took a step closer, her face beet red.

"And maybe you shouldn't do things that make you look guilty," Seth shot back.

"You really think I could do something like . . ."

The back door blew open with a crash and Uncle Pete hurried inside breaking the tension. "Good, I'm glad you're all here. I need to ask you some questions. Where's Shirley?"

Chapter 9

"She's upstairs in my office. Why?" Cat had a bad feeling in the pit of her stomach. If Uncle Pete wanted to talk to Shirley, it couldn't be about Kevin's demise. It had to be about Michael's. They'd talked about his death during their first dinner, and Shirley had become obsessed with finding out what had really happened to Cat's first husband.

"Seth, go get her. I need to talk to her too." Uncle Pete hung up his clothes and knocked any snow off his boots. "I can't stay long. I just wanted to go over Shauna's statement with her."

He pulled out a notebook. "This won't take long. Mainly, I need to set up a timeline of the night Kevin was murdered."

Cat moved to the door and paused. "If you need me, I'll be in the study."

"Don't go too far. I need to talk to you as well." Uncle Pete narrowed his eyes at Cat and she felt guilty, like she'd been caught sneaking out with Seth during high school class. Her uncle had that way of making you confess even if you hadn't been caught yet.

She returned to the study and saw the desk. That was when she remembered the flashlight. She knew exactly where one was, in the shelf next to the kitchen door. She sighed and glanced at the bookshelves. She'd look through the books one more time to make sure she was sending everything economics-related to the library.

She pulled out several books that she'd missed earlier because they had been lying down flat on the top shelf. As she set them on the desk, she realized they were annuals from Covington. Michael had gotten one free of charge every year as a faculty member. She'd boxed up all but the ones that covered the years she'd attended and taught at the school. She looked at the dates. They were from the mid-nineties. Michael hadn't started teaching at Covington until 2005. Why did he have these?

She paged through the first one and realized Michael had been an undergraduate at Covington. Had she known that? He'd always talked about getting his masters at Harvard, but she didn't remember one time when he'd mentioned going to Covington as a student.

She turned to the student pictures and found him, dark brown eyes, dark brown hair, a lady-killer even then. She ran a finger over the professional shot and smiled. She'd loved him once. And for many reasons, not just because of his looks. She looked at the list of clubs and organizations. Just a few. Cross country, which made sense since Michael had kept up with his running, even through their marriage. Some business fraternity, probably because he was ultra-smart. And another one, Kappa Alpha Beta. Cat flipped through the pages until she was in the organizations section and found the fraternity. There was her ex-husband, grinning with his arm around another frat brother. One with blond hair and what looked to be green eyes. She knew who the man was even before her eyes dropped to the caption and she read his name.

Dante Cornelio.

He'd been friends with Michael when they'd both attended Covington.

Why hadn't Michael ever talked about Dante? What else hadn't she known about their relationship? And had they stayed friends?

She sat down in her reading chair with a notebook and made a note of every time she saw a picture of Michael or a picture of Dante. She put two stars for any pictures of them together.

After she was done, Uncle Pete still hadn't called for her. She looked at her list. Over a hundred mentions over the four years. The men had been popular with the annual's photographer during their time at Covington. The photographer had been there for all the highlights. There were candid shots of Michael at a football game. Or running track. Shots of the two men in the library, books piled next to Michael, but Dante always seemed to be waiting for him to finish. No books, no notebooks, no studying for the blond.

Michael had mentioned being a scholarship kid. He'd had to keep his grades up, not like the son of a rich mobster. But that hadn't stopped Dante from hanging around.

"They were friends," she said aloud to the empty

room, wondering what that really meant in regard to the recent events she'd uncovered, if anything.

A knock sounded at the door, causing her to jump. Seth poked his head inside. "Your uncle wants you back in the kitchen."

She tucked the notebook into the top book and hurried to the door. Seth waited in the hallway. He pushed her hair out of her eyes. She shivered as she remembered Dante doing the same thing earlier. "You all right?"

Nodding, she paused and looked at him. "I'm fine. I'll be glad when this is all over though."

"The retreat?" Seth tilted his head as he watched her reaction. "I thought this one was going well. No one's ended up dead or missing yet."

"Except for Shauna's boyfriend." She leaned against the wall. "But I wasn't talking about the retreat. I want to find out what happened to Michael, once and for all. Good or bad, I need to know."

He pulled her toward him and they started walking to the kitchen. "Sometimes you don't want to open Pandora's box, babe."

He opened the kitchen door and they walked in. Shirley and Uncle Pete were at the table, looking at something. And Shauna was at the stove, frying hamburger.

"I thought we'd have taco salads for lunch." She glanced at Cat as she entered the room. "Will that work?"

"Perfect. A salad at lunch means I can pig out at the restaurant tonight." She tried to gauge Shauna's discomfort. How bad had the questioning been?

She didn't have much time to analyze the situation. As soon as her uncle saw her, he waved her over to the table. "I want you to be careful. Dante Cornelio's in town."

Cat sank into a chair across the table from her uncle. "I know."

This apparently wasn't the answer Uncle Pete had been expecting. Both he and Seth turned toward her. Uncle Pete closed his notebook. "What do you mean, you know? I was just informed a few minutes ago by the school."

"I know he's in town because he stopped by the house." She glanced at Shauna, who shrugged. Apparently, if Cat wasn't going to report Dante for breaking and entering, her friend wasn't going to rat her out either. She saw by the look on his face that Seth had caught the unspoken conversation and wasn't happy about it. "He said he wanted to warn me off of investigating Michael's death. He said it wasn't safe for me."

"Well, at least he's smart about the situation." Uncle Pete narrowed his eyes at Cat. "Have you been investigating?"

Cat squirmed uncomfortably in her chair. "I haven't been doing anything wrong, if that's what you mean. I've been going through his notebooks and books before I donate them to the school, but that's all. And, I talked to Dean Ngu."

"Maybe it's my fault, Pete?" Shirley tapped her pen on the table, trying to break the stare down between Cat and her uncle. "I've been talking to people about Michael and looking at his published works at the library. I could be stirring up the pot here."

"You"—Uncle Pete pointed at Shirley—"I'm not worried about. You're a trained law enforcement officer. You know how to handle yourself if things go wonky. My niece on the other hand . . ."

Cat interrupted his tirade. "Your niece is sitting right here and can talk for herself. I don't know why Dante is concerned. All I've done is try to figure out who Michael was working for before he died. It's a simple question."

"A simple question that, to the wrong person, could get right back to the people who had Michael killed in the first place." Uncle Pete's voice raised, and Cat leaned back, away from the anger.

Shauna set a brownie and a cup of cocoa in front of Uncle Pete. "You haven't eaten all day, have you?"

"What's that got to do with anything?" he grumbled, but took a deep breath in, and even Cat could see the effect the smell of the chocolate had on him. He picked up the brownie and took a large bite. After sipping down some of the cocoa, he nodded and squeezed Shauna's hand. "That's good, but food doesn't solve all the problems."

"Don't take your frustrations out on Cat. You just have a lot on your plate right now. I'm the one who called you in on this whole Kevin thing." Shauna sighed. "I really thought we'd find him stranded out on the road with one of his cars or motorcycles. Not dead."

"I'm sorry things turned out this way." Uncle Pete finished the brownie and drained his cup. "Thanks for the food. I've got to get back to the station."

Shauna went to the fridge and filled a bag. She met him at the door as he pulled on his coat and handed him the bag. "Here's some soup you can warm up in the microwave. You can't keep going on just chocolate alone."

Uncle Pete kissed her cheek. "You're an angel, you know that, right?"

Shauna nodded and then returned to the stove. "Feeding people is what I do. It makes my heart feel better. Even after all of this."

Shirley excused herself to catch up with Uncle Pete outside. Cat watched through the window in the kitchen door as the two of them talked and wondered if Shirley had already found something. Seth followed her gaze, then moved his chair in front of her to block her view.

"Hey!"

"Hey yourself. I think you have some explaining to do. Why didn't you tell me that Dante was here? And when? I've been here just about twenty-four-seven for the last few days." He waited for her response.

"This morning. You were still asleep." Cat shook her head. "Don't give me that look. Shauna was up and in the kitchen. It wasn't like I was completely alone. One scream and I'd have people running out of the woodwork to save me. Besides, he's really not that dangerous."

"You're kidding me. You don't think Dante's dangerous? Your uncle made a trip over here out of his busy day investigating a murder just to warn you, and you think the guy isn't dangerous?" Seth took a breath. "Seriously, Cat, what does he have to do, show up with a gun, before you realize the guy has people killed? He put a hit out on Tommy O'Neil last month."

"He knew Michael. They were friends." Cat's face

felt hot and she wanted to kick something. Who was
Seth to tell her who she could or couldn't talk to? It
was just talking, for goodness sake. "Anyway, I've
told him not to come back without permission. It's
not like I'm inviting him into the parlor for tea."

"But your insistence on figuring out what happened to Michael, that's what's bringing him around."
Seth stood. "I've told you to let sleeping dogs lie.
He's told you to let it go. Your uncle's told you. You
need to listen."

"And you need to find your friend and fix the
attic heater." Cat pushed down the anger she felt at
him telling her what to do and tried to change the
subject. "Wasn't Hank supposed to be here by now?"

"He was. I'll go give him a call." Seth glanced at
his watch, then back up at Cat. "You know I'm just
worried about you."

Cat watched him walk out of the kitchen. Shauna
set a bowl of taco salad in front of Cat, complete
with a homemade tortilla shell. "Eat—you're just
like your uncle. Have you had your blood sugars
checked? Maybe that's what makes the two of you
so grumpy without food."

Cat sniffed, trying to hold back the tears. "I'm
not grumpy. Besides, I didn't start that fight. Seth
did."

"So your man is feeling a little uncomfortable
with a wealthy, handsome guy showing you attention. I can't really blame him. What does Seth have
to offer that even comes close to what Dante can
provide?" Shauna got her own salad and sat at the
table with Cat.

"You're kidding, right? Seth is kind, funny, intelligent. I never said I wanted someone who could

buy me the world, especially since the source of Dante's money is, well, questionable. You know me—why would I go for that type of man?" Cat watched as her friend drizzled homemade Thousand Island dressing over the top of her salad.

"You wouldn't. But does Seth know that?" She set the small jar down and slid it toward Cat. "The last time he lost you, you fell in love with a college professor. Maybe he thinks Dante might have a chance because he's more like Michael than Seth is?"

When Cat didn't respond, Shauna went on. "Don't get me wrong, I'm still ticked at him for telling you about the poison and making me look all Lizzie Borden. Now Pete has to explain away the fact I was seen with the murder weapon."

"The lab tests came back?"

Shauna nodded. "And what's worse is they found my prints on the bottle. Which of course would be there, since I was the one who bought the stuff."

"What aren't you saying?" Cat realized her relationship problems weren't significant when she compared them to Shauna's current issues. "Why did Uncle Pete want to talk to you?"

"Cat, there was poison in the Irish stew. The food I fed him was what actually killed him." Shauna laid her head on the table, crossing her arms around herself. "I guess the fight in the barn just finished him off. If he would have stayed in bed, I would have found him and maybe. . ."

"But he didn't stay in bed and you didn't know." Cat put a hand on Shauna's head. She was just about to say more when Shirley came back into the house.

"Brrhh. I should learn to slip on a coat when I

head outside. I do the same thing at home. Go to get the mail from the mailman, then stand around and talk until my teeth are chattering." She stomped the snow off her feet. "I'm heading upstairs to get my computer, then I'm going into town for lunch. You need me to pick up anything?"

Shauna raised her head, wiping her eyes. "We're good. Are you sure you don't want to eat with us? I made plenty."

"Oh, no. I'm looking forward to some pizza. That crust is addicting. I may just need to have them ship me some when I leave for home." Shirley disappeared into the hallway.

"Crap, I wanted to ask her if she'd found anything in Michael's papers." Cat looked at the door, knowing Shirley was probably already near her room by now. The woman moved quickly. No moss grew under her feet.

"If she'd found something, she would have told you." Shauna pushed a tomato around in her salad. She didn't look up as she spoke. "You don't think I could have killed Kevin, do you?"

"What? No!" Cat set her fork down. "There's no way Uncle Pete believes you could hurt anyone, let alone kill someone. He loves you like family, you know that."

Shauna set her fork down and took a sip of water. "He asked me a lot of questions, like where was I that night. Why didn't I notice Kevin get up? If I'd stopped him, had him come back to bed and forget about that stupid text, he might still be alive. Or at least just in the hospital getting his stomach pumped."

"Maybe. Or at least, he might not have died *that*

night. From what I've heard, whoever killed Kevin was angry. And that kind of anger doesn't go away because someone misses a meeting. More likely, the killer might have tried to enter the house and you might have been hurt." That thought hadn't occurred to Shauna, Cat could see from the fear on her face.

Then she shook her head. "The entire area around the cabin is fenced. There is a security guard at the gate. No one could get into the house without setting off an alarm. Kevin had that place wired, and he always turned on the alarm before we went to bed. He was obsessive about it. And how did someone get into the house to put the poison in the stew? We were home all evening, watching a video."

Cat thought about what Shauna had said. "Then the killer probably snuck into the house after coming on the property through the grazing fields. That's why he had to get Kevin to come to him."

"That makes sense." Shauna had picked up her fork again and was worrying that one lone tomato wedge with it.

"It tells us one more thing." Cat took a bite of her salad. She was beginning to see a way to help Uncle Pete solve this.

Shauna speared the tomato and paused with it midway to her mouth. "What?"

"Not only did the killer know Kevin, but also"— Cat broke off a bit of the crunchy shell and used it as emphasis on her next words—"the killer knew Kevin's security system."

Shauna's eyes widened. "You're right. The horse barn is too far away from the house for anyone to get picked up on the cameras that the gate guard monitors."

"Well, now we know how he got into the compound. Now, we just have to figure out why he wanted Kevin dead. And how he got into the house without being caught on the cameras." Cat finished her salad and took the plate to the sink. "You got any idea if he was fighting with someone?"

"Besides Paul about our engagement?" Shauna shook her head. "That's the only person he told me that he was angry with. And, boy, was he peeved. That's why he asked me not to wear the engagement ring around the house. He didn't want Paul to see it."

"The guy did have a vested interest in Kevin staying unmarried." Cat leaned on the counter, watching Shauna. She looked even thinner and paler than she had the day before. Maybe she should take some time and go visit her parents. Cat would suggest it tonight at dinner. She could manage the rest of the retreat by herself. And she had Seth here this week.

"I know you see all kinds of neon warning signs pointing to Paul, but seriously, there is no way the guy would do anything to hurt Kevin. They were like co-conspirators in everything. Kevin joked that they shared a brain. They go way back, to college fraternity days." Shauna looked at the clock. "I didn't realize it was that late. I need to get the dining room set up for afternoon treats. What time are we going to dinner?"

"Our reservations are at six. I'll drive since Seth doesn't want to tag along." Cat smiled. "That way, you can have a glass or two of wine."

"After the last few days, I'm not sure I could go a day without a little something in my bloodstream to keep me going." Shauna smiled. "And my bottle of Irish whiskey is almost all gone. I'll have to have Chase at the grocery order me a couple more bottles. Maybe a vat. They don't carry my brand in stock."

Cat took a deep breath. Hopefully her friend would find her way out of her grief before she started floating in alcohol. "Well, let me know if you need me to do anything. I'm here to help too, you know."

"I like staying busy. It keeps my mind off thinking about things." She stood and went to the sink, where she busied herself rinsing her plate. "Who would have thought buying a simple bottle of rat killer for the ranch would have caused so many problems?"

Cat left the kitchen, feeling the weight that Kevin's loss had placed on her friend. She glanced left toward Michael's study and the uncompleted mystery there. Then she glanced up the stairs to her office. She wanted to do some research on Kevin. There had to be something in his past that had brought him to this end. Something besides her friend. Uncle Pete may not believe Shauna had killed Kevin, but if that was what the evidence said, he'd have to follow it. So she would just give him a nudge in a different direction.

Instead of going to either Michael's study or her office, she grabbed her wallet. Turning back into the kitchen, she put on her coat and boots. When Shauna looked at her with a question on her face, Cat announced, "I'm going out for a walk."

She hurried out the door before Shauna could ask where and headed toward town. She had two stops. The first one was just down the street to a large house recently remodeled from its lovely Victorian bones to a mansion fit for a prince. She rang the doorbell and a face appeared at the monitor.

"May I help you?" The face of a man who must be the butler, or could play one on a British television show, filled the screen. The door opened wide, and he motioned her inside. "Oh, Ms. Latimer. I'll tell Mr. Cornelio you wish to see him."

"How did you know who I was?" Cat glanced around the large foyer. Her boots were snow covered from the walk so she stayed near the door, hoping to avoid melting all over the marble floor.

He held out his hand for her coat and handed her a pair of slippers that appeared to be straight off the store shelves. "Oh, I have a lot of time on my hands running this second home for Mr. Cornelio. I'm a big fan of your books."

"Thank you." Feeling as if this whole thing were surreal, Cat shrugged out of her coat and took off her boots. "I'm really not staying long. I just have a question or two to ask Dante."

"No worries. I'll keep these close at hand." He smiled at her one more time before he left her in a sitting room next to the foyer. "I'm going to have to tell my granddaughter I met you. She'll be so jealous."

Cat walked around the large room, anxious now that she'd decided to confront Dante about his relationship to Michael. A large bookshelf covered one wall of the room, and she glanced through the titles. Pulling out one, she noticed it was a signed first edition of a popular mystery author. Not highly valuable, at least not to anyone who wasn't a collector. She'd bet that all of the books on display were signed first editions. Except for the row that had three lonely mass-market paperbacks. Her books.

"I'd hoped I could get you to sign those to me one day. Maybe you can be so kind to do me that favor today since you have arrived unannounced." Dante stood at the entrance of the room, watching her.

"I think my books don't quite fit into your library." She turned toward him. "You have quite a collection of current authors."

"You never know who is going to be classic in the next generation. I'd rather get all the books now than realize I missed out when I could have bought it cheap when it was first released." He came over and picked up one of her books and took a pen out of his pocket. "Can I impose?"

What the heck. She took the pen and scribbled her name in all three of the books. "Now, you owe me."

"Anything. I thought I'd made that clear." He returned the books gently to their place on the shelf.

"Why didn't you tell me you and Michael were friends?"

Dante pointed to the leather couch in front of a large fireplace. "Let's sit."

"Are you going to answer my question?" Cat crossed her arms, feeling a little silly standing in deep blue slippers in this room that looked like an old-fashion gentlemen's club. It felt like she was trying to be at home in a fancy library.

"Catherine, please. Come sit, and I'll tell you what you want to know."

When she left, twenty minutes later, she thought about the bond Dante and Michael had had while they were young adults. Before Dante had told Michael who he really was. Before they'd agreed to set aside their friendship in order to protect Michael from the stigma of the crime family.

"And yet, somehow, he got dragged back in," Cat murmured to herself as she walked toward town. Had Michael known who he was working with when he'd taken the job from Dean Ngu? So many unanswered questions.

Chapter 10

Aspen Hills Hardware appeared to be empty when she entered through the doorway. A bell on top announced her appearance, and a voice called out from the back, "I'll be right there. Let me know if I can help you find anything."

Cat wandered through the aisles until she found the shelves of pest control items. She'd had Seth purchase no-kill mice traps last month, and so far, they'd caught and released five of the little guys. They'd probably come to tragic ends after Seth released them at the edge of the park, but at least they'd had a chance and she wasn't responsible.

The products on the shelf were all standard and, from what she could see, didn't contain the cyanide that had killed Kevin.

"Anything specific you need?" The same man's voice that had called out when she entered the shop was now in the aisle with her. She turned to see an older man, dressed in jeans and an Aspen Hills Hardware T-shirt standing next to her.

"I was wondering about a stronger poison for

mice. My mom always used a brand with cyanide as the main ingredient." Cat waved her hand at the shelf. "Do any of these have that?"

"Now that's old school. Most folks around here are more into the no-kill traps nowadays. Well, except for the few ranchers that still run outside of town. I might still have a bottle in the back. It's been a popular product the last two weeks. I don't think I've sold one bottle for years, but now, I've sold two, maybe three." He turned toward the back again. "Let me check."

Cat felt bad lying to the guy, but weaving in a little fiction seemed the easiest way to get the information she needed. She wandered up to the counter.

When he returned, he shook his head. "Sorry, we're all sold out. But I can order you a bottle."

"Who bought the product recently? Maybe I can ask them if they thought it was useful."

The old man scratched his head. "I didn't know either of the women. Both had red hair, I can tell you that much. I always was a sucker for red hair."

"Thanks. You've been helpful." She turned and headed out the door.

"Do you want me to let you know if I get some more in?" he called after her.

Cat spun around. "I'll stop back in a few weeks."

So when Uncle Pete went to talk to the hardware store owner, he'd find out that a cute little redhead bought the poison. Another finger pointed at Shauna. But who had the other woman been? Cat needed to find out, and fast.

Back home, she headed straight to her office. Entering, she noticed the changes. Shirley had set up a little workstation on the couch and coffee table. There was a box on each side of the couch, one half empty, the other about a quarter full, and a pile of Michael's workbooks sat on the table. One was open and Cat ran a finger over his tight, neat handwriting on the page. He'd always said she should have been a doctor, her handwriting was so hard to decipher. Seeing his notes, reminded her that she still had some good memories of her marriage.

She stepped away from the impromptu desk and went to her own, where she powered up her desktop. A lot of the writers she knew worked solely on laptops. Cat liked the feel of the real keyboard and the consistency that came from sitting down at the desk and writing. She could write anywhere, but she was most productive here, in this room, on this computer. It was her process. But today's work wasn't a word count.

Today she needed to research Kevin Shield. She started by requesting a Google search with his name and *Aspen Hills, CO*. The search engine returned two hundred and fifty hits. Cat pulled out a clean notebook and wrote *Who Killed Kevin* on the top of the first page. Then she started searching websites, writing down anything that seemed interesting. Like who he had been dating before Shauna. Or what projects he'd been rumored to be part of. About halfway through, she found his company website. It was publicly owned, which meant Kevin had stockholders. Cat put a star next to that note, but didn't find much else on the company website except for a list of prior successful developments.

Kevin liked to build skyscrapers, that was for

certain. She clicked through a photo gallery of the apartment complexes he'd built in Denver over the last five years. Upscale condos where the young professional could entertain or just cuddle up on the couch with a drink and the television after a long day. The rooms were modern, highlighting glass and chrome. So not Cat's style.

She'd gone through most of the links when she came upon a holiday picture at a Denver charity event. It was several years old. Kevin and Paul flanked a black-haired woman in a long red dress that highlighted her cleavage, along with the obvious baby bump in the center. This must be the accidental pregnancy; however, from the way she was smiling and holding on to Kevin in the picture, Cat didn't think the woman thought the soon-to-come babies were an accident. The photo's caption identified the three as Jade, Kevin, and Paul.

Jade was much taller than Shauna, the dark to her friend's ginger lightness. The woman was gorgeous and powerful—you could feel her strength through the picture. Cat wondered how handsome the two boys were, with such good genes from both sides of the family.

Shirley came into the room behind Cat. "Oops, I'm sorry. Were you working?"

Cat closed down the Internet window and then turned off the computer. She could finish this later, maybe in her room on the laptop. That's where she should have been. Somewhere she could have locked the door. "No, just web searching. It's a bad habit, especially when I'm not in a current book. I skim sites where teens hang out and see what they're talking about. It helps me stay current in today's lingo."

"Virtual voyeurism. I like it." Shirley smiled. "Do you mind if I get back to work? So far, all I've found out about your husband is how much he loved economics. What are you doing with these papers after we're done? It would be a shame for them to go unread."

"I'm donating them to his former department. As you know, the dean is very anxious to get his hands on them. He can be a jerk, but I guess they're missing Michael's keen brain in the academic discussions." Cat looked at her calendar. If she focused all next week on the project, she could have most of Michael's workbooks to the college by mid-month. And the rest as soon as she determined if they held any clue to what he'd been working on when he died. Kevin, Michael—there were too many must-dos in her head on both their investigations. Investigations she'd been warned off by more than just her uncle.

Shirley set a new carafe of coffee down on Cat's drink station and poured herself a cup. "You want some coffee?"

"I'm good." Cat stood and stretched, grabbing the notebook before she stepped away from the desk. "Don't spend too much time digging. I want to see your own project get some of your dedication too."

"Don't worry. I finished a chapter this morning, and I'm mulling over the next one as I work. It's funny what gets your creative muse busy." She sat down at the table and picked up the notebook she'd left open and started reading.

Cat had been dismissed. From her own office. She grinned and headed down the hall to her room. Glancing at her watch, she had an hour left before she had to get ready for dinner. She'd do some research on Jade and see what her story was. Or at least her story without Kevin.

By the time she gave up and got into the shower, she thought she knew everything there was to know about Jade, at least what was online. She was an avid supporter of a local T-ball team the boys played on. She had an open Facebook page, where Cat was able to see pictures of the boys over the years. They both looked like Kevin. Focused, determined, and rarely smiling. Cat thought about the man she'd met just a few times. He'd smiled some, but mostly it had been directed at Shauna. Cat had believed Kevin loved Shauna, despite his inability to be a good boyfriend and keep dates or show her off in his social circles.

"Kevin, you kept as many secrets as Michael did." Cat spoke the words aloud as she closed up the laptop and put her notebook underneath it. No need for Shauna to see the book and be curious about what Cat was working on now. Even though she'd known about Jade and the boys, the fact they were around had to remind Shauna of what she lost. She smiled at the comparison between Kevin's secrets and her own. But there was one difference. The only person she was trying to protect was Shauna. Kevin had hidden his other life to protect himself.

"Keep telling yourself that," she chided herself as she stepped into the warm water.

* * *

The drive to the restaurant was clear. The highway department kept the major roads in and out of Aspen Hills plowed so unless they had snow fall while they were eating, Cat shouldn't have any problem getting them back to the house.

Now, they were seated at a table near the fireplace with drinks and a warm loaf of bread to share for the table. The lighting was subdued and the dining room was filled with couples. Cat was glad she had brought Sasha too. Maybe the company would keep Shauna's thoughts from going to Kevin and what she'd lost. She took a thick slice and passed the basket to Sasha. "This place is heaven."

"I do love a restaurant where you walk in and they throw a hunk of bread at you. It's like being at grandma's, except at my grandma's, it was cornbread." Sasha took the basket and her slice of bread and then sent it on to Shauna. She grabbed her phone and quickly found what she'd been looking for. "Speaking of grandmas, my mom sent me a picture of Olivia today. She's reading her favorite book."

Cat took the phone and smiled at the little girl perched on a too-big-for-her recliner, a book of fairy tales open on her lap. She had a pink ribbon woven through her hair like a headband. Cat handed the phone to Shauna. "She's adorable."

"Thanks. I'm kind of taken with her. I mean, it's been hard, being a single mom, but I have my family and for a while—well, let's just say I've learned men can be more than just a good time." Sasha tucked her head into her menu, clearly uncomfortable with the conversation.

"So, you're dating someone?" Shauna set the

phone next to Sasha's plate. She smiled sadly at
Cat. "Tell me about him. I'd like to think some fairy
tales come true."

"You don't want to hear about this, not now, not
after . . ." Sasha lowered the menu and stared at
Shauna. "I'm so sorry for your loss."

Cat saw the tears well up in her friend's eyes.

"Actually, I do want to hear about happy things.
The world goes on, right? We grieve, we make
peace with the new reality, and the world goes on."
Shauna sniffed, then started buttering her bread.
"We're not talking about my sad story tonight.
Tonight is about good food and finding out what's
been going on in your life since we last met."

Sasha watched Shauna before she spoke, maybe
judging the sincerity of her words. Finally, she
nodded and Cat could see she'd made a decision.

"Okay, my story's not so happy. I was dating this
guy in South Cove. Toby. He's a deputy and also a
barista. That's where we met, at the coffee shop.
He's hot. I mean totally crazy hot. And he draws in
the women. I think he could sell ice cubes to at least
female Eskimos." Sasha took a sip of her wine.
"He's nice too. Olivia loved him. But when I moved,
I broke up with him. I didn't think it was fair to try
to do the long-distance thing."

"That must have been hard." Cat thought about
her own love life. She'd had only two boyfriends,
Seth and Michael. And now Seth, again. She wasn't
an expert on the whole love thing.

"It was, but it was a good decision." She re-
arranged her silverware. "Anyway, I met someone a

few weeks ago. It's still early and he hasn't met Olivia yet, but I think he might just be the one."

"Seriously?" Cat grinned. "So you tell us the first part of the story to get sympathy and then hit us with the new, hot boyfriend? He is hot, right?"

"He's smart, and funny, and caring." Sasha grinned at her table companions. "And yes, he's hot. But I don't know if I would have even accepted the first date with him if I hadn't been with Toby last year. Toby taught me so much about being in a real relationship. I should send him a thank-you card."

Shauna shook her head. "I don't think men like being told they were the reason their ex-girlfriends are with Mr. Right."

The three broke into laughter, and the waitress came up for their dinner orders. The rest of the evening flew by, and while Cat was busy signing the check, Sasha leaned over to Shauna. "Don't look now, but that woman is checking you out."

"Well, she has good taste, but I don't play for that team." Shauna finished off her glass of wine and leaned over toward Sasha. "Which one is looking at me like I'm a goddess?"

"Over there, the brunette in the black dress. The guy she's with just went to the bathroom." Sasha pointed to a small table in the corner, away from the fireplace.

Cat tucked her copy of the receipt into her purse, then leaned over to see what Sasha was looking at. Her jaw tightened when she recognized the woman at the table. She stood and waved her dinner companions toward the door. "Let's go."

"What on earth is going on? What's your hurry?"

Shauna looked around the room, then leaned closer and whispered. "Is Dante here?"

"I think I just saw him go into the men's room," Cat lied. She was grabbing straws, but she wanted Shauna out of the restaurant before Paul came back to his table and her friend understood the real reason why the pretty brunette was staring at her.

When Shauna gasped, Cat knew that directing her attention toward the restrooms had been a mistake. Paul strode toward his table, and as he sat, Cat saw the woman jerk her head toward their table. He turned in his chair, an arm casually draped around the back, waved at Shauna, then turned back to his sister. But she didn't follow his casual example.

Jade stood and rushed over to their table. Cat took an instinctive step between the two women, stopping Jade's charge.

"You. You are the reason he is dead." Jade was shaking from head to toe, and Paul had joined the group standing around the table. "My poor boys, what are they going to do without a father now?"

"Sweetheart, you're causing a scene. Come back and eat your dinner." Paul put his arm around her and tried to move her away from the women. "I'm sorry for the disturbance."

"Why is everyone trying to protect her?" Jade tried to shrug out of Paul's control. "She's the one who killed my Kevin."

The woman burst into tears, and Paul gently folded her into his arms. He murmured something into her ear and then turned his head back to us, fury on his face. "I'm sorry for the disturbance. My sister is distraught over her loss."

"As we all are . . ." Shauna's words cut through the scene, and as Cat looked at her, she saw the fire dancing in her friend's eyes.

"Let's go." Cat took a step toward Shauna and watched as Sasha did the same. They gathered their belongings, and when they reached the lobby area, Cat handed Shauna her coat. "That was intense."

"The woman is crazy. I wonder if Pete has checked into her alibi." Shauna jerked on her coat and flipped her hair back out of the collar.

"I shouldn't have pointed her out. I mean, I thought the way she was staring at you that she was digging your look." Sasha slipped her own coat on. "I'm sorry for the mess."

Shauna put her hand on Sasha's shoulder. "You didn't cause this mess. Kevin was the one who put this in motion. Once when he slept with that woman. Then when he proposed to me. You would have thought he might have thought twice getting involved with me after his experience with Mommy Dearest over there. And Paul must have been upset about losing the leverage he had on Kevin and his assets. Worse, the guy tried to hide all traces of me from his sister. Whoever killed Kevin just pulled open all the doors on his secrets."

As they made their way home, Cat thought about Jade's reaction. If she'd killed Kevin, would she try to play the angry wronged woman? Especially in public? Of course, that would be the perfect place to convince a jury pool. She had the trump card, the children. No matter what might have happened in the future between Kevin and Shauna, she was still just his girlfriend today. Cat glanced at her friend.

Shauna sat next to her in the passenger seat, staring out into the night, lost in her thoughts.

Arriving home, they went into the house through the kitchen. Sasha yawned. "I'm heading upstairs to bed. I want to be up early to work on my presentation and do a run-through one more time. Thanks for dinner. It was great being able to talk to adults for a change. Olivia keeps me busy getting all the pre-school drama."

"Enjoy it while you can. I hear by first grade they don't tell their parents anything." Cat stood in between the door leading upstairs and Shauna, who was filling the tea kettle. "We're the ones who are thankful you took time to come to the retreat. I've enjoyed getting to know you better."

"Well, we have one more day. Unless I really bomb this presentation and you want me to leave early." Sasha grinned. "Which is one of the reasons I need to get upstairs now. Besides, if I hurry, I can catch Olivia before Mom puts her to bed."

They said their good-nights and Cat sat down at the table. Shauna put two cups of tea down in front of Cat and joined her at the table. Cat ignored the plate of cookies sitting in the middle of the room. She was stuffed, but they were her favorites, Mexican wedding balls. "I take it you want to talk?"

"This is going to sound stupid, but I don't want to regret not telling someone. Especially after tonight." Shauna pulled the cookie plate closer and popped one into her mouth. "Sorry, I've been starving all day. I can't stop eating. I thought grief was supposed to make you not want to eat?"

"I think it affects people differently." Cat reached for one of the cookies, just so Shauna wouldn't be eating alone. Okay, so that was a bald-faced lie, the second one of the evening, but they were great cookies. "What do you need to tell me?"

Shauna took a sip of her tea, then blew out a long breath. "I think Paul has someone following me."

Chapter 11

"I don't understand." Cat set the tea down. It wasn't fully brewed anyway, but the warmth of the hot water had made her hands stop shaking. "Just because they were at the same restaurant as we were? It's not like Los Angeles—Aspen Hills is pretty small."

Shauna brushed the powdered sugar off the table and onto a napkin. "I know. I've lived here for over six months now. No, it's not that he and his sister were at the FarmHouse. I saw a small blue compact waiting when we left, and whoever was driving followed us back home."

Cat thought about the possibility of someone following them before she answered. "It could be a coincidence."

"I'd think that too, except this same car followed me out to the ranch this morning and then back home. The guy at the gate noticed him hanging around when I was being refused entrance." Shauna picked up a second cookie. "And before you say there's more than one blue compact, this one has a dent in the driver's side and a Wall Drug bumper sticker on the back. Unless that's a favorite South Dakota hangout for Aspen Hills residents, I'm pretty sure it's the same guy."

"Did you tell Uncle Pete about this?"

Shauna popped the cookie in her mouth and shook her head. "Nope," she said after she swallowed. "I didn't think much about it until tonight. I think it's a guy, but I couldn't see his face."

"And you think Paul set him on you." Cat took a second cookie as well.

"Who else would? Paul is the only person with a horse in this race, which you've pointed out several times. I just don't understand what he thinks he'll find on me if he keeps watching."

"Maybe he's hoping you have a secret lover you'll go running to now that Kevin's gone." Cat licked powdered sugar off her finger tips. "Or maybe a huge drug addiction so he can petition the court to set aside any bequests from Kevin's will."

"Okay, stop it. I told you it was going to sound stupid." She sighed. "Maybe I'm just brain dead from lack of sleep. Something feels off and I can't put my finger on it. Of course, I've never had someone die on me before."

"No one? Not a grandparent or aunt?" Cat stared at her friend. She'd lost her grandpa when she was six. Then her grandmother had died a few years later. Death had always been a part of her life.

Shauna shook her head. "Both sets of grandparents are still active and even live on their own. Kevin's the first person I've loved that has passed on."

"I'm sure you're just experiencing grief your way." The door to the kitchen opened and Collin walked in. He looked at Cat and Shauna, then flushed. "I didn't think anyone would be up."

"Come on in. We're just chatting." Cat smiled at the obviously flustered young man. He was so nice. "Can I get you something? How's your retreat going so far?"

He seemed confused by the question. "It's been fine. I mean, I'm getting a lot done and I really have enjoyed the breakfasts. I was looking for a bottle of water."

"I'll get you one." Shauna stood and walked over to the fridge. She handed him the bottle. "Anything else?"

"No, this is great. Just looking for some water." He backed out of the doorway.

"That was weird." Cat shook her head. "The kid acts like he's afraid we're going to yell at him all the time. He's so nice though. He volunteered to walk the group back from the library every day. I don't even have to check in. They all have his cell and text when they are ready to leave. This group doesn't even seem to need us."

"Except for the food and drinks." Shauna looked at the door and frowned. "Although there is one thing I don't understand."

"What's that?" Cat yawned. She was ready to climb the stairs and go to sleep. This week had been a killer.

"I filled the drink fridge before we left. There should be enough water in the dining room for the rest of the retreat." Shauna looked around her kitchen. "Maybe he was looking for something else?"

"Like liquor? Could be." Cat covered her mouth,

hiding another yawn. "Although we don't leave a lot out here in the kitchen."

"You go upstairs to bed. I'll close up the house. I feel like I haven't been keeping up my share this week."

"You always do more than your share. Well, you typically do more than your share." Cat stood and stretched, feeling like a heel for what she'd thought about Shauna at the beginning of the retreat. She should have learned by now that teamwork meant give and take. "But I will let you close up. I'm beat for some reason."

"See you in the morning."

Cat wandered into the lobby area, checking the front door as she went. She peeked into the living room and saw Pamela and Melissa on the couch, their laptops open and fingers flying. They must have been doing sprints, as Cat saw Shauna's kitchen timer sitting between them. She eased out of the room, unwilling to disturb their progress.

She rolled her shoulders and was up the first two steps when the front door swung open. Shirley and Cat's uncle stepped into the lobby. She leaned over the railing and called to them, "Hey, I didn't realize you two were out tonight."

"Just dropping Shirley off after dinner." Uncle Pete stamped his feet on the rug, but Cat didn't see any snow on his boots.

"I'm heading up to my room." Cat paused. "Unless you need me for something?"

Uncle Pete shook his head. "Nothing I can think of."

Cat smiled to herself as she made her way upstairs. Her uncle and an Alaskan cop. *Retired cop*, she corrected herself. Anyway, she liked the fact he was getting out again. Maybe Shirley wasn't the perfect candidate for a long-term relationship, but at least he was dating someone.

She paused at the second floor and listened for any signs of trouble. Water was running in one room, the faint sound of a television in another. But nothing out of the ordinary. Satisfied, she went up another flight to her room. Within a few minutes, she was tucked into bed, the idea of Uncle Pete on the prowl flitting through her mind. With a chuckle, she turned off her light.

Wednesday morning came bright and cold. Cat pulled open her drapes to look down on the backyard. The snow had a frozen top layer that sparkled in the sunlight. Two more months, maybe three, before she'd see grass growing. Then, as soon as spring would come, the vegetation would spring to lift. Shauna had been planning on starting a herb and vegetable garden soon. Cat wondered if, with the loss of Kevin, Shauna might find Aspen Hills filled with too many memories. She'd been worried about Shauna leaving the retreat for weeks for different reasons. First, it had been Shauna's pending marriage. Now it was Kevin's death.

Cat got dressed and headed downstairs. Even though she wasn't currently writing, the new story she'd been plotting was messing with her muse and Cat wanted to get at least a few pages down, especially since she could see the opening scene clearly in her mind. Funny how she could write about warm summer days when the actual temperature outside was closer to single digits than triple ones.

She knew Shauna was up long before she reached

the bottom floor. The house smelled like warm baked bread and chocolate muffins. And coffee. Always coffee. Shauna bought her beans from the local coffee shop, The Morning Bean. When they'd first opened, Shauna had made some sort of trial agreement with them, but last week, Shauna had set up a promotional contract with the small shop. The Morning Bean had an ad in their program that got writers coming in during the day, and the retreat had amazing coffee all the time. Cat pushed open the door and called out, "Good morning."

But Shauna wasn't alone in the room. Collin stood near the table, his fingers tapping out a song of sorts. Shauna turned from the stove and smiled. "Good morning, Cat. Collin came in and begged for an early special order of over-easy eggs. Do you want something now?"

Cat went to the coffeepot. "Nope, my muse is talking so I'm heading upstairs with go juice and one of those chocolate muffins." She turned to Collin. "What are you working on so early?"

"What?" he stuttered, turning his attention from watching Shauna to Cat. The words must have sunk into his brain because he answered. "Oh, I'm working on a chapter about college organizations and extracurricular activities. Did you know Covington has over a hundred campus clubs? And bigger colleges offer even more."

"I was asked to be a faculty sponsor of ten different clubs my first week as a professor. Most of them weren't in my wheelhouse though, so I turned a lot of them down." She held a cup up toward Collin. He was back to watching Shauna. The boy either had a major crush or was very particular on how his eggs were cooked. "Want a cup?"

"Actually, I'm good." He must have realized she'd caught him staring, as his face turned beet red. "So what were the clubs you turned down?"

"It's been a while. Let's see if I can remember." Cat brought her coffee mug over to the table and grabbed a muffin. "Campus yoga lovers, the travel club, and, now that I think of it, I turned down the Covington Society for Wiccan learning. I should have jumped on that since my heroine in the books is a witch."

Shauna plated the eggs and then set the plate in front of Collin. "Seriously, you turned that one down? I thought you were writing by then?"

"I was, but no one knew I was writing genre fiction. I would have been kicked off campus."

"Thanks." Collin grabbed the plate and bolted out the door.

Shauna met her gaze. "That was weird. I found him in here when I came back from running upstairs to grab my laptop."

"Maybe he's been the one messing with your supplies?" Cat realized she still hadn't read Harry Bowman's background checks. But then she remembered she didn't even order one on the graduate student. "I swear, we have the worst luck with retreat guests."

"Or maybe we're seeing zebras because we have had bad luck in the past. It could be that he really just wanted some eggs." Shauna sank into a chair. "I've got to work on the accounting today. What's on your schedule after you drain yourself of words?"

"I'm sitting in on Sasha's presentation at ten, then

my schedule is free. I want to talk to each of the
guests and check in at some point today. It feels like
they've been working pretty independently, and I
want to make sure they don't need anything from
me, or us."

Shauna laughed. "You're the one who is always
saying that everyone's process is different. Maybe
this group just wants to be left alone?"

Cat stretched and then grabbed her stuff. She
also wanted to talk to Uncle Pete about the case,
but she wasn't going to tell Shauna that. "Maybe, but
I still want to talk to them."

"You know, they have a word for people like you."

She paused at the doorway. "Helpful, considerate?"

"Control freak." Shauna opened her laptop and
started working.

"You're funny." Cat turned into the hallway
and ran straight into Seth.

"Good morning sunshine." He nodded to the
door as he held her arms to steady her. "You and
Shauna are fighting? She must be feeling better."

"We're not fighting. She's just calling me names.
Before you wonder, I asked her about the poison. It
was for rats at the ranch."

Seth looked toward the door, like he could see
inside to the woman cooking there. "That's a logi-
cal answer."

"But you don't think it's an answer—you think
it's an excuse." Cat looked up into his brown eyes
and swallowed the sigh that wanted to ease out of
her mouth. She took in a deep breath and got a
head full of Seth's soap. She loved the smell. Blink-
ing her eyes, she focused on the anger she'd been

building up before she'd gotten distracted. "There's no way Shauna killed Kevin."

"You know that for a fact?" Seth challenged.

"I do. And I'm going to prove it. Two people bought the same rat killer in the last month. It had to be the second person."

"Who's the other person?"

Cat shrugged. "A woman with red hair."

This time, Seth didn't answer. He just raised his eyebrows.

"Okay, so it's a little vague. I didn't want to push because he didn't have to tell me anything, but I thought I'd call Uncle Pete and see if he's got any kind of video surveillance of the hardware store." Cat started to list the questions she'd ask her uncle.

"I think you have a problem there. Most of the town security tapes are dumped periodically and none of them are in color. So red hair isn't much to go on." Seth reached out to touch her arm, but Cat stepped back.

"I'm still going to prove Shauna didn't kill Kevin." She decided it was time to change the subject before Shauna came out of the kitchen and found them talking. She asked, "What's going on with the attic furnace?"

"Hank's waiting for the part to come in and then he'll be over. The game went into overtime last night so I got in late. Everyone except the two girls was already in their rooms by the time I got here." A lazy grin curved his lips. "Even you."

Cat took a step toward the stairs. "I was beat. And now, I'm heading upstairs to write. Let me know when the attic isn't an icebox."

He put his hand up to his head in a short salute. "Yes, ma'am."

"I am not a dictator." Cat headed up the stairs. "You both need to get over that."

She heard the laughter coming out of the kitchen all the way up to the second floor. Instead of being mad, she felt thankful that Shauna was starting to return to the land of the living. Even though she hadn't dated Kevin long, Cat knew her friend. And Shauna had fallen fast and hard for the guy. When she reached her office, Shirley's piles were on the coffee table. Apparently, the woman had spent several hours here last night, as many of the boxes had been moved from under the window to a neat pile next to the couch. She glanced at the open notebook on the table, but even though Shirley's handwriting was neat and legible, she must have used some sort of shorthand because the words strung together didn't make any sense to Cat.

Cat's grandmother had been a secretary over at Covington for years. Grandpa said she'd worked for mad money, but Cat wondered if her grandmother had needed the intellectual stimulation from a job. She'd left Cat her books, and one of the older ones from her high school days was a course on shorthand. Cat had loved the wavy lines and precision of the images and how they turned into words. Shirley's shorthand wasn't based on images but instead on abbreviations that Cat didn't understand. Maybe it was a cop thing.

She abandoned the project on the coffee table and went to her own desk. She'd left the notebook in which she'd made notes about Kevin and his life on top of the desk. Had it been moved? She was sure she'd left it to the right side, but now it was more centered. Maybe Shirley was a little snoopy, just like Cat had been.

She pushed the book aside and opened a blank document. Thirty minutes later, she closed the Word program in frustration. Whatever she'd thought she'd had in her head for this next story had been crowded out by thoughts of Michael and Kevin. Cat picked up the notebook and opened it, reading over what she'd found. When she got to the last page, the one where she'd started listing information on Jade, a page was missing.

She turned back to the page before, where she'd left off in mid-sentence describing the photo of the three of them at the party. The next page was completely blank, and yet, Cat knew she'd written down at least a few paragraphs about Paul's sister, including where she lived and the names of her children with Kevin. Why would someone take just that page? Cat took a pencil and tried to do a lead rub. Some of the words appeared, but others were gone forever. She thought of Collin standing in Shauna's kitchen. She didn't know why the guy was being a creeper, but she was going to find out.

Digging in her desk drawer, she found the envelope from Bowman Investigations. She took out the report and started reading. When she'd finished, she tossed the papers on her desk. The one person she didn't have a report on was the one she had concerns on. "Over a hundred dollars and not a speeding ticket between them."

"I wondered if you pulled background checks on your guests." Shirley stood in the doorway, watching her. She held out a hand as Cat spun around in her chair. "Don't get me wrong—I would do the same thing if I was bringing people into my house. And your uncle said you've had some problems with guests lately."

"I'm still not comfortable with doing it. It feels like I'm prying." Cat closed the notebook where she'd been making notes on Kevin. No need for it to get back to her uncle that she was snooping into Kevin's life.

"You have to face it, the world isn't as safe as it once was. Taking a few precautions isn't a bad thing." Shirley pointed to the couch. "You mind if I work a little up here? Your ex-husband was a fascinating man. I'm always surprised at what you can learn about someone through their work product."

"Go ahead. I'm not working anyway." Cat turned off the computer. "I don't believe in writer's block, but sometimes, it's hard to write fiction when your mind's on other things."

Shirley sighed. "How is your friend? She seems so sad, like a beautiful ghost in a castle."

"Shauna's better." Cat didn't correct Shirley. If she wanted to assume Cat's concern was over the state of her friend, she'd let her. Besides, it would be better told to Uncle Pete that way. "I know Kevin's death was a shock to her and I'm sure she's not done grieving, but having people to cook for is helping her get past the initial shock."

"I guess I can see that. Although, even when I was married, I never cooked. I knew how to order from any place that did takeout or delivery in Anchorage though." Shirley opened one of Michael's notebooks, then glanced at her watch. She hit a button, then looked at Cat. "What time is the bookseller talking?"

"Ten." Cat picked up the notebook and headed to the door. "Do you want me to come up and get you?"

"No need, I just set an alarm. I love this watch. The city gave it to me when I retired, although I would have rather have had a pension." She turned back to the notebook.

Cat went to her room and put the notebook on her desk. This room was locked and no one except Shauna had a key. She needed to find out who had been snooping and why before something worse happened.

Chapter 12

"Hey, Cat?" Shauna's voice echoed up the stairs.

Cat hurried down to the second-floor landing. She'd just left her room after making sure she not only locked her door, but set up a booby trap on the notebook, just in case someone did somehow get in. This time she'd know for sure.

"I'm coming down. What's wrong?" She leaned over the railing, trying to see her friend. When there was no answer, she hurried down the rest of the stairs. "Shauna?"

"Over here." Shauna was at the registration table talking to Paul Quinn, one of her uncle's officers. Or was he a detective now? Cat couldn't keep the chain of command at the police station straight. Today, Quinn was dressed in a suit instead of an Aspen Hills police uniform. He'd insisted on being called by his last name since junior high. Cat frowned as she walked up.

"Everything okay?"

Quinn shook his head frantically. "No, Mrs. Latimer, everything is not okay."

"You *can* call me Cat." She had gone to school with Quinn. He knew her name. What the heck was going on?

He ignored her request. "Mrs. Latimer, your house is a robber's haven. You have no security cameras on your doorways and you host these writers' retreats where people come and go all the time. You are just asking to be robbed." The sales pitch had begun. He put his briefcase on the desk and flipped open the brass locks. "I'm here to make you sleep better at night."

"I sleep fine, Quinn." Cat wasn't much for the hard sell. "What is it you want to sell me?"

"Peace of mind, Cat. I'm selling peace of mind." He handed her a pamphlet.

"Does Uncle Pete know you're selling these things?" Cat opened the flyer, which advertised a security system that had cameras situated over the entire house. "I don't know, Quinn. I'm not ready to put in something this expensive."

"Of course he does. He told me to report my sales but so far, they've been pretty limited. I've had a lot of people just pull out their hunting rifle and tell me they had a security system in place. Any way, you need to ask yourself, how do you put a price tag on peace of mind, Cat?" Quinn pointed to the bottom of the flyer. "Our system monitors your house even when you're not in town or when you're asleep. You can't do it all yourself, especially with the number of strangers you have in your home, month after month."

He had a point there, and she had been considering a system. She just hadn't done any research into costs or what she really wanted. "Look, I'll keep this flyer and I'll call you in a few months to give you my decision."

"You may not have a few months. Look what happened to Kevin Shield. The good thing is he had invested in the security system just a few months ago."

"And yet, he's still dead." Cat didn't want to point out the obvious, but Quinn's system hadn't saved Kevin's life. "Unless you're telling me that you have pictures of the person who killed him and you've turned them in to my uncle."

"Don't you think I would have done that first thing?" Quinn ran a hand through his prematurely thinning hair. "Geez, Cat, I'm not an idiot, no matter what people say."

"I didn't mean to say you were an idiot. Did anyone show up on the video feed?" She'd assumed Kevin had had his own private security system, not one he'd bought off of Paul Quinn.

"There was a shadow outside the horse barn. Kevin said something to them, looked around, then pushed the person into the doorway. They didn't have cameras installed in the barn. They should have. I told them it would be more protection to have cameras in all the buildings, but he didn't care about the barn. He only has one horse in there now anyway." Quinn looked around, then lowered his voice. "I think he only kept that one around for Ms. Clodagh."

Shauna loved to ride. When she'd found out that Kevin had a horse, she'd spent hours out at the ranch, riding and taking care of the horse. It had been a sore spot in their relationship since Shauna had felt like Kevin hadn't been taking care of the horse before she'd arrived. Probably one of the toys that he'd purchased, then forgotten about once he'd lost interest in the item. She wondered what would happen to the horse now that Kevin was gone and Shauna had been banned from the ranch.

A shadow at the barn. Cat wondered about the house. The killer would have had to get into the house with the poison sometime after Shauna had arrived. Cat froze. If Shauna had been hungry, she would have eaten the stew as well, instead of her salad. Her friend had almost died too, but no one was thinking about that.

Quinn was still talking, and Cat wondered what she'd missed. Finally, he took a breath.

"Did you look at the images of the house that night? Are there cameras there?" Cat broke into his descriptions.

"Unfortunately, no. Kevin didn't want the house on surveillance. The man had privacy issues." Quinn shook his head. "If he'd listened to me, that place would have been covered in cameras and this might not have happened. So when can I schedule your walk-through? I'd like to get started setting up the system as soon as possible. If I get one more sale this quarter, I'll hit bronze level. It doesn't even have to be the whole house. Kevin's system almost set me on bronze all by itself."

"Look, I'm just not able to afford a system right now. I hate to waste more of your time."

The sigh that followed her announcement went through Quinn's entire body. "I'll convince you, I promise."

He closed his briefcase, then handed her a card. "You can reach me at this number if you have any questions."

"I know where you work, and where you live. I'm pretty sure I could find you without this." She held out the embossed card.

"Keep it. The security company makes me give these out on every cold call I make. It's a pain and they cost an arm and a leg, but I guess it's the cost of doing business." He glanced around the large foyer and pointed to two spots on the ceiling. "I think putting the interior cameras there would be best. That way, your guests don't even know they're being watched."

Cat waited until Quinn was out of the house before reaching down to throw both the pamphlet and the card in the trash.

"You sure you want to do that?" Shauna's voice came from behind her. She stepped around and took the card and flyer out of the trash can. "It's a good system. Paul and Kevin were talking about how much cheaper it was to get this set up than hire a private team."

"And look where it got him." Cat squeezed her eyelids shut. "I'm sorry—that was rude and uncaring."

"You forgot one thing." Shauna tucked the flyer with the card into the desk drawer. "It was also true. Look, we need to get past this. I'm really tired of being treated like some hothouse flower, ready to fall apart at a moment's notice. Seth's even being weird around me since Kevin died."

Before Cat could respond, Sasha came running down the stairs. "Oh, gosh, I'm so sorry."

"Why are you sorry?" Cat and Shauna turned toward her.

Sasha stopped in front of them, her breath heavy. "Aren't I late?"

"No, it's not quite ten yet." Cat glanced at the grandfather clock. "You still have fifteen minutes. Have you eaten anything?"

Sasha ran her hands over her jeans, then pushed back her hair. "No, and I don't think I should. I don't think I could keep it down. I'm so nervous."

"Don't be." Shauna took the girl by the shoulder and gently moved her toward the dining room. "Let's get you some tea."

Cat went into the living room to make sure it was ready for Sasha's presentation. The last thing she needed was problems with the setup. Of course, these groups were small and intimate. They didn't use microphones or projectors. Just a portable whiteboard that Cat kept hidden in the closet and some markers.

She glanced around the room when she was done setting up the podium area. The room looked warm and welcoming. As she finished checking the markers, Jordon Hart came in and took a seat on the couch.

"I wasn't expecting to get to talk to a bookseller. Of course, I don't even have a contract yet, so anything she says will be for future use." He tapped the notebook she'd seen him carrying around all week.

"She's very knowledgeable. I think you'll enjoy listening to her talk about her book club groups." Cat adjusted one of the wing chairs to aim toward the front of the room. "Of course, you can also go talk to Tammy Jones, here in town. She might have a different perspective since she owns the business. We're all in this crazy business together—we might as well learn what works for all of us."

Jordon nodded, opening his notebook to a fresh

page. "I'm really interested in how you do your marketing. Are you going out to talk to schools? Youth groups?"

"That's actually how I met Sasha. She used to work for an independent bookstore in South Cove, California. So I got to talk to over a hundred teen readers who either liked my first book or had heard it was good. Of course, the first step is to complete your manuscript." Cat sat down on the couch next to Jordon. She'd planned on talking to everyone about the retreat. This way, it seemed more conversational and less intense. "How's your writing going this week?"

"I've gotten three chapters done. The five of us are doing a word-count challenge—did you know that?" When Cat shook her head, he continued, "Whoever writes the most words in a day gets their dinner paid for by the others. I've almost won, but Collin's taken the prize twice. To be honest, I think he needs the free meal so he really hustles during the day. Being a graduate student is tough, especially since he's trying to send money home to his mom too."

Collin seemed to be a sweet kid. No wonder he'd been concerned about Shauna and how she was feeling after losing Kevin. The guy had his own problems trying to support his mom. Empathy was a learned skill, not an inherited one. "I didn't know that."

"Well, don't tell him I told you. We were drinking a few beers last night and he let it slip when he stopped at just one. I bought him a couple, but I'm sure he doesn't like to feel like he's getting charity."

"My lips are sealed." Cat looked up as the rest of

the guests entered the room chatting quietly. Cat stood and walked around the coffee table, freeing up another seat. "Looks like it's time to get started. I'll go get Sasha."

She passed through the group as Collin spoke to Melissa, overhearing his words. "If you ever want to go into Denver for some sightseeing, I can borrow my roommate's car. It's not pretty, but it gets you where you need to go."

Smiling, Cat left the living room and went to track down Sasha. She was sitting at the table with Shauna, a cup of mint tea in her hands. "You're up! I know you'll be amazing."

Fear showed in Sasha's face as she turned to stare at Cat. "I can't do this. I'll pay for my plane ticket and the room and board. I'm sorry. I thought I could, but I can't."

Cat slipped into the seat next to her and took Shauna's cold, shaking hand in her own. "Calm down. You can do this. Now, tell me what you were going to say."

"That's just it. I've already forgotten and I don't want to just read what I've prepared." A tear fell from her eye and plopped on her floral dress.

"Okay, then, how were you going to start?" Cat threw her an encouraging smile. "Just your opening line, nothing else."

Sasha started and Cat could see the nerves fall away as she started talking about where she used to work. Cat held her hand up after the first sentence. "Stop. Now take a deep breath. That was lovely and informative. What was going to be your next sentence?"

They went through the first five minutes of the speech, and Sasha's shoulders dropped as she realized she did know the information. She took a deep breath and smiled at Cat. "That was pretty tricky."

"Tricky is my middle name—just ask Seth." Cat stood. "You ready to go slay this?"

Sasha nodded and made her way to the door. "If I don't come back, tell Olivia that mommy loved her."

"They're writers, not lions," Cat called after her.

Shauna moved the cookies toward Cat. "Nicely done. Want a treat?"

"If you keep rewarding me with food, I'll be as big as a house." Cat took the butter cookie off the plate and took a big bite.

"That's why I keep telling you we need to set up a home gym in the basement. It's clean and dry down there. The guests would love it," Seth said as he entered the kitchen and sank into a chair. He took a cookie and wagged it at the two women. "Besides, with all the crazy, fattening treats you make, you need something at the retreat that's a healthy option."

"You're right. I do need to do it, but I'm focusing on the attic right now. When will that project be complete?" Cat moved the cookie plate out of Seth's reach.

"I've got some bad news. The part Hank ordered came in wrong. He's on the phone getting the right one, but it will be tomorrow before we can finish up." Seth got up and poured himself a cup of coffee. "Which means . . ."

Cat interrupted him. "Which means you can't take Sasha to the airport."

"Give the woman a stuffed bear. She got it on the first try." Seth turned the chair around and sat on it backwards, leaning on the railed back. "I'm really sorry, Cat, but the good news is the roads should be clear. There's no precipitation expected until this weekend. And Sunday when I drove to the airport, the roads were mostly free of ice."

"It's the mostly that always worries me." Cat took a second cookie. "Bad news always seems better after a sugar rush."

"I can take her." Shauna sipped her coffee. "You don't have to do everything, you know."

Cat shook her head. "I don't want you to be out of town in case anything happens."

"What, you think I'm running away after killing Kevin? Do you and your uncle think I'm the Lizzie Borden type? I don't even own an axe." Shauna held her hands up in claws and made a wooing sound. "I'll get you and your little dog too."

Seth and Cat exchanged a glance.

"Guys, it was supposed to be a joke. Seriously, what is wrong with the two of you?" Shauna looked back and forth between her two friends.

"It's just that you had access to the poison. And, honestly, you were upset at him when you left that day." Seth blurted out the words.

"Well, aren't you the trusting type. I can't believe you think I'd do something like that. I thought we'd gotten past this. It was a perfectly good Irish stew, except, well, no matter." Shauna looked at Cat. "I suppose you agree with your boyfriend that I'm a stone-cold killer?"

"No. And Seth doesn't believe it either. We just have to figure out what really happened so you won't be sent up to the big house with your Aunt Lizzie."

Shauna's lips twitched. "She wasn't really my aunt. Did that whole thing happen around here though? I thought it was in the west somewhere."

"Sorry, no. Lizzie Borden was back east. Not that it's important," Seth added quickly as both Shauna and Cat glared at him. "What? I thought we were talking again. It was nice for a few minutes."

"Anyway, we both know you didn't kill Kevin. But if Uncle Pete needs to talk to you, now would be better than later. My uncle can be a bit of a taskmaster when he wants to get something done and out of his hair." Cat shrugged. "Besides, if we get a freak snowstorm while you're gone, I'll have to cook for the guests myself."

"Now that argument I agree with." Shauna glanced around the warm and cozy room.

Cat noticed the room had started to take on Shauna's personality. It *was* her kitchen. When Cat had been married to Michael, he'd been the one to choose the paint colors and decorations. She'd been too busy, first with finishing her graduate degree and then with teaching. Shauna had added more personal touches in the last six months than Cat had during all the years of her marriage.

"Now that I've delivered the bad news, I've got to get back to Hank and see what the progress is on that part. I've told him I'll take him to The Diner for dinner tonight, then we'll probably hit Bernie's. I might just crash at the apartment if you don't mind." He looked at the two women. "I'm willing to come over if you need me, but it will be late."

"No need. I'll see you in the morning sometime." Cat stood to leave. "Wait, did you ever take those books to the library?"

He shook his head. "Sorry, I've been knee deep in this furnace disaster. I think we've torn that furnace apart and put it together so many times in the last few days that I could build them as a career. Do you think Miss Applebome will be at the library on Friday?"

"No, you can take them on Monday." Cat pondered the idea. "Maybe I'll come with you. I'd like to know what she thinks of the donation."

"She should be thrilled with getting all those. Some of them looked positively ancient. Are you sure you don't want a collector to look through them before you donate them?"

"I didn't think of that." Cat pondered the idea.

"Think about it. We can always take them over next week. It's not like the library is hurting for books. They'll probably sit in those boxes until Miss Applebome finds a work-study student with some time." He put his fingers to his forehead in a two-finger salute and disappeared out into the hallway.

"Professor Ngu has just been so insistent that anything of Michael's belongs at the school."

"Why *is* that?" Shauna put up her hand. "Don't get me wrong. I'm sure Michael was brilliant, but he hadn't made a name for himself in the field. Why does the dean want his papers at the school?"

Shirley joined them in the kitchen, looking behind her like she could see through the wall. "That man of yours is nice to look at."

Cat turned Seth's empty chair around facing the table and patted the table in front of it. "Come sit with us. We're talking about Michael and his legacy."

Shauna stood and grabbed a bag of cookies off the counter. "I'm not really concerned with Michael's legacy. I'm just wondering why Dean Ngu is so insistent that the library and the college get a hold of Michael's papers. Seriously, why does he care where they wind up?"

Shirley held up the notebook in her hand. A blue spiral notebook, one of Michael's. "I think I can answer at least that question."

Chapter 13

The group gathered around the table as Shirley opened the notebook to the second page. "This appears to be the workbook for the secret project that you told me about. He writes about the work, what the assignment was, and then, here, mentions who had hooked him up with this job."

Cat followed Shirley's finger and read the name out loud. "Dean Ngu!"

"That's the guy who was so pushy with you on Sunday, right?" Shirley asked.

"One and the same. I knew he was the one who referred Michael. I could tell by the way he didn't answer my questions directly. The bigger question is who was he working for?" Cat took the notebook out of Shirley's hands and flipped through the pages, looking for names or meetings, or anything that would lead to more information. She paused on a page at the end. "This was the address on the card Michael left for me."

"What card?" Shirley scanned the address. "You didn't mention a card."

"One of our other guests found it in the research books Michael had collected about the area." Cat stood and went to the kitchen desk. She opened the drawer where she kept the office stuff and dug through until she found the envelope. She'd been meaning to check out the place the next time she was in Denver, once spring arrived. She handed the envelope to Shirley, who opened it and slipped out the small sheet of paper. "It looks like your husband's handwriting."

"It is," Cat agreed, but Shirley moved the paper over to the notebook to double-check.

"Did you check out where this address is?" Shirley stared at the loose sheet like it was a treasure map.

"Yes." Cat shook her head. "It's a dry cleaner. I thought Michael might have just been sending me to pick up his shirts and the envelope got lost in all the divorce stuff."

"That could be right." Shirley set the page aside. "I'll do some research on who owns the property first thing tomorrow. Maybe that will reveal more."

"Or, maybe it will just be one of Michael's to-do lists." Shauna glanced at her watch. "You're missing the bookseller talk. If you hurry, I bet you'll catch most of it."

Shirley stood. "I wanted to drop this off before I went into the living room. You go over the notebook and see if anything jumps out at you. I'll take the Denver address and do some more digging. Maybe we will wrap this case up before I leave on Sunday. I have a good feeling about this lead."

Shauna pointed at the door and said to Cat, "You need to get in there too. Sasha needs your support."

"I already asked and she didn't want me to come."

Cat flipped back to the beginning of the notebook. "I'm going to go into the study and read this. Do you need anything from me before I leave?"

"Like what?" Shauna narrowed her eyes. "Just because I'm grieving Kevin's loss doesn't mean I'm not capable of handling my retreat responsibilities."

"I never said . . ."

Shauna didn't let her get the words out. "Sorry, gut reaction. I don't know when my emotions will settle down and go back to normal. I'm okay one moment, then I'm sad, then I'm mad as hell."

Cat put a hand on her friend's back. "You're one of the strongest women I know. I can't believe you're getting through this as well as you have. I would have been a melted pile of mush by this time, especially after the crap Jade pulled last night at the restaurant."

"I can't really blame her. She's grieving too. And I'm an easy target as the other woman." A small smile curved Shauna's lips. "The man's going to have a lot to account for when he meets Saint Peter, including giving up on not one, but two families. I'm kind of feeling like I might just have dodged a bullet there."

Cat poured herself another cup of coffee and took it and the notebook into the study. She curled up in her chair rather than behind the desk and set the cup down on a granite coaster. After opening up the notebook, she read through 'til the end. Turning the last page, she realized either Michael had moved the rest of the story to another notebook, or this one had some pages missing. She looked closely at the spiral wires where little bits of paper clung after the page they'd been attached to had been ripped out of the notebook. Pages were definitely gone.

What she'd thought might be the answer to one mystery had ended in another one. Who had ripped out the pages? And if it had been Dante's nephew who had been sneaking around the house, why hadn't he taken the entire notebook? No, there was something more to this than met the eye.

She tucked the notebook under her arm and took her empty cup to the kitchen. When she emerged with a bottle of water to take upstairs with her, the lobby was filled with people pulling on coats.

Collin stood by Pamela and Melissa, putting on his coat. Cat heard him repeat his earlier offer. "Seriously, if you two want to take a trip to Denver to see the city before you leave, just let me know. My roommate has a car we can borrow. All we have to do is fill it up with gas."

The girls giggled and put on hats and gloves.

Collin pulled a ski cap over his blond hair. "It's kind of a beater, but the engine is solid and it's great on gas. So it won't cost us a lot to go. I know a few good dance clubs we could check out."

Cat heard Melissa's one-word answer before they headed outside. "Maybe."

Sasha held back when she saw Cat. "We're going for pizza. Want to come along?"

"No, I was just checking to see how the talk went." Cat figured it had been successful, mostly because of the size of the grin plastered on the young woman's face. She waved her toward the open door. "But we can chat later. Just come find me when you get back. I'd love to hear your take on the session."

After everyone had left, Cat went into the living room and was surprised to see Jordon Hart still in the room, scribbling into his notebook. She glanced back at the doorway. "You know the rest of the group just left for lunch, right?"

He finished a line, then looked up at her, not moving his pen away from the page. "I know. I told them to order for me and I'd be down as soon as I get this scene out of my head."

"That good, huh?" Cat moved the podium out of the walkway and into its permanent spot next to the bookshelves.

"Does that happen to you where you think, 'that would be perfect'?" He started writing again, but at a slower pace. Having Cat in here had interrupted the flow of words.

"Sometimes. I'm a pantser so I have to find my way around a story, but when I start thinking about a problem, it always reveals the solution in time." She wiped down the whiteboard and folded it up, putting it away in the closet on the other side of the room.

She wasn't sure if Jordon had heard her since he continued to write rather than keeping up his end of the conversation. She didn't mind. She knew she was equally laser focused at times during her writing. And Shauna and Seth still put up with her. She had a lot to be thankful for. She walked around the room, picking up cups and trash. Behind one of the bookcases, she found a tray that Shauna used to bring in treats. She filled it with the discarded items she'd found and started to head out of the room, giving Jordon his privacy.

But instead of continuing to write, he stood and

followed her. "This was perfect. I got a great start on one of the reveal scenes, but I still need to layer in hidden clues for the reader to find."

"You think about that while you're writing? Couldn't you just add them in later?" Cat hadn't studied the writing process of mysteries and she was undeniably curious.

"It doesn't work like that, at least not for me. Finding the clues has to be organic, part of the whole story. And when something happens in chapter four, it affects all the chapters before and after." He patted his notebook. "With the reputation this place is getting for being murder central for Aspen Hills, I would have thought you knew that."

Cat groaned. "Please don't say that. I've been hoping that would be our little secret."

"Don't get me wrong. It's not like people think they're going to be killed when they check in." He waved his hand toward the dining room. "Except maybe someone could die of overeating. You guys put out a great breakfast. I hardly need to eat the rest of the day."

Cat set the tray on the registration table and looked around. She wondered if being attached to so many murders recently would start to affect retreat registrations. She really didn't want to lose the house, not a second time. "Now you have me worried."

"Believe me, writers are more likely to come to a place with a little backstory than some boring white-walled motel for a retreat like this. You've got it made." He glanced at the clock. "I've got to get moving or my pizza will be cold—or worse, half eaten by Collin before I get there. You would think that kid had been raised by wolves. He eats constantly."

After Jordon left, Cat took a quick peek into the dining room to see if anything needed refreshing, but apparently, Shauna had already taken care of that task. The retreat week was busy but between the three of them, they had most of the tasks down to a science. As long as no one was killed or kidnapped, that was. She took the tray into the empty kitchen and grabbed another cookie and a bottle of water. She decided to head up to her office to start going through the boxes that Shirley had finished. She wanted to know just what she was handing over to Dean Ngu, especially now that she knew he'd had a hand in referring Michael to his second job.

A knock came at her door after she'd finished reviewing the papers in two of the boxes. Shauna came in with a tray and what looked like enough sandwiches and pasta salad for the writing retreat guests. "What's all this?"

Shauna set the tray in the middle of the coffee table, and then grabbed a stack of papers. "I'm setting these down on the floor right underneath the table. That way, we don't mess with your system."

Cat grabbed another set she'd already gone through and moved it to a box marked DONE. "Who's we? Don't tell me I forgot about a session I was supposed to lead."

"No, you have a guest. And I invited him to eat lunch with us." Shauna looked at the doorway.

Cat held her breath. Had Dante returned again, this time through the front door like she'd requested? She needed to get him to understand that she wasn't interested in dating him now, or ever. Cat heard heavy footsteps hit the third-floor landing, and then her uncle came into the room.

He slipped his phone back into his pocket. "Sorry about that. Katie was calling with an update on a project I'd given her."

Cat eyed him suspiciously. "You just came over in the middle of your workday to chat?"

He sat down next to Shauna on the couch and took the plate she held out to him. "Come sit down and eat with us. We need to talk."

Cat sighed, knowing that nothing good ever followed that phrase. She pulled up her office chair and took a plate that Shauna now held out for her. "About what? Kevin's death? Or Michael's? Or did Reno's Pizza blow up?"

Uncle Pete's hand froze as he was reaching for a sandwich. "Not that I know of. Why? Someone calling in bomb threats? It's a little early in the semester and, typically, it's in the math department on a test day that the shenanigans happen. I swear, I'm going to start having Homeland come in and do a scare assembly first thing every semester."

"No, I mean, you don't usually just come by and talk. And the gang's all down at Reno's for lunch. The way things are going, I thought maybe you were here about them." She took her sandwich and balanced her plate on her knees. She didn't want to mention her trip to the hardware store, not in front of Shauna. Cat decided she'd wait to ask her uncle more about that when they were alone.

"Sometimes I think you're a pessimist." Uncle

Pete shook his head. "You know, there are times I visit for no reason at all."

"And yet, why do I have the feeling this isn't one of those times?" She took a bite of the ham sandwich, watching his reaction.

He glanced at Shauna, who was focused on eating and pointedly not looking at either of them. "Okay, you're right. I am here on a mission. And the investigation into Kevin's death is still pretty new so I don't have much to go on. Yet."

"What did I do now?" Cat thought about the last week. She hadn't put herself in any danger that she could remember.

"It's not what you did. It's what I worry you're planning to do." Uncle Pete took a bite of the pasta salad, then set down his fork. "Shirley told me what she found out about the Denver address. Why didn't you tell me?"

Cat set her sandwich down on the plate. "I didn't tell you because I didn't know if it was important. And I still don't. Who cares who owns a dry-cleaning shop?"

"You should." Uncle Pet pulled a piece of paper out of his pocket and set it on the coffee table. He pushed it toward her.

"Why?" She stared at her uncle, but when he just pointed to the folded paper, she set her plate down and picked it up. Unfolding it, she read the first page. She looked at her uncle in shock. "You have to be kidding."

"I had Katie go down to the county courthouse this morning and pull a copy from the records. I knew you wouldn't believe it unless you saw it."

Uncle Pete took a bite of his sandwich, watching Cat read the entire document.

Shauna dished up the last of the pasta salad, dividing it among Cat, Pete, and herself. She set the bowl down, then looked at the two of them. "So do I have to guess, or is one of you going to spill the beans?"

Cat shook her head and handed Shauna the paper.

It only took a few seconds for her to find the relevant part. "You own the building? Why?"

"That's the question, isn't it?" Uncle Pete took the paper from Shauna and turned a couple of pages. He pointed to a part near the signatures. "It was put in your name a couple years ago, while you were still in California. Katie said she tracked down the title company on the deal and talked to them just now. Michael transferred the property from his name into yours just months before his death."

"I don't understand." Cat scanned the document again. "What does a lot in Denver run? At least five figures, right? Where would Michael have gotten that kind of money? We had our retirement funds, but professors don't make a lot of money."

"I never had the opportunity to look into Michael's financials when he died, the ruling that it was a heart attack was so quick. Bob Jenkins did the autopsy and closed the file on the same day." Uncle Pete took out his notebook and scribbled a note. "The district attorney and the mayor were all concerned about me since Michael had been your husband. I should have looked more closely at the evidence. Instead, I took Bob's findings at face value."

Cat thought about Michael's love of running.

The man often trained for marathons and had even talked about doing an Ironman one day. "Both of his parents died young, he told me it was a car accident. He went to both Covington and Harvard on a mix of scholarships and student loans. And that's about all I know of my ex-husband's humble beginnings. Kind of scary now that I think of it."

Uncle Pete stopped writing. He looked at her strangely. "Michael went to Covington?"

"I just found that out when I found the yearbooks in his study. I don't think he ever talked about where he got his undergrad, now that I think about it. I mean, we talked classes and campus life stuff, but he never once said he went to Covington. In fact, I had the impression he was back east for college." Cat picked up her sandwich, studied it, pulled off a sliver of ham, and set the rest down. Thoughtfully, she added, "So you didn't know either. You must have worked at the police station back then. You didn't run into him?"

Uncle Pete shook his head. "I don't see or meet up with every student at Covington, especially not, what? Ten to fifteen years ago. I was just the beat cop for the town. My chief was handling all the sensitive Covington stuff."

"By sensitive, you mean meeting with the Mob families?"

When her uncle nodded, Cat sat back, trying to piece together all this information and whether it even mattered. One, Michael had gone to Covington—that was a fact. He'd been friends with Dante during that time, another fact. Michael died. That was a fact. Of what—now, that was more of a question. Where had he gotten the money to buy the land? And, for some reason, Cat now owned a building in Denver that must be leased to a dry-cleaner business. Things weren't adding up at all.

"Are we looking for zebras here?" Shauna's voice was quiet as she grabbed the lunch remainders and stacked them on her tray.

"I don't understand." Uncle Pete stopped scribbling in his notepad and turned to her, his confusion clear on his face. "Why would we be looking for zebras?"

She shrugged. "It's an old thing my mom always said. It goes something like, 'When you hear the sound of hoof beats, it's more likely to be horses than zebras.'"

"So you think we're reading too much into normal things." Cat put her own plate on Shauna's tray with her half-eaten sandwich. She'd lost her appetite.

Shauna shrugged. "The one thing I've learned about Aspen Hills in the short time I've lived here is nothing is normal."

Uncle Pete and Cat didn't talk until Shauna had left the room. Then he leaned forward and focused on her. "You're sure you didn't know about the property or any money Michael might have stashed away for such a purpose?"

"When we divorced, my lawyer gave me an entire list of everything Michael had, just in case I would change my mind about not wanting support after seeing the figures. The only two big things he had were the house and his retirement. He took a loan out of the 401K, paid me a settlement, and we were done." Cat set the paper down.

"What did you do with the money?"

"Bought my Jeep and put the rest on my student loans. That's why I should be able to pay them off next year." She held up a hand. "Before you ask, it was forty thousand dollars. My share of our marital assets, including the value of the house. But he had to take out a loan to get the money."

"I wasn't going to ask you how much you got, niece." Uncle Pete patted my hand. "I was going to ask who Michael's attorney was for both the divorce and the estate. Maybe I need to go chat with them."

She shook her head. "No. Let me. If a cop shows up asking about Michael and this guy is connected, they might just tip our hand. If I go, I can play dumb."

"Darling, you can never play dumb." Her uncle chuckled. "But I'll let you do some Nancy Drewing here as long as you take someone with you. I don't want you going alone."

Cat filled him in on what she'd learned at the hardware store, which wasn't much, but Uncle Pete wrote it down in his notebook. If he could find this other red-haired woman, maybe Shauna would be okay. She walked her uncle to her office door. "I think I know just the person to help me with this."

Chapter 14

By six, the guests were all at The Cafeteria for dinner and Seth and Hank had left to spend the evening at Seth's place. Shauna, Cat, and Sasha sat around the kitchen table eating dinner. Cat was writing a list of questions to ask the attorney. She'd called as soon as Uncle Pete had left and the guy's secretary had squeezed her into a ten o'clock cancellation. Which still gave Cat plenty of time to get Sasha to the airport.

"So, maybe I start with the money in Michael's 401K. What happened to it? Maybe see if I can get it?" Cat worried her bottom lip.

"You want to play the greedy ex-wife?" Shauna nodded, appraising her friend. "I can see that working. But you need to wear something expensive. Like big jewelry, and I'll loan you the black mink Kevin gave me for Christmas. It's a total Colorado look of wealth. Jeans, jewelry, boots, and the black fur bomber jacket. He won't know what hit him."

Cat had seen women like that around Denver and a few in Aspen Hills, but their town was too small to attract the people with real money, unless they were visiting their kids at Covington.

"Make sure you ask about property. Let him tell you that you own that lot. Then drill him about where the income from the rentals is going and when can you sell it." Sasha pointed to Cat's paper.

"And life insurance. If Michael didn't take you off the house, maybe you're still on his life insurance," Shauna added as she swirled pasta around her fork.

"Guys, I'm not really looking for more money from Michael's estate. The point is to find out where the money to buy the property came from." Cat frowned at the list of questions. She really would look like a greedy ex-wife if she asked all this.

"You don't care what you look like—you have to get him talking. And then at the end, you could be surprised that Michael even had enough money to buy the lot. Since when you were married he seemed to be broke all the time. Heck, you even had to pay for the heat for that drafty old house he left you." Sasha glanced around the room. "I bet the place costs a lot for utility bills."

"That's good." Shauna pointed at Sasha. "What she said. You need to get the guy feeling sorry for you. Maybe he isn't connected, but who knows in this town. Besides, everyone thinks authors are rich. You can just play that card too."

"It's going to take a bit to get me to remember all this. Sasha, why don't you come into the office with me. You could play someone who found that there were two properties in my name because you were doing a practice search for one of your business law classes."

"Oh, I like that. And that way, if you forget to ask something, I can be like, 'hey, remember you wanted to ask this too.'" Sasha held up her phone. "And I can tape the conversation while I'm pretending to be bored and play on my phone."

Cat narrowed her eyes. "Is that legal?"

"I'm not sure, but at least your uncle will be able to hear what the guy says, even if he can't use it in court."

"While you're in Denver, I'm going to do some research on Kevin. I guess I can play the greedy fiancée and call up his attorney to see if the guy left me anything. Maybe I can find out who is really profiting from Kevin's death and point your uncle in that direction."

Cat studied her friend. "Are you sure you're up to talking about this? Michael and I were over long before his death. Kevin and you . . ."

"Were going to get married. If someone killed him, I want to help put that person behind bars." Shauna pushed the food around on her plate. "We may not have lasted, but it feels unfinished, never being able to have a chance to try."

"So, let's do something else besides think about the former men in our lives." Sasha pushed away her plate. "Chick flicks?"

"Sounds lovely. I'll go set up the DVD player in the living room." Cat took her plate to the sink.

"I'll pop us some popcorn, along with a bowl for the guests' treat table." Shauna stood and started clearing the table.

"And I'll do dishes." Sasha took her own plate to the sink and opened the dishwasher.

"You don't have to. I can manage," Shauna protested.

Sasha didn't even pause. "I know I don't have to. I want to. Go make popcorn. I call first dibs on movie choice."

"I'm beginning to feel like we should have a nickname like Spies R Us. Maybe we should watch *Charlie's Angels* or something." Cat headed to the kitchen door. "I'll pull out all the romantic comedies I have and, Sasha, you can have first pick."

They gathered a few minutes later in the living room. The treat room was set up for the guests, the kitchen was cleaned, and all they needed to do was pick a movie. When Sasha had finished, the trio relaxed into the couch and spent the evening laughing. Melissa and Pamela joined them when they arrived back from dinner, but Jordon, Collin, and Shirley said their good-nights and headed upstairs to their rooms to work.

Cat liked the way the house felt, filled with people. Some people she loved, some she barely knew, but she liked all of them. By the time the group broke up for the night, it was after eleven. Sasha gave her a quick hug on her way out of the living room.

"Thanks for a lovely few days. I really needed some girl time and some me time. You don't get that a lot raising a five-year-old. If I don't tell you again tomorrow, I want you to know I really, really appreciated the invitation to visit."

Cat watched as Sasha made her way up the stairs. Books. They brought people together. She was lucky to be in this crazy business. Shauna walked back from checking the lock on the front door.

"She's pretty special. The kid's going to go far in this world."

Cat nodded and walked next to her friend up the stairs. "I know. I'm just hoping she'll be happy along the way."

When Cat got to her room, she saw a text message on her phone. She opened the message from Seth and read the words aloud. "Sweet dreams."

Cat decided to take him up on the offer, and crawled underneath the covers.

The next morning, she woke early, nervous about the upcoming day's events. Driving into Denver to drop off Sasha was enough to set off her nerves, but visiting Michael's attorney? She wondered if she could trust the guy or if Michael had. She guessed there was only one way to find out.

She ate breakfast with Shauna and Seth, not mentioning the detour on her trip. When Shauna started to bring it up, Cat gave her a slight shake of the head. Seth didn't need to know what she was up to today. He'd complain about her putting herself in danger and ask her not to do it. Cat didn't see this as danger. Besides, Uncle Pete had told her to go. One way or the other, she really should have talked to Michael's estate attorney about what happened to the rest of his belongings. Maybe she could pay for a better heater than the one that didn't seem to want to work in the attic.

"Hank's picking up the part right now and we should be up and running by midday." Seth seemed to read her mind about the attic issue. Or maybe he thought she was quiet because of the problems. He unwrapped a peppermint Life Saver and popped it into his mouth. "He's not charging for this fix. It's under warranty."

"I should hope so," Shauna exclaimed. She appeared happy to have a topic she could talk about that didn't deal with death or murder. "I mean, we paid the guy an arm and a leg for the system when he installed it last month."

"Hank's not the bad guy here. Some appliances just have ghosts you have to work out of the system before they work correctly." He glanced around the kitchen. "Anything you need me to do before he gets here?"

Cat shook her head. "Nothing."

He paused, leaning on the door frame. "If I get done before noon, I can take Sasha into Denver and save you a trip. Or she could hitch a ride with Hank. He's going back tonight anyway."

"That's okay," Cat said quickly. "I've got some errands so we're going in early to do some shopping before I drop her off."

His eyes narrowed and Cat could feel his suspicion.

"You're shopping with the retreat in session?" He rubbed at his face. "And I can't even get you to go out to dinner with me during a retreat week?"

"That's not fair." Cat's face burned. "I'm working. This is work too. Sasha needs to do some marketing research for a class before she goes back. So what if it's at the regional mall?"

Seth shrugged his shoulders. "Whatever. I can see where I stand in your priorities."

"Seriously? You want to get into this now?" She

set down her cup and stood, wanting to take the conversation to another room. She didn't like fighting. And she hated fighting in public.

A grin curved Seth's lips. "Gotcha."

"What?" Cat furrowed her brows. "What are you talking about?"

"I was messing with you. You guys have been pretty serious this week, and I get it. Shauna is grieving and the heater went out, but we need to be able to laugh. At least just a little." He gave her a quick salute. As he turned out of the room into the hallway, he called back, "Have fun shopping."

"That man is infuriating sometimes." Cat took her dishes to the sink and turned on the water to rinse them.

Shauna laughed, turning the water off. "He knows how to push your buttons. I can't believe you let him get to you so quickly. Anytime you have something you don't want him to know, he sees right through you."

"Do you think so?" Cat leaned against the countertop.

Grabbing the wash rag, Shauna nodded. "You two are like two parts of a brain. Together, you're whole, but separate, you have your limitations."

Cat refilled her mug. "I'm going upstairs. I've got a rhythm going with those papers. I should be done by early next week and then we can get them out of here and over to the college. Tell Sasha I'll meet her in the lobby at eight-thirty."

"You don't have long to work." Shauna glanced at the clock. "It's already six-thirty."

"I have long enough. My clothes are already laid

out for the transformation, and I don't want to be walking around here in the costume." Sasha and Shauna had raided Cat's closet last night once the plan had been set. "Besides, thinking about economics will keep my mind off what we could be walking into by meeting this lawyer." Dante's warning echoed in her head.

"He'll never know your real mission." Shauna started stacking dishes in the dishwasher. "You are a natural snoop. You have the gift."

Cat wondered if what her friend had said was true or if she'd just been lucky so far. Figuring out who might have wanted to kill someone was easy. She didn't have to worry about a jury or evidence or chain of custody. Not like Uncle Pete did. She could cast aspersions with immunity, even if the person she suspected wasn't the killer. But even she knew she was playing a dangerous game with trying to solve Michael's murder. Dante's warning hadn't been necessary. Not after she'd realized the Mob was involved with Covington. Uncle Pete might be told everything was above board, but every college had its secrets. And Michael must have found out one that got him killed.

All she needed was a clue. And she hoped this trip to the lawyer's office would provide her with at least some information. She settled into her office and started scanning the pages in yet another one of Michael's notebooks. At least this would be over soon. The faster she got through all this stuff, the sooner she could close the door on her first marriage and Michael.

* * *

She and Sasha had gotten out of the house without anyone but Shauna seeing them leave. Which was good since Cat felt ridiculous in the clothes she wore. The black fur kept flying up and tickling her nose. When she got into the driver's seat, she put the coat and the felt hat onto the back seat. When Sasha looked at her questioningly, she swiped at her face, hoping she wasn't messing up the overdone makeup. "I'll put it on before we get to the lawyer's office. I just can't breathe in that thing without fur going up my nose."

"I've never seen a real mink before." Sasha leaned back and stroked the soft fur. "It's amazing."

"I don't know why anyone would want to wear a dead animal." Cat started the car and pulled out of the driveway.

"You wear leather boots. That's a dead animal."

Cat laughed. "True. But for some reason, the fur just seems different."

They talked about Cat's books and writing for most of the trip to Denver. When they got close to the office, Sasha pulled out the list of questions the three of them had made up last night. "You know, if I'm your assistant, I probably could be checking these off as you ask them. He would think I'm just making sure you got what you wanted answered."

"That's good. I was going to say you're my friend, but your age might make him suspicious." Cat eyed the young woman appraisingly. "You're good at this sleuthing thing too."

"In South Cove, you have to be." Sasha pointed to a lot next to a large building. "Park there and get your disguise on. It's time to go fishing."

"Fishing?" Cat pulled on the hat, then checked it

in the mirror. She had to admit, she looked good, in a truly high-maintenance way.

"That's what Toby called it when they interviewed someone and didn't have any evidence to follow up on. You just hope they give you something to use." Sasha got out and stared at the building.

"Remind me, is this Toby old boyfriend or new?" Cat walked around the car and hit the remote lock.

Instead of answering, Sasha pointed to the sidewalk going through the two buildings. "I believe we're looking for the one on the left."

Definitely old boyfriend. Cat adjusted Shauna's fur and started to power walk toward the building opening. She felt Sasha's hand on her arm.

"Slow down," she whispered. "You don't have anything to do except go shopping after this. And probably a late lunch."

Cat looked sideways at her. "What are you talking about? We have to get you to the airport, and then . . ."

Sasha shook her head. "Not this Cat. She's a different person, remember?"

Cat rolled her eyes and slowed down, trying to stroll instead of the fast-paced walk she was more comfortable with. At least the fur kept her warm. If she power walked too long in this thing, she'd be sweating up a storm. She rehearsed her questions silently as they made their way into the building. A large reception desk and security guard stood by the only bank of elevators visible. The rest of the floor must be accessible from another vantage point.

"Can I help you?" the receptionist asked, her

phone headset looking more high-end pop star than office worker.

"I have an appointment with Thomas Charles at ten." Cat didn't trust men who had two first names. It was odd.

The woman looked down at what Cat guessed was a computer screen and nodded. "Ascia added you to the schedule just a few minutes ago. You're Cat Latimer, correct?"

Cat nodded, feeling the hat bobble on her head. She wasn't used to wearing anything but a ski cap, and that was only on the slopes. Her fingers itched to reach up and take it off, but she resisted the urge.

"And my assistant, Sasha Smith." Cat smiled, but kept the action small. "I think sometimes she's my external hard drive with all my memory."

The woman at the desk blinked, but nodded, apparently used to odd statements like the one Cat had just blurted out. "Tenth floor. Ascia will meet you at the elevator and take you to Mr. Charles." She nodded toward the shiny silver elevators. "Have a wonderful day."

When the elevator doors closed, Cat turned and adjusted the hat in the glass mirror. "Stupid thing."

"Be careful," Sasha warned and glanced upward toward the camera in the corner of the elevator.

They were being monitored. Or could be monitored. Cat didn't know what was worse, thinking people were watching or knowing they were. She gave the hat one last tug. "I told you that we should have bought the other one. This hat doesn't want to set correctly. You can't trust something that doesn't come from a designer's label."

Sasha pressed her lips together, trying to keep in

the laughter Cat saw in her eyes. Apparently she'd nailed the role. At least for the moment.

The doors opened and a tall young woman in a black skirted suit stood in the lobby to greet them. She held a file and looked up and smiled when the doors opened, right on cue. "Mrs. Latimer. So nice to finally meet you. I'm so sorry for your loss. Michael was a lovely man."

Cat took the offered hand and shook it. She kept her answer short. "He'll be missed."

The woman nodded, taking Cat's brief answer as a sign she didn't want to engage in small talk. "Mr. Charles will see you in the small conference room. It's this way."

An older man sat at the conference table, a tablet in his hand, poking away at the screen. When Cat walked in, he looked up, closed something on the hand-held computer and then set it aside. "Sorry, too many emails for a twenty-four-hour day, much less an eight-hour one. But here I am complaining about being busy. Catherine, I'm Thomas Charles. I was Michael's attorney for many years. I handled his parents' estate as well."

Cat blinked. Maybe this guy was on the up and up. Still, she didn't know what she didn't know. "Call me Cat." She reached out a hand and then nodded toward Sasha and made the introduction. "I didn't know Michael had an attorney. At least not until I got your letter."

"Well, now you know. If there's anything you need, I'd be glad to help you as well. Keep it in the family, so to speak." He opened the file that his assistant had brought in and left on the table. "So what can I help you with today? Is there a problem regarding the house?"

Cat sat at the chair nearest the man and the file. Sasha flanked him and sat across from Cat. "No, the house is fine. I was just wondering about the rest of Michael's estate. Where did that go?"

"The rest?" He looked down on the file. "The house was the majority of the estate."

"What about his life insurance? What about the retirement funds?" Cat nodded at Sasha, who took out a pad and pen, waiting to take notes. "Who got those?"

Thomas frowned and glanced down at the file. "Are you sure they existed?"

Now Cat felt her temper rising. Even though the trip was supposed to be just a fact-finding mission, now she was invested. Michael had no responsibility to leave her his estate, but this guy didn't even seem to understand what Michael had owned. "I worked for the same college. I know what benefits employees have."

"Well, you must be right. I'm surprised he didn't mention these things when we were making out his will." The lawyer paged through the file. "Oh, here it is. It wasn't included in the will because both assets had beneficiaries set up."

Sasha leaned closer, trying to look over his shoulder. "Who was the beneficiary?"

Thomas Charles closed the file. "I would suspect you'd need to go to the college to find that out. But I would have thought they would have contacted you before this."

"You're saying I'm the beneficiary?" Cat sat back, stunned.

He looked at her, obviously trying to read her emotions. "Unless he changed it after the divorce. I only know what the will said, and that was executed a year before the divorce. In fact, I don't think I saw Michael after the divorce was final. I was just about to have him come in for an update of his estate papers, but then"—he swallowed hard—"it was too late."

"Yes, his passing was unexpected." Cat looked at Sasha, hoping to get away from the emotional moment.

"Okay, so we'll check into the college stuff." Sasha made some notes on her list. "What about bank accounts, stocks, maybe other property?"

Thomas turned in his chair, his back toward Sasha, and addressed Cat. "You still have a joint checking and savings at Aspen Hills bank, but that's everything, I'm afraid." He pulled out an envelope and set it on the shiny walnut surface. "Unless he has something hidden in this envelope. Michael asked me to give this to you when you came. I'd sent a letter to your attorney in the divorce, but I guess it didn't get passed on. He appointed you to be the executor."

Chapter 15

"Don't bother parking. You can just drop me off at the terminal." Sasha checked her watch. "I've left your notepad here with everything I saw in the file listed. Darn, I wish I could stay for a few more days and see this thing through. I thought Mr. Charles was really nice, even though he thought I was a gold-digging friend. Did you see the way he turned away from me?"

"Yeah, I think he told us everything he knew. So if Michael's attorney didn't set up this land purchase in my name, who did? And maybe that is where the life insurance went to, to buy this land? No, the timeline's off on that. He would have had to be dead to get that money." Cat sat through a second light, waiting to turn into the terminal's departure line. The envelope sat unopened in her purse. "I don't think he had another policy he could cash in to get that much money."

"My grandpa always said that you can't print more land. Maybe that's why he wanted property instead of cash. Maybe this other job paid him in property?" Sasha adjusted her shoulder strap and watched as Cat turned toward the line of airlines that flew out of Denver. She pointed to the next area. "There's my airline."

"If so, he was charging them an arm and a leg. I don't think he could have made that much just reviewing corporate accounting records." Cat pulled the car over and stepped out into the cold winter day. "I'll get your bag."

Sasha met her at the back of the SUV and gave her a quick hug. "Again, thanks for everything. I hope you figure out what happened to your ex. Not knowing is the absolute worst."

"Take care and call sometimes. You have our email addresses. Let us know how things are going with this new flame." Cat took out the suitcase and set it next to Sasha. "And thank you for coming. I know the guests enjoyed hearing another side of the publishing business."

"Keep doing these. Everyone loves the process. I even want to start writing just so I can come to a retreat." She waved good-bye and went inside the terminal.

Cat got back into the car and made her way out of the airport grounds. The trip into Denver hadn't given her the answers she'd hoped for. If she could believe Thomas Charles, and she had the feeling the guy was being truthful, he hadn't handled the property transfer. Instead of pulling onto the highway that would take her south and back to Aspen Hills, she went east into the city. She programmed her navigation system with the address from Michael's note.

The street the system led her to was one of the

up-and-coming neighborhoods in the city. Signs advertising high-priced lofts were on the large brick buildings that had been factories once upon a time. She found a parking spot on the street in front of One Hour Cleaners and started taking pictures of the building. It was huge. The cleaner shop took up half of the street-side first floor with a chain coffee shop next door. She counted the floors. Ten. She owned a ten-story building in the middle of Denver?

No way Michael had bought this free and clear off his salary as a professor. And his estate attorney hadn't known of any large pots of gold in Michael's life. Since she'd moved back, all thinking about Michael had brought her was one question after the other. She thought she'd put him and his life into a box and buried it in her past.

And yet, too many things weren't staying in the box. Maybe Dante had been right. Maybe she should stay out of any and all things Michael. But even as she tried to put the questions away, she knew she had to follow the leads to wherever they took her.

She needed to talk to Dante again, with her own list of questions for the guy.

A sign in the second-floor window caught her eye: SPACE FOR LEASE. Shield Holdings had a local number with a 303 area code. Was Shield Holdings Kevin's company? Cat tried to remember if Shauna had ever told her the name of Kevin's business. But if that was true, why would Michael own a building that was part of Kevin's company holdings? Too many questions.

She put the car in gear and headed away from Denver, toward Aspen Hills and home. She had a retreat to finish up. Three more days and the guests would be flying home. She needed to make this retreat special for each and every one. Then she could fall apart or dig in to this crazy mess.

When she got home, Shauna and Seth were sitting down to lunch in the kitchen. "You have excellent timing." Shauna got up and dished a couple of stuffed cabbage rolls onto a plate and set it at the empty spot between her and Seth. "Come sit down and tell us what you found out."

Cat hung up her coat and glanced at Shauna. "I took Sasha to the airport."

"You can stop the code. Shauna told me about your trip to the lawyer's office." Seth didn't look up. "So you might as well spill. I know you want to tell."

"It wasn't my fault." Shauna met Cat's gaze as she slipped into the chair and picked up her fork. "Your uncle was here talking to Shirley and assumed Seth knew about your little side trip. Blame him."

"There's no need for blame. I'm sure Cat was going to tell me as soon as she came to her senses." Seth stretched his neck. "Come on, spill. I'm ready to go upstairs and take a long shower and maybe sneak in a nap. Getting that heater back online was more work than I'd expected."

Cat pulled out the envelope and set it in the middle of the table. Then she filled them in on what Thomas Charles had told her, including the direction on the 401K and life insurance. "Apparently, I'm still on the joint accounts and whatever Michael had left in there is mine as well."

"Are you a rich widow? I've always wanted a sugar mama." Seth's lips curved into an easy smile, helping Cat relax a little. Seth might not have been happy when he'd found out about her sleuthing, but he wasn't holding a grudge.

"I don't know. If I am, you'll be the first person I tell." Cat cut a piece off the roll and popped it into her mouth, the warm rice and meat filling her senses. She'd needed this. "Then he gave me the envelope."

She opened the envelope and dumped its contents onto the table. She glanced through the paperwork and found a copy of the life insurance policy, a sheet of paper from the Covington College employment manual, copies of older joint bank account statements, and a small gold key.

"Can't we have one lead that doesn't turn into just another piece of the puzzle?" Shauna glanced at the key and shook her head. Then she slid it down the table toward Seth. "Any idea what this might fit? Some chest in the basement maybe? Or a locked cabinet?"

He picked it up and then set it down. Standing, he went to the stove and refilled his plate. "I know exactly what it fits. Lunch is excellent, by the way."

Cat waited until he returned to the table. When he started eating again, she lightly kicked him in the shin. "Stop teasing us. What does the key fit?"

He pulled a key ring out of his pocket and matched the key on the table with one on the ring. Satisfied, he looked up at the two women. He held up the two keys so they could see the similarity. "This key opens a safety deposit box. Probably over at either Aspen Hills Financial or the college credit union."

Cat stared at her boyfriend.

"What?" He looked between the two women.

"Why are you both staring at me? Do you think I'm wrong?"

She shook her head. "No. I just didn't peg you as a guy who has a safety deposit box. What do you keep in yours?"

Seth's face turned beet red. "I've had it for a while. I got it while I was still in the service. I've put things in there I don't want to lose."

"I get that." Shauna slipped off the engagement ring Kevin had given her. "This thing is worth a lot of money, but the promise behind it is gone. Maybe I should put it and Jake's ring in a safety deposit box. You still have room in yours?"

"Sorry, it's full." Seth quickly ate the last bit of cabbage roll on his plate. "I'm heading upstairs for a shower. Tell me you two are staying put for a bit."

Cat held up the key. "I told myself I'd check out the bank, but I guess I can make a few calls." She looked at the calendar. "It's Thursday and the retreat's almost over. I'd like to spend at least some time with the writers."

"You should wait until Monday. Or at least until I wake up tomorrow. I'll drive you to the bank if you decide you need to go in." He put his plate in the sink and left the room.

Shauna played with the food on her plate for a few minutes before they heard Seth's footfalls on the steps. Then she whispered to Cat, "So what do you think he has in his box? Something he got in the service?"

"It has to be. I mean, Seth's folks are both still alive, so it's not anything they gave him." Cat stared at the key. "Maybe that's what's in Michael's box. Stuff from his parents."

"Or the key to this whole mystery about his death." Shauna played with the ring and then seemed to make a decision. "I'm getting a box next week, and this thing is going inside right after Kevin's funeral."

Cat wanted to challenge her friend about trying to box up her feelings on losing Kevin with the ring, but she left it alone. Then what Shauna had said hit her. "Wait, who's Jake?"

Shauna stood, taking her own dish to the sink. She kept her back to Cat as she packaged up the leftover food for another meal. "I thought I told you about him. He was the manager of the first bar I worked at when I moved to California."

"And you were going to marry him?" Cat hadn't heard this story. "What happened?"

Her friend turned, wiping her hands on a dish towel. "I met his current wife."

"Seriously? He was married and you didn't know?"

She shook her head. "I had no clue. She came into the bar one day before we opened looking to surprise him with an early dinner. Wife and three-year-old son."

"What did you do?"

"I went into his office, told him his family was there, and then quit. I told him to send my last paycheck to my post office box. I got a new job and then I did have to move since we'd spent a lot of time at my apartment. I loved that place too. Within a week, I had a new life. And a two-carat engagement ring that I wasn't giving back." Shauna's gaze dropped to the ring on her left hand. "Maybe I'll just start a collection of great rings from bad engagements."

Cat knew Shauna was trying to keep the conversation light, but she felt the hurt in her friend's words. "Well, if I can keep the box, I'll let you put your rings in there. At least they'll be safe. Quinn was right—we do have a lot of people running through the house at times."

"Is he still trying to sell you a security system?"

"I told him I'd call him. But I'm not sure I'll be able to hold him off too long. I guess his system is as good as any. Did Kevin have any problems with it?"

Shauna rolled her eyes. "Besides there not being any camera set up in the horse barn, you mean?"

"Well, yeah, there's that." Cat felt like a heel. But then Shauna smiled and she realized she was being played. "Did you find out anything from Kevin's attorney?"

"I didn't even get to talk to the guy. His assistant took down my questions and promised to call me later today with the answers. She seemed hesitant to even talk to me." Shauna sank back down in her chair at the table. "Paul has probably put a gag order on all of them."

"Isn't there a reading of the will? Paul wouldn't be able to stop that, even if he was in charge of the children's trust. By the way, I found something curious." Cat took out her phone and showed Shauna the picture of the leasing sign. "Is that Kevin's company?"

She pointed to a logo in the corner of the sign. "Shield Holdings is Kevin's company. That's the horse logo that Kevin had on all his marketing. Where did you see the sign? He has a lot of properties in Denver and Aspen Hills he leases out."

"That's the building I apparently own in Denver." Cat waited for the implication to settle. "So why was Kevin involved in the mystery building that Michael owned?"

The kitchen door swung open, and Pamela peeked her head inside the kitchen, scanning the room. When she saw Cat and Shauna, she smiled. "There you are. We're all in the living room waiting for your talk on being a working writer. It's still on, right?"

Cat glanced at the clock. Two p.m. already. She'd forgotten about the scheduled seminar where she took questions and answers from the guests. "Of course. I'll be right there."

"Hot apple cider and cookies are on their way too." Shauna gave Cat a we'll-talk-about-this-later look and then went to the fridge to start up the afternoon treats.

"No worries, we just got back from lunch. Man, I'm going to miss that pizza joint when I get home. We don't have Chicago style at home." Pamela disappeared back into the hallway.

Cat followed her out, thankful she'd given this presentation at every retreat so far. She didn't need notes or prep time to talk about her author job. And she could talk forever on the subject. She just needed to push Michael and Kevin out of her head.

Shirley, Pamela, and Melissa were on the couch chatting. The two men were standing by the wall-to-ceiling bookshelf, talking. The conversations stopped when Cat entered the room, and for a brief second, she wondered if they'd been talking about her, or worse, Shauna. She pulled a chair over to near the coffee table and waved Collin and Jordon over to join them. "Shauna will be in with some cookies and cider in a few minutes, but I thought we'd start talking about Sasha's presentation yesterday. Was anyone surprised at what they learned about the whole book-selling process?"

Melissa held up a hand. "I didn't realize how many books they hand sell. I guess I thought every book had the same chance at being sold. But she said they did Staff Picks and just being chosen for that could increase a book's sales."

Cat nodded. "That's why a lot of us do in-person signings. We want to be talking to librarians and booksellers so they remember us and our books. All of the magic that creates a bestseller isn't just in the writing. There's a lot of personal attention and a good deal of luck to the process. What else?"

"I didn't realize I'd be marketing so much. Don't the publishers do that for us if we get a good deal?" Pamela closed her laptop and leaned against the back of the couch.

Cat smiled, knowing that the answer was going to burst the girl's bubble about what her potential life as a working author would entail. By the time she finished her discussion of the marketing she had to do and continued to do, the writers had started to make notes in their notebooks and looked a little pale.

Shauna set a tray on the coffee table. "Well, now, it looks like we need a bit of sustenance before we go on with Cat's lecture. What did you tell them?

The truth about marketing? Or the royalty rates and what that means in real dollars?"

"Marketing." Pamela groaned as she took a cookie. "When do you find time to write?"

Cat took a mug of hot apple cider from Shauna and leaned back in her chair. "You don't find time to write—you make it. Writing is your number-one job. If you were a farmer and you did everything but plant the seeds, you wouldn't have a crop. If you're a writer, your writing is your seeds."

"So why haven't you been writing this week?" Shirley sipped her cider, watching Cat's reaction.

"I'm between books. So I'm mulling over the plot for the next one. I know how long it takes me to write a first draft, and I've got a few months before my deadline. Sometimes, you need the brain space too." She took a cookie. "I don't believe in writer's block. We need to work to get better. And if that means writing crap, you write crap until you understand why it's not working."

They talked for several minutes more about the process of writing their way out of a hard scene or a place where they didn't know what was going to happen next. Collin smiled after Melissa told her story of having nothing to move the plot. "That's why writing nonfiction is easier. I don't have to make up the stuff. I'm more of a reporter."

"Sometimes that's the way fiction feels too. Like we're reporting on the lives of our imaginary friends." Cat glanced at the clock. "We've been talking for over two hours. I can stay and answer some more questions, or if you all have dinner plans, we can schedule some more time tomorrow to handle any follow-ups."

"Wait, I want to know what Shauna meant about royalty rates?" Pamela looked around the room. "We're the authors of the story. We should be getting most of the sale money, right?"

Shauna had opened up a can of worms that new writers never considered. "I'll be happy to talk about standard contracts in today's publishing world. I won't give you specifics, but you'll get a good idea of what's being offered out there."

"We were going to The Cafeteria." Shirley glanced at the clock. "We have reservations at six."

"Then let's meet back here at two tomorrow. That way you should all have time to make your word count in the morning. Bring any and all questions. I may not have an answer, but I bet the group can answer most everything." Cat finished the last of the cider in her cup.

"You're more than welcome to come with us. You and Shauna." Collin stood next to her. He added quickly, "And your boyfriend too."

"Thanks for the offer, but we have a few things to discuss about the house." She followed Collin out to the lobby. "I appreciate your friendliness with the group. I know fiction writers can be different."

"They're funny. I'm really enjoying the week. At Covington, everyone is really focused on grades and projects. It's pretty stressful. These guys are more laid-back, yet they get a lot of work done." He paused at the foot of the stairs. "I didn't have any siblings growing up. Mostly it was my mom and me, and she was at work all the time. This is what I thought a family might feel like."

Cat watched as the young man headed up the stairs. She'd felt the same about the closeness that happened during the retreats, but she didn't know if the guests felt that way. Now, she knew it wasn't just her imagination.

A scream came from the kitchen. She ran into the room and saw Shauna standing by the open back door. Cat ran up to her and moved her aside to see what she was upset about. On the back step, a rat had been stabbed, the knife still stuck inside.

Chapter 16

Cat closed and locked the door and led a shaky Shauna to the table. She pointed to the bottle of whiskey, and Cat brought it over with a shot glass and her cell. "Call Uncle Pete. I'm going to make sure the guests have left for dinner and wake up Seth."

Shauna poured out a bit of the whisky with a shaky hand. "Maybe it's just a prank."

"If that's a prank, I still want to know what type of sick person would think that was funny." She moved the phone closer and repeated her instructions. "Call Uncle Pete. I'd like to get him here and gone before the guests get back from dinner."

Shauna picked up the phone, but Cat saw her hands were still shaking.

In the lobby, the five retreat guests were pulling on coats. Shirley narrowed her eyes when Cat approached. "Everything all right? I thought I heard something."

"Shauna thought she saw a deer in the backyard. They sometimes sneak in during the winter. I'm going up to get Seth to see if he can make sure it's going back toward the mountains and not the highway." It was close to the truth. Cat made sweeping movements with her hands. "Go on now. I'd hate to think you missed your reservation because I kept you all talking too long."

Cat watched the group make their way to the sidewalk, then turned to go upstairs. She had taken the first step when she heard footfalls on the stairway. Looking up, she met Seth's gaze. His slow smile and teasing look dropped as he took in Cat's tenseness.

"What happened now?" He took the stairs two at a time and then pulled her into his arms. "Your uncle okay? Your folks? Shauna?"

Cat pushed away the tears that wanted to fall just because it had been a really, really bad week so far. She took in a deep breath and lifted her head from his chest so she could see his reaction when she told him. "Someone killed a rat."

The confusion registered on Seth's face. "Isn't that a good thing?"

"They left it on the back door with the knife sticking out." Cat could see Seth's jaw tighten.

"Let me see."

They moved toward the kitchen, but before they could step inside, Paul Quinn flew through the front door, his laptop open in his hands. His wild gaze searched the lobby, and when he found Cat and Seth, a grin fell on his face. "I told you that you needed a security system."

"Why, so people like you just don't barge into the

house?" Seth walked over and shut the door Quinn had left open.

Now Quinn was chattering at Cat and pointing to the screen. "Just look. I told you."

Cat made eye contact with Seth, who shrugged. She needed to get back to Shauna, but it was apparent that Quinn wasn't leaving until she dealt with his discovery. His idea of a sales call was a little too extreme. "Fine, Quinn, what do you want me to see?"

He punched a key on his laptop and a video started. A view of a snowy back porch came into view, and as Cat focused, she realized what she was looking at. "Wait, that's my back door. Who said you could put a camera on my house? Isn't that against the law?"

"Good question, and yes, it is." Uncle Pete had come in the front door and was taking off his coat. "What's going on, Cat? Shauna sounded horrible when she called. And why can't I use the back door?"

Quinn pointed to the laptop. "Because of this. Look." He waved Uncle Pete over to where he stood with Cat.

"Let's go into the kitchen." Uncle Pete pointed to the door. "I want the whole story and my feet are killing me since I had to do a walkabout on campus today with the new security team over there."

They moved into the kitchen, where Shauna sat staring at the empty shot glass. Instead of sitting down at the table, Cat took the bottle and glass away from her friend and set a cup of coffee in front of her, hoping that she hadn't taken more than one or two shots. "Anyone else want coffee?"

Quinn raised his hand, but Uncle Pete shook his head. "Let's see what we have here first. So, Shauna, why did you call me?"

Instead of answering, she pointed to the back door. Cat already knew what was out there, but Uncle Pete, Seth, and Quinn went to look. After a few minutes, they came back to the table. Cat had taken the time to fill a carafe with coffee and set out cups on the table. She filled her own and wrapped her fingers around the ceramic mug, hoping to ease the chill she felt.

"So that's what she left." Quinn filled his own mug and was about to take a sip when he felt the weight of Uncle Pete's stare. "On the video, I saw a woman drop something off at the door, then leave. When I was walking here from my car, I heard her scream."

"The woman's?" Uncle Pete moved the laptop closer and peered at the screen. "How do you make this work?"

"Not the woman in the video." Quinn pointed at Shauna, then leaned over and hit a button on the laptop. "Hers."

They all watched as the snowy-white scene played on the small screen. A woman bundled in a too-large parka with the hood covering her face came into view. Or at least Cat thought it was a woman from the way she walked. And the parka was pink with a ruff of fur around the hood. If it was a guy, he was fine boned and liked his outerwear a little feminine. Her/his hair flowed out of the coat and it was a deep red. The kind you were more likely to get from a box than be born with.

The woman arranged something she'd pulled out of her pocket on the doorstep, then stuffed the bag back into a large pocket, glanced around, and hurried off.

The scene went back to the way it had been before, a beautiful Colorado winter garden, except the walkway had a few footsteps in the snow.

Quinn hit another button and rewound the video to where the woman's face was almost visible. "Female, red hair, probably five-five from the angle, and maybe a hundred and seventy-five pounds?"

Uncle Pete didn't look at his officer. "Maybe. Or could be a male of that size with a red wig and wearing a woman's coat. But you go into the lobby and call Katie and get a BOLO out for this person." He paused. "Then you come back here and explain to me why you are videotaping my niece's house."

Quinn swallowed hard but nodded and skirted out the doorway.

Uncle Pete looked at Shauna. "I take it you found her little gift?"

When she nodded, he glanced at Cat. "Where are your guests?"

"The Cafeteria for dinner. If we're doing the whole search thing with more cops and flashing lights, I'd like you to be done before they get back." Cat didn't know if she should be scared, or angry. Maybe both. Emotions were fighting inside her. "I bet that's the woman who bought the poison at the hardware store."

"We didn't get any video from the town cameras. Too bad I didn't know about this sooner." Uncle Pete looked up from the laptop. Now she felt the heat of her uncle's stare.

"Don't gripe at me about it." She glanced around at Shauna and Seth. "I told you what I heard. Besides, Seth told me about Shauna having the rat poison so I went to ask who else had bought it recently. Like I was looking to get rid of a problem in my house."

"The point is, I don't like you going around poking your nose in my investigation." Uncle Pete returned his gaze to the laptop.

"I was trying to help," Cat muttered.

"There's no use calling out a CSI team from Denver. I'll have Quinn take pictures of the footsteps and the rat before we bag everything up. He can drive everything down to the office and wait for the results because, apparently, I'm not keeping him busy enough. I'll deal with this camera thing in a second." He moved the laptop and poured himself a cup of coffee. "Shauna, can you tell me everything that happened?"

She worried her bottom lip, then answered. "I was here, starting dinner, when I heard a noise outside. I figured it was Seth and he'd gone out the front without grabbing his keys. We keep the back door locked." Her eyes glazed over a bit as she remembered the moment. "When I opened the door, no one was there, so I went to close it, but that's when I looked down."

"So you didn't see anyone or hear a car start up?" Uncle Pete spoke slowly, calmly.

"No. I even looked toward the drive, thinking it was Seth and he'd gone to his truck, but no one, and no car sounds either."

Quinn cleared his throat from the doorway. "I

ran from King Street and didn't see anyone, nor did I see or hear a car."

When Uncle Pete turned his head, shooting his officer a hard stare, Quinn stepped into the room. "Katie's on it. I wanted to see what you needed next."

Cat knew that look. Apparently Quinn had learned to read her uncle's unspoken communication as well as she had.

"I want you to go process the scene. Then take everything to Denver's crime lab and wait for processing." Uncle Pete tapped the table. "And I want all the cameras off this house before dark. You're lucky she's not pressing charges."

"I was just trying to help. Besides, I'm not on duty today." Quinn's face fell. He stepped back and reached for his laptop. "I mean, sure, Chief."

Uncle Pete closed the laptop and moved it closer to himself. "I'll take this back to the station since it's evidence."

"I could send you the file." Quinn kept his hand outstretched.

Uncle Pete didn't move. "No need. I'll have Katie transfer the file into evidence when I get back to the station. You just go process the scene. I'd like to have at least a little natural light to see the photos when they're done."

They waited for Quinn to leave before anyone spoke. Cat focused on her uncle. "So do you think this is about me looking into Michael's death? Do you think the lawyer was connected?"

"I've done some research on Thomas Charles and no, he doesn't have any apparent ties to the family." He rolled his shoulders. "I guess it could be about Kevin, but what message was it supposed to send? It's just weird."

"No, what's weird is Paul Quinn setting up cameras and watching the house." Seth spoke a little too harshly and his face was red. "What are you going to do about that?"

"I told him to take them down." Uncle Pete sighed. "Look, I know he overstepped, but the kid has a good heart on him. And we wouldn't have a clue on what happened this afternoon if he hadn't put them up to prove his system was useful. Although I may need to put a halt to this moonlighting position. The lines are getting a little murky."

"I still think . . ." Seth started, but Cat laid her hand on his arm.

"Uncle Pete's right. Quinn's video has given us at least a clue to finding out who did this. I'm sure it's not connected to Michael. Dante told me that he'd dealt with Martin on that problem." Cat didn't mention the fact that Dante had told her specifically to stop snooping. She looked over at Shauna. "Besides, whoever did this expected you would be the one to find the body. Maybe they've been watching the house?"

"You think this is about Kevin? Maybe someone thinks I killed him?" Shauna glanced at the bottle of whiskey and licked her lips.

"Stick with coffee." Cat nodded to her cup. "We know Jade thinks you killed Kevin. She told you that. Although she's probably at least five-foot-ten, so she didn't leave your little present."

"Then who else was that involved in Kevin's life that would know about our relationship and how he was killed?" The question hung in the air.

Finally, Uncle Pete stood up. "And that's why they pay me the big bucks to find this stuff out. I want to hear about your trip to the lawyer soon, but I need to get back to the station and see if we can find this woman on any of the street cams in town. Maybe she's local."

The three sat around the table sipping coffee, and soon, Seth stood and glanced out the window, then opened the back door. He returned to the table. "They're both gone."

"With the rat?" Cat knew the answer but wanted confirmation before she opened the back door again. If she ever did.

Seth gave her a quick hug. "Yes, the rat's gone. But seriously, who would do this?"

"Does Paul have a shorter sister?" Cat asked.

The stricken look on Shauna's face softened and turned to laughter. "Not that I know of. Of course, as rude as his lawyer's assistant had been today, it could have been her."

"Jealousy is a cruel master." Seth took out his phone. "I don't mean to be callous, but I need to ask a question. A meat lovers and a veggie?"

"What are you talking about?" Both women turned to look at him.

He glanced around the kitchen. "Dinner. It's almost seven, and I don't think Shauna wants to cook tonight. So is pizza okay?" He smiled a little wider. "I'm buying."

"Didn't you have pizza last night with Hank?" Cat wondered if Seth had lived on pizza and hot wings before she'd moved back to Aspen Hills.

"Are you saying you want a salad instead?" He paused, his finger hovering over the phone.

"No. Get pan crust, not that thin stuff." Cat glanced at Shauna. "You want anything else?"

"Besides a case of good stout beer?" She shook her head. "Pan veggie will do nicely."

A knock sounded at the back door. Cat stood and waved Shauna back down. She frowned at Seth. "Did you already call?"

"Nope." He stood and followed her, pausing at the sink to look out the kitchen window. "No new cars in the driveway. Maybe it's one of the guests?"

Cat inched the door open. Mrs. Rice stood on the step, right where the dead rat had been a few minutes ago. Cat opened the door a little wider but not enough to invite her neighbor inside. "Mrs. Rice, what are you doing out on such a cold night?"

"I saw your uncle here." She tried to look around Cat. "I just wanted to remind you if Shauna leaves or is, well, arrested, I'm available to start at a moment's notice. I know you have guests this week and not having someone to help would be catastrophic."

"Well, thanks for the offer, but Shauna's still here and I still don't need to hire on additional staff at this time." She turned a bit so Mrs. Rice could see Shauna at the table. When Shauna waved, Mrs. Rice blanched just a little. "Anyway, we're getting ready for dinner so I hate to run, but I need to go."

"Remember I came to you first." Mrs. Rice stepped off the porch. "Be sure to tell your mother hello. And remember, I've won more blue ribbons at the county fair than anyone in Aspen Hills."

Cat rolled her eyes after the woman's back was turned and called after her as she went to close the door, "Have a good night, Mrs. Rice."

"That woman has a lot of gall." If it were possible, steam would have been rolling out of Shauna's ears, just like in the cartoons. "She acts like she knows I killed Kevin. Or at least I'll be convicted of the crime."

Seth put in the call for the pizza, then sat down at the table. He tapped a finger on the table. "Who knows more gossip about Aspen Hills residents than anyone else?"

"Mrs. Rice," Cat and Shauna said in unison.

"And so the question stands, why does the gossip queen think that Shauna's going up the river for this murder?" He leaned back in his chair.

Cat groaned. "I'm going to have to go talk to her, aren't I?"

"Only if you want to find out what she knows." Seth went to the fridge and took out three sodas. "We can sit here until the pizza comes and try to guess what she knows, but going over tomorrow for a few minutes might just give you another piece of this puzzle."

Cat leaned back into her chair and listened to Seth and Shauna list off all the possible things that Mrs. Rice might know. She was hungry and getting a headache. All she knew was she had to go visit her neighbor tomorrow, maybe with a plate of cookies to eat along with the crow she'd have to swallow to get Mrs. Rice to spill her secrets.

Chapter 17

The next morning, Cat sat at the kitchen table, making a list. Her day had just become too busy. She'd agreed to meet with the retreat guests at two, and before that, she needed to talk to Mrs. Rice, call the human resources department about Michael's life insurance and 401K, and go visit the bank. Maybe she should have thought about these things when she found out about him leaving her the house, but she'd been shocked he was dead. Thomas Charles had said he'd sent her several letters as Michael's executor, but either they'd gotten lost in the mail, or she'd thrown them away thinking they were junk. She should have dug deeper when she'd come back instead of letting the rest slip her mind.

She decided it was a good thing. The fact she wasn't that money-hungry ex-wife looking for a free ride made her feel good about who she was as a person. However, now she was playing catch-up with information she could have known for a while.

Shauna put a plate of waffles in front of her with

a cup of warmed maple syrup. "Eat. You look like you're going for a job interview rather than just visiting the bank."

Cat pushed her list to the side and dug in to the waffles. She hadn't eaten a lot of pizza last night. After the guests had come back from dinner, she'd excused herself to her room, feeling like she couldn't pretend there was nothing on her mind. She had taken a long bath and curled up with a mystery novel she'd been trying to fit in reading time for.

Her stomach growled as she took the first bite of the warm, crunchy, sweet waffle. Then she remembered the other visit she'd planned for the day, seeing what her neighbor knew about Kevin's death. Shaking away the sour feeling, she focused on eating her breakfast.

She had almost finished, the last bite on the way up to her mouth, when she heard voices coming from the lobby.

"Hello, is anyone here?" A slightly familiar voice called out a greeting.

Cat and Shauna made their way out to the lobby. Cat's stomach sank when she saw Paul and Jade standing just inside the door. Their coats were still on, and Jade held a Michael Kors bag out in front of her like she was afraid someone would steal it.

Cat heard Shauna's quick intake of breath and cut off whatever her friend had been planning on saying. She stepped closer and decided to try the high road. "Good morning, Jade, Paul. What can we do for you today?"

Paul pushed his sister closer. She looked back and, from what Cat saw of her face, gave her brother a look that she must have hoped would hurt him, if not kill him. Jade recovered nicely and when she turned back to face Cat, no trace of the anger remained on her face. She held out her hand. "I'm sorry, I don't think we've been introduced. I'm Jade Addison."

"Cat Latimer. I'm Shauna's friend." Cat let the words echo, mostly to let Jade know where she stood in the war.

Paul stepped closer. "We wanted to let you all know about the funeral arrangements and Jade wanted to say something." He squeezed his sister's shoulder, just a little too hard. "Didn't you?"

Jade swallowed hard. "I'm sorry about causing a scene the other night at the restaurant. I, of course, knew about you and Kevin. And your relationship. Sometimes it was just hard to be part of Kevin's past rather than his future." She glared at her brother. "Especially since I'm raising his children."

Shauna stepped around Cat. "I know this must be hard on you as well. I've been alternating between crying uncontrollably and being royally ticked off. I don't understand this grief thing. It's worse than PMS."

A small smile curved Jade's lips. "It does make one an emotional wreck."

Cat could see Jade's body relaxing. Jade was accepting Shauna. Cat felt like she was watching two cats fighting in the street. Or calming down and not fighting would be the better analogy. "Can I offer you some coffee? Maybe we should sit and talk a bit? I'm sure Shauna has questions."

"That would be lovely, wouldn't it, Jade?" Paul

looked down at his sister, then glanced up to follow her gaze. "What is he doing here?"

Cat turned to see which of the three men in her house Paul was referring to. Collin Adams stood halfway down the last flight of stairs, seemingly frozen in place. "Collin's one of our retreat guests this week. He attends Covington."

"I know exactly where he goes to school since Kevin's been having me pay the bills for the last four years." Paul glared at Shauna.

"I bet one of you killed him and the other is diverting the police chief's attention so the old fart doesn't even look in your direction. Why else would you be together?" Jade spat out the words like she was trying to turn them into daggers. She whirled on her brother. "I told you we couldn't trust her. Now we find *him* here, probably feeding her lies about Kevin and his life."

The volume of Jade's voice had shot up a few decibels. Cat was still totally in the dark about why the woman was upset now. Honestly, Cat was beginning to think that she was unhinged and maybe she'd had something to do with Kevin's death. But her grief seemed real, at least as much as she'd seen.

"Look, I don't know what you're talking about, but no, we weren't involved in Kevin's death." Cat tried to calm the woman using her quiet voice. She'd had to take a physical safety class when she'd started teaching, and honestly, this was the first time she'd ever used the technique.

It wasn't working.

Jade started shouting and pointing at the young

man still frozen on the stairway. Paul turned her toward the door, whispering in her ear, trying to get her to calm down, but nothing was working. He glanced up at Collin as he pulled the door closed. "You better not be involved in this."

The door closed and Paul was hurrying Jade back to the Land Rover that sat running at the curb. Paul and Jade had used a driver. The guy had moved up in the world, taking over Kevin's toys as if they were his own. And maybe now they were. Shauna really needed to talk to an attorney to protect any interest in Kevin's estate he might have left her.

"I'm sorry about that." Collin now stood at the bottom of the stairs looking miserable. "She's always hated me. And Paul, well, he just saw me as competition for Kevin's attention." Collin shuffled his feet, keeping his eyes cast downward. "At least all that's over."

"How do you know Kevin? And why would Jade and Paul hate you so much?" Cat rubbed her temples. She'd wanted a slow morning; instead, she was in the middle of major drama about Kevin. What a surprise. She was actually glad the guy was dead. Shauna would have been miserable with him.

Collin didn't look happy, but he looked at Shauna. "Kevin was my dad. He and my mom went to high school together and well, I happened. He sent us child support for years, but when I turned eighteen, all he would do was help with college costs. Mom, well, she had to make it on her own. It's been really hard."

"You're Kevin's son?" Shauna croaked, staring

at the young man in front of her. "Why are you here in Aspen Hills? Didn't Kevin grow up in Philadelphia?"

"If I wanted his help with schooling, I had to come to Colorado and go to Covington. He made that crystal clear when he came to my high school graduation." Collin rubbed his shoulder. "I hadn't seen him in years and I thought maybe he wanted me close so he and I could have a relationship, but instead, I never saw him. That guy, Paul, he always came at the beginning of a semester, looked at my grades, and then handed me a check for room and board, tuition, and some spending money. And now, with Kevin dead, I'll never have a real dad."

Cat watched as the kid wiped at his eyes. Collin had never looked so young and vulnerable as he did in that moment. What had Kevin been thinking, bringing him out here like a favorite toy, then casting him aside and letting Paul deal with the details?

"I didn't expect this," Cat muttered as she took in the scene. Jade and Paul clearly thought Collin was involved in Kevin's death and that Shauna had played a part. Instead, the two had been thrown together by one thing: Collin's drive to attend Cat's writers' retreat.

"I'll go pack and go back to the dorm." Collin turned toward the stairs. "Tell the group how much I enjoyed meeting everyone."

"Why?" Shauna's voice stopped him in his tracks.

He didn't look at her when he answered. "I knew you were dating my dad—I mean, Kevin. I wanted to meet you. I guess I never understood why he and my mom split up. She keeps holding on to some dream that they might get back together. Or did, before he died."

"I didn't mean that." Shauna waved away his explanation for being at the retreat.

"I don't understand." Collin looked as confused as Cat felt.

"I'm asking, why are you leaving?" She walked toward Collin. "You didn't do anything wrong. Jade and Paul can just deal with the fact you're here. Besides, I'd like to get to know you better."

Collin looked dumbstruck. "Seriously? You want to get to know me?"

"I do." Shauna put her hand on his arm and gave it a gentle squeeze. "I loved your father. I'm not sure why he didn't do right by you, but that doesn't mean that we can't be friends. Stay for the week, finish out the retreat. And when you're not writing, come into the kitchen and we'll talk."

Collin swallowed hard, then nodded. "I'd like that."

"So let's start now. How about some eggs and bacon for breakfast? Or maybe waffles? After that blowup, I feel like I need some crunchy pork products to make me forget what a witch Jade can be."

Cat watched the two go to the kitchen. She followed and quickly finished her own breakfast. When she was done, she grabbed her list and a cup of coffee and left the two alone to talk. She considered going upstairs to her office, but with Michael's papers all over, she changed her mind and turned left toward his office. If anyone came in to work, she'd send them upstairs to the attic library, where Seth had promised the temperature should be tolerable by now.

A sharp rapping on the front door caused her to turn. Quinn stood at the doorway, with what looked like a brand new laptop in hand. He yelled something through the window.

"What?" Cat put a hand around her ear, indicating she couldn't hear him.

He shook his head, then pounded harder. This time, she heard the words.

"Let. Me. In." He stood staring at her and waiting.

One more thing to deal with on her list. She walked over to the doorway, unlocked it, and stood blocking his entrance. "What do you want, Quinn?"

He glanced around her, standing on tippy-toes to look past her to the lobby area. "I wanted to check and see if you were okay. I saw them coming in while I was taking down the last few cameras. Do you want to press charges?"

"For what? Accusing Shauna of murder?" Cat shook her head. Quickly, she made up a new explanation for Jade's outburst, one that didn't include Collin. His parentage wasn't something that Quinn needed to know about, at least not from her. "From what I saw, it was more about the ownership of certain properties she might be entitled to inherit."

"That's not what I saw." Quinn narrowed his eyes. "What do you know that I don't know?"

"From town gossip, lots of things." Cat wasn't going to share her secrets even though he worked with her uncle. "Anyway, thanks for taking down the cameras and checking on us."

She watched Quinn leave, then went into the study. She dialed the college's general number and asked for the human resources department. After working her way through the automated prompts, she finally got a live person.

"Good morning, this is Agatha. How can I help you?" the cheery voice asked.

Cat told her about Michael's employment and subsequent death last winter. Then she got to the point. "I was wondering if I happened to be the beneficiary on his life insurance and the 401K."

"Let me check." A pause came over the line and Cat could hear the clicking of keys. Finally, Agatha came back on the line. "I'm sorry. I can't tell you."

"Why? Is it because I'm not the beneficiary?"

"No, I mean I don't know if you are or not. It looks like those files have been archived out of our current system. And I don't deal with separation issues anyway. Can I have Carolyn give you a call this afternoon? She's at a chamber meeting this morning."

Cat left her name and number and then pressed Agatha on when the elusive Carolyn would be back in the office. "You promise I'll get a call back before two? I have a meeting at two and I'll be unable to take the call for at least an hour, maybe longer."

"I'm sure she'll call as soon as she has information for you."

Obviously, this woman was done talking to her and ready to get on with the rest of her day.

"Thanks for all your help," Cat muttered, laying on the sarcasm. "You've been extremely informative. I look forward to hearing from Carolyn."

She didn't expect the HR representative to actually call her back today or even before Cat reached out again. But a girl could hope. She put a check mark beside the *call HR* note and then glanced at the next step. She had dressed up a little for this bank visit. She didn't have to play the money-grubbing widow, but she thought something besides yoga pants might make a better impression. Which meant she'd borrowed another outfit from Shauna. As soon as this retreat was over, she was heading into Denver. Apparently, her wardrobe needed a bit of restructuring. And she would take Shauna with her so she didn't come home with more stretchy jeans, yoga pants, and several T-shirts in not so bright colors, the author's work uniform.

A knock came at the door and Cat looked up, expecting to see one of the retreat guests looking for a place to write. Instead, Seth stood in the doorway. Dressed in his usual rock concert T-shirt and jeans, he looked good. And when he smiled at her, she remembered all the reasons she'd fallen in love with him in high school. He'd always been there for her. Carrying her books, listening to her gripe about Mr. Higgins, their English teacher who was not willing to see anything written after 1960 as being worthy of discussing in class. She smiled as she thought of the long debate she'd had with the teacher about the advantages of teaching more modern and popular books, like Stephen King. In a way, the teacher had molded her own teaching style when she became a professor. An influence that he wouldn't like to be associated with.

"What are you thinking about?" Seth came over to the desk visitor chair and relaxed into it, easing his long arms around the back. "It must be your next book. You get that look when you're somewhere else, playing with Tori and the rest of your imaginary friends."

He knew her too well. Cat smiled. "Actually, this time you're wrong. I was thinking about high school and Mr. Higgins."

"The English teacher." Seth chuckled. "You hated that guy and he still gave you A's in the class."

"Probably because even though I fought him on every assignment, I turned in well-researched and thoughtful papers that didn't include reading the book via CliffsNotes."

Seth's grin widened and he gave that shrug that meant everything from *Whatever* to *Yep, you caught me, so what.* "CliffsNotes were the bomb. I would have flunked English for sure without them. I'm so glad I went to that Denver bookstore with you to hear that really boring guy."

"It's cheating," Cat reminded him. "But at least you didn't buy your papers off some term paper mill. I bet twenty percent of my freshman English class bought their first paper off the Internet." She smiled. "But when they got an F for a paper they paid good money for, they got the point and wrote their own for the next assignment."

"You became Mr. Higgins. You do realize that." Seth glanced around the room, his gaze settling on the box of books in the corner. "You're sure you don't want me to take those over to Miss Apple-bome today?"

"On a Friday? You're kidding, right? She'd shoot you."

"What are you doing today? Anything I need to help with?" Seth drummed his fingers on his jeans.

Cat knew sitting around made him jumpy, but

he was here more as backup, not as a handyman this week. "I'm heading over to the bank. And no, I don't need a lift. Why don't you check out the basement and see if there's any way we can set up a gym down there. I want it to be easy access for the guests and clean and bright, so it doesn't look like a basement. Give me an estimate on the remodel and then we can talk about a budget for the project."

The smile on his face looked like she'd just given him a train set for Christmas. "You'll love it when I'm done."

"Well, Shirley pointed out the need for it especially during the winter. In the summer, people can go hiking or running around the neighborhood. I think we need to have a place for the writers to get physical during winter as well." She bit her lip, thinking about the cost of the project, but pushed it away. Maybe she'd find enough money in their joint accounts at the bank to cover the expense without adding to her remodel loan.

Seth didn't move. "I was thinking that maybe this summer we could do a hiking trip at the beginning of the session, like we did the ski day in November. If we had an extra day like that for all of the sessions, you could charge more for people who wanted the full Colorado experience. Maybe even a ghost town visit for one of the summer sessions?"

"That's a great idea." Cat's eyes widened as she thought of the marketing plan she could set up around the different sessions. Shauna could even lead a day on cooking Colorado specialties during the winter.

Seth's chuckle brought her back to today. "You always sound so amazed when I have one."

"One?" She'd lost the train of the conversation.

He stood and walked toward the door. "A great idea."

After Seth left, she put her notebook into her oversized tote and headed to the lobby to grab her coat. She didn't want to leave without letting someone know where she was heading so she poked her head into the kitchen. No one was there. Shauna and Collin must have finished their breakfast bonding time and gone on with their day. Cat wrote a note on the kitchen whiteboard and then left through the back door. She thought about Shauna's new role as almost stepmother to the unclaimed child her murdered fiancé had basically ignored. Yep, that had trouble written all over it.

"It's a good thing real life doesn't follow novel plots," Cat said to no one as she walked out into the cold morning air.

Chapter 18

Cat sat in the bank's waiting room, the leather wing chair and dark wood making the area to look like she'd stepped back into time. Except the leather was fake and the old-timey pictures and wanted posters on the wall were framed replicas that she knew hung in every branch of the Colorado-based bank. Aspen Hills Financial was part of the Bank of Colorado. Every branch took the name of their neighborhood or town rather than the parent name. That way, people thought they were banking with a small community bank, not the corporate financial giant Bank of Colorado really was.

A woman in a black pantsuit with a dark blue shirt came out of her office. "Sorry about the wait. The corporate office always wants to hold a conference call Friday morning first thing. I guess they want to get the bad news off their desks and onto ours before the weekend." She held out her hand. "Karen Williams. And you don't have to introduce yourself—I've read all your books. My daughter keeps asking if she's old enough for her magical powers to have shown up. You're raising a generation of wannabe magical creatures, Miss Latimer."

Cat stood and took the woman's outstretched hand. "I suppose there's worse things she could be focused on. And call me Cat."

"Tara will be ecstatic when she finds out I met you. Last summer, when we came into town for a youth day at the college, she made me drive by your lovely bed-and-breakfast, just so she could see where you lived." She motioned to the office's open door. "What can I help you with today?"

Cat pulled out a postcard she'd had made with the trilogy's covers. She grabbed a pen out of her purse and signed it, *To Tara, good luck with your initiation.* She handed it to Karen. "I'll give you this before we get started since I'll probably forget after we start talking."

Karen beamed at the inscription and then set it aside. "You've made one little girl very happy today. How can I make you happy?"

"I've got a few questions. My ex-husband and I banked at this branch when we were married. I assumed he'd closed our joint accounts, but his estate attorney tells me that they were left open. Can you see if I'm still on the accounts?" She took out her notebook. "His name is—I mean was—Michael Latimer."

"You are Catherine, legally?" The branch manager listed off a birthdate, and Cat nodded. "It looks like he never changed the account. You are still active on the savings, the checking, and the safety deposit box."

Cat dug out the key from her wallet. "And this is the key to the safety deposit box?"

Karen reached out her hand, examined the key, and then returned it. "That's our key." She frowned, looking at the account. "I'm sorry for your loss. He must have just recently passed away. I'm sure, even with your divorce, you must be still grieving."

"No." Cat saw the shock in the woman's eyes. "No, I mean . . . this is coming out wrong. What I'm trying to say is he didn't pass recently. Michael died early last year."

"And you weren't aware of or using the account?" Karen watched Cat's face carefully.

Cat knew something was wrong from the tightness in the woman's face. "I didn't think about the rest of the estate until recently. I knew he'd left the house to me, but I didn't realize he hadn't closed out our accounts. Is there something wrong?"

Karen turned the computer screen so Cat could see what she was looking at. A long list of transactions filled the screen. Mostly deposits, but Michael liked to use the credit card for his expenses so he got points. Cat briefly wondered about what happened to credit card points. Were they available for her to use too? She realized Karen was waiting for a response, but she couldn't see anything wrong with the picture. "The amount's kind of high. When we were together, Michael only kept a minimal amount in the account, sweeping the rest into savings so we wouldn't be tempted to spend it. Is that what's concerning you?"

Karen shook her head and ran a printout. She handed it to Cat. "This lists the amounts and the dates of recent deposits. If your husband has been dead for almost a year, why is he still getting regular deposits put into his account twice a month?"

Cat checked the deposit dates, then the amounts. "Fifteen hundred dollars? Where's the deposit coming from?"

"It's an automatic deposit. I don't recognize the coding, but I can do some research and let you know." Karen hit a few keys. "And to answer the question you had earlier, yes, you are still active on the account along with the savings. I can make you a debit card today, but if we order checks, those will take a few weeks."

Cat didn't know what to say. She thought about the accounts and who might have continued making deposits. Was this where the lease income from the building she "owned" was going? Was the money really hers? She'd need to get Uncle Pete looking into this. But for now, she thought the best course of action was one of protection.

"A debit card would be great. But I want to move all of the savings and all but five hundred of the checking into a new account only in my name. Can I do that?" Cat took out the card Thomas Charles had given her earlier. "Do you need permission from Michael's attorney?"

Karen picked up the card, glancing at the information, then pushed it back toward her. "Your name is on the account. You have full access. You can do whatever you want with the money in the account, including moving it to a new account. Let me just set it up. Do you want me to mirror the personal account you have with us?"

Cat nodded and, while she waited, she texted her

uncle about the deposits. When he didn't respond, she figured he was busy with something else. Finally, Karen printed some papers. "I need your signature here, here, and here." She pointed to three spots. "I'll be right back with new debit cards for both accounts.

As she signed the papers, she glanced at the amount. Frowning, she waited for Karen to return. Cat wasn't sure if all of her accounts would add up to that amount, but she didn't want to mess up the accounting system Shauna had set up for the writers' retreat by closing out the account. When the woman returned, two plastic cards in hand, she pointed to the deposit receipt. "I think there's a mistake, the new account has over three hundred thousand dollars in it. You didn't combine all my accounts together, did you?"

Karen put a sticker on each card and wrote a quick note. "No mistake. I took all of the joint savings and all but five hundred of the checking just like you asked."

"Michael had over three hundred thousand dollars in our joint accounts?" Cat tried to sound normal, but she felt her voice squeaking from her throat squeezing together so tight.

"Did you not want to transfer all of the savings?" Karen looked at the paperwork she'd already completed. "I could do a transfer back into the account if you want."

"No." Cat just needed to talk to her uncle. She took a deep breath. In for a penny, in for a pound, whatever that really meant. Today it meant she was checking out the safety deposit box as well. She might as well know all the secrets Michael was hiding. "Can I check out the box now?"

Karen handed over the debit cards, explaining that the one with the sticker was to the joint account. "You may want to keep this separate, just until you decide to totally close out the account. I'll call you as soon as I have the information about the deposit source."

They walked back to the lobby, where Karen called over a teller who wasn't engaged with a customer. "Kim will get you into the box. Thank you again for the postcard and the inscription. Tara is going to explode when I get home and give this to her."

She followed Kim into the vault. Rows of numbered boxes surrounded a chest-high table. The teller held her hand out for the key, checked the number, and then put her master and Cat's key into a lock under number 545. She turned the keys, opened the door, and pulled out the box. She left it hanging halfway in and halfway out, taking her key out of the lock. "When you're done, just put the box back, shut the door, and take your key. It will automatically relock."

Cat waited until she was alone, then took the box out of the slot. She set it on the table. It was light, so visions of it being stuffed with coins or even packets of money disappeared. She flipped open the lid and looked inside. The box was empty except for three sheets of notebook paper. She'd found the missing journal pages.

She ran her hand back inside the box and felt a hard small item. She curled her fingers around it and pulled it out and held it up to the light. Just like she'd guessed, it was a flash drive. Just one. Along with the pages, it was the only thing in the box. She tilted the back of the box up, just in case something had made its way to the deepest regions of the box. But nothing else came out.

A flash drive. Cat didn't even want to know what was on it. Whatever it was, Michael had given his life for the information. She didn't want to think about what would happen to her if anyone found out she had the flash drive, especially if it had something on Michael's project.

Dante had been right. She should have kept her nose out of this whole thing. Blissful ignorance was called that because you really were happy not knowing. Her gut told her she didn't want to know. But her head told her that if she wanted to solve Michael's murder, she needed to know.

She pulled out the tablet she'd put into her tote bag, inserted the flash drive, and downloaded the files. She opened each one, just to see if they had transferred and saved, then closed down the tablet and put it away. Then she flattened the pages on the table and took several pictures of each one.

Should she put them back into the box? Or what? She stared at the items. She looked at her phone. No bars here in the vault. She made a quick decision.

Cat wrapped the flash drive in the pages and tucked it into her pocket, then put the box back and took the key. At least now, she had her own box to keep her contracts in. Those were her only items that were valuable enough to keep away from the house. Well, those and now Shauna's new collection of engagement rings.

When she left the warmth of the bank, the bright winter morning that had greeted her during her walk to downtown now felt cold and cloudy, the clouds covering up the bright blue sky she'd enjoyed so much on her way there. Now, the chill around her seemed to match the chill she had in her bones that seemed to be radiating from the flash drive. Instead of turning left and heading home, she turned right and went to the police station.

She wanted this thing off her hands and into her uncle's sooner than later. The station was only a few blocks away, but Cat had to keep from running toward the building. When a car came up behind her, she froze in place, pretending to be window shopping in the bookstore window. The owner, Tammy, waved at her and she waved back, thankful to have the attention of another human being. The car passed without slowing, and Cat let out the breath she'd been holding. *Calm down*, she told herself. No one knew what she had in her pocket because no one had been in the vault when she'd gone inside.

And no one but Kim the bank teller and Karen knew she'd even known about the box. She could make it another block to the police station. She took a deep breath and started walking again. Her mind told her it was fine; her heart rate refused to listen however and showed her fear.

She reached the station and went up the stairs quickly, jerking open the door to hurry to the front desk. Katie Bowman watched her entrance.

"What's got your feathers all ruffled?" Katie's

southern drawl became more intense when she was agitated.

Cat looked around the empty police station. Katie had a romance novel sitting on her station. It appeared to be a slow day. "Nothing, just trying to get out of the cold. I didn't think it was this bad when I left the house."

"A front's coming in. We're supposed to have three inches tonight. But you never know. Weathermen are just guessing like the rest of us." She covered the novel with a loose sheet of paper. "Did you just come in to warm up, or do you need something?"

"Is Uncle Pete here?"

Katie shook her head. "He was called to the college. The security team is having fits trying to figure out how to work the new camera system they just got installed. Seriously, don't buy the toys if you're too dumb to use them properly."

Her words made Cat smile. Katie had worked at the station long enough to remember back before the college even had a security team. She had called the college guys rent-a-cops for years before her uncle had asked her to stop. Then Cat felt the flash drive poking her leg and the humor of the situation left her.

"I need to leave something for him. Do you have an envelope and a pen?" Cat waited for Katie to pull out a small manila envelope and hand it to her. Cat scribbled on the front the words, *Call Me!* Then she lowered the envelope out of Katie's sight, dropped the pages and the flash drive inside, and sealed the flap. If it had been back in the day, she would have gotten wax and pressed her seal into the wax to make sure no one opened it except

Uncle Pete. She would have to hope the gummy seal would do the same thing. Besides, the police station was a safer place than anywhere else in town. Except maybe the safety deposit box she'd taken it from.

Katie set the envelope on the side of her desk. "I'll give it to him first thing when he comes inside."

Cat was having second thoughts. Maybe she should have studied the information more closely before giving it over to her uncle. She'd been so frantic about getting here to the station, she hadn't taken the time to really look at what she'd copied. It could be Michael's private papers, maybe the beginning of the memoir he was always talking about writing. Something simple and not the clue she was looking for. But it was too late now. Besides, she'd had trouble walking two blocks with it in her pocket without thinking she was being followed. How would she have gotten home?

She realized Katie was watching her. She probably looked crazy, standing here thinking. Cat forced a smile. "I'm not looking forward to the walk home, not in this weather."

"You could call a cab. Danny's probably awake by now. He tends to sleep in on the weekends since he knows he'll be called out late when the bars close." She flipped through her Rolodex on the counter. Katie was the only person Cat knew who actually still had the paper contact filing system. Of course, she didn't have a cell phone that Cat knew about. If you wanted to reach her, you had to call the landline at her house or call the station. Cat had heard the woman say that no one needed to be that connected to the world at all times. Sometimes, she wondered if stepping back in time wouldn't be the best solution.

"I'll just walk fast."

Cat said her good-byes and started thinking about what moment in time she'd choose to start over in as she walked home. Would it be before she and Seth broke up the first time? Would it be the day of her wedding and she could choose to run away with Seth to a new life in Washington? Or would either of those things change the outcome for Michael? Would he still have gotten involved with this thing that had gotten him killed? She had herself twisted in the lines of thought that always surrounded statements that began with *If only* when she heard the car pull up behind her and a door slam shut.

Chapter 19

Cat spun around, certain she'd be face-to-face with men in black suits pointing guns at her. Instead, Seth stepped toward her. "I thought you were going to the bank? Where have you been?"

"I went to the bank, and then to the police station." She blew out a breath, trying to calm down as she walked back toward him. "Why are you asking? Did something happen?"

"Shauna's on a tear. Apparently, she finally got a hold of Kevin's lawyer. He told her Kevin was in the middle of changing his will before his death. The lawyer advised her to get her own attorney because Paul was trying to block the filing of the new will. She thinks it's proof that Paul killed Kevin."

"Do you think he did?" Cat hurried over to the passenger side and climbed inside. She turned up the heat and put her hands over the vent. "There's a difference between fighting over money now that he's dead and actually killing the guy."

Seth got into the car and pulled back out onto

Main Street. "Paul doesn't seem to be the type who'd kill his best friend. He and Kevin were tight. Everyone knew that. I asked Brit about any rumors on family connections to the murder, but she says she hasn't heard a thing. And she was certain she would have heard."

"You've been asking around?" Cat's hands were starting to thaw. Finally.

"You know I consider Shauna a friend too. I don't want her going down for something she couldn't have done." Seth turned the corner. "There's one thing that still bugs me about that afternoon when she went over to Kevin's that last time."

"What? The poison? We've already found out someone else bought an identical bottle that same week. A woman with red hair. Like the woman Quinn caught on tape dropping off the dead rat." Cat watched the houses pass by as they drove up the street to home.

"No, it's not the poison that bothers me." Seth snuck a quick glance at Cat. "She was just about to put the lid on the casserole dish with the stew. I started to grab a bowl to get some before she left. She told me I couldn't have any."

"Maybe she didn't have enough." Cat turned in her seat to watch him.

"You know she always cooks too much. It was awkward for a moment, but then she told me to grab something out of the fridge to heat up if I was hungry." He pressed his lips together. "It was like she didn't want me to taste what she'd made for Kevin."

Neither one of them spoke. Finally, Cat shook her head. "No. There's no way she could have done something to hurt him. I don't know what she was thinking, but Shauna's no killer."

"I hope your uncle finds this mystery woman. I like Shauna."

"There's no way Uncle Pete would arrest her. He loves Shauna." Cat aimed the heat toward her feet.

Seth looked at her as if to say, *He would so*, but at least he didn't say it. "That doesn't help find out who killed Kevin."

"So, it's not the Mob. And it wasn't Shauna. And we don't believe it's Paul." Cat counted people off on her fingers. She filled him in on the scene that had transpired earlier with Paul and Jade, including the discovery that Collin was Kevin's son. "We still have Jade and Collin and anyone who'd ever been in business with Kevin."

"You've narrowed the field down to no more than two, three hundred people, tops." Seth grinned. "Are you sure you're even related to your uncle? Maybe you should just sit this investigation out. It might be safer for all concerned. Let's change the subject. Why were you at the bank?"

Cat showed him her tablet. "I found something in the safety deposit box. The original is at the police station."

"There was a tablet in the box?" Seth pulled the car into the driveway and turned off the engine.

"No. I downloaded some files that were on a flash drive. The original flash drive is at the police station. Try to keep up." Sitting in the car, Cat stared at the house Michael had left her. With the money she'd just transferred into her name, she'd be able to buy one just like it. If her uncle would let her keep the money. It might be seized as Mob money. Or the person who had given it to Michael may come back to reclaim it.

She needed to know what was on the flash drive. She hoped it would tell her what had gotten Michael killed. Popping out of the car, she waited for Seth to join her. "And that's not all I learned at the bank."

As she quickly ran down her morning, they walked to the kitchen door and opened it. The room was empty. Seth glanced at the row of keys. Shauna's car keys were still on the hook in the middle. "She's somewhere in the house."

They didn't have to look far. Shauna was digging through the desk in the front lobby. She looked up when Cat approached, her eyes wild. "I know it's here."

"What's here, honey." Cat kept her voice quiet and hoped she could calm her friend. "What are you looking for?"

"Quinn's phone number. I got to thinking that if he put up extra cameras here to prove to you that the system could help, well, maybe he did the same thing at the ranch. That system isn't that old."

Cat stared at her friend, then dug through the papers herself. "You're so smart."

"I just pay attention when people talk." Shauna grabbed some papers and set them on the desk. She started lifting each page slowly, one at a time, looking for the small card.

When Cat found the business card, she held it skyward. "Here it is. . . ."

Shauna snatched it out of her hand. "I'll call him. I don't want you to go off on him."

"He put up cameras on my house without my approval. I don't think I was in the wrong asking him to take them down." Cat followed Shauna into the kitchen. "So do you know what you're looking for?"

"Any camera that isn't looped into the ranch's security tape. I'm thinking Quinn might have some film he hasn't watched or maybe he's afraid to say anything to your uncle." They sat at the table as Shauna dialed the number. When Quinn answered, Shauna got down to business, rapid-firing questions. Finally, she hung up.

"What's going on? Does he have more film of that night?" Cat leaned forward, watching her.

"He agreed to come over. He wants to talk to you first before he says anything. But he can't be here until Saturday night after his shift. I guess your uncle put him on extra shifts this week." Shauna got up and grabbed a cup of coffee. "I told him we had dinner with the guests, but that we would be back by ten and we'd wait for him to get off."

"Leave it to Quinn to make this all cloak and dagger." Cat turned toward Seth and, out of the corner of her eye, saw the kitchen door swing close. Had someone been watching them? Listening? She stood and went to the door, scanning the hallway for anyone. But it was empty.

"Looking for someone?" Seth asked when she came back to the table.

Cat ignored the question and took her tablet out of her purse. "I guess we should look at these files. I don't want to do this alone."

The three crowded around the small screen as

Cat opened the first file. It was filled with charts and graphs outlining the profit margins of different properties.

"This looks like a profit comparison sheet." Shauna pointed to a few columns. "There's costs and potential income. I guess that was what Michael was working on?"

"I guess." Cat closed the file and opened another one. This seemed to be a list of properties with no comparison chart attached. She glanced through the street names and saw 846 Willow Lane on the list. She pointed to the line on the screen. "That's the one that is in my name."

She opened the last file. This one was a list of numbers, dates, and amounts.

"Well, that was illuminating." Cat looked at Seth and Shauna. "You guys got any ideas? Because I'm stumped."

"Nothing. I guess it could have been working documents for Michael's final report. But without that report to decipher the numbers, we're shooting in the dark." Shauna sank back into her chair.

"Tell her about the money," Seth prompted.

Shauna listened as Cat went through the visit to the bank. "So you're rich?"

Cat shook her head. "I think it's more likely I'm holding on to laundered Mob money and I'll be killed in my sleep for moving it."

"He should have taken your name off his account before he died." Shauna tapped her fingers on the table. "Wait, didn't you say the building on Willow Lane has some vacancies?"

"Yep. Shield Holdings is the leasing agent. We already know that."

"Maybe we should see who *is* actually working that property." Seth chewed on the side of his mouth. "We could learn more about who they're saying owns the property."

"What, you want to just call them for a showing?" Cat shook her head. "Shauna's too noticeable."

"I'm not." Shirley's voice came from behind Cat. She swept into the room and joined them at the table. "Look, I'm the perfect choice to go undercover. No one knows me in Denver. Are these apartments or commercial? I need to get my cover story down."

"Were you listening in? You need to be writing." Cat felt a twinge of distrust. Had Uncle Pete asked Shirley to watch over the three of them, especially when it came to doing any investigation on the side? "You paid us to attend a writers' retreat, not to go investigating some cold case."

"Honey, this *is* book research. I've already gotten my words in for the day. Now I need to stop thinking about it and do something else. Investigating your ex-husband's demise keeps me busy." Shirley took out her notebook and held a pen to a blank sheet of paper. "So what are we doing?"

It took a few minutes researching the building to build her cover story. As she took notes, Cat tried to think of any questions this stunt might answer. "Ask who owns the building because the last apartment you leased went condo a few months after you moved in."

"That's good." Seth nodded his approval. He grinned at Cat. "That should get them talking about the owner and her plans. Of course, she's actually a very hands-off property owner. Probably doesn't work with tenants or fix problems."

"You realize I didn't know I owned this place, right?" Even though she knew he was kidding, she felt defensive at his statements. Someone had been acting on her behalf for over a year. "Wait, can we use that? 'Tell me about the owner' kind of questions? Is she/he active in the property? Maybe they own the penthouse?"

"Good line of questioning." Shirley scribbled several points down. By the time she was ready, Seth had the car warmed up again. He would pose as Shirley's nephew helping her look for a new apartment. Cat and Shauna would stay in Aspen Hills and see if there were any other loose strings to pull at regarding Kevin's murder.

"I'm not a hundred percent sure this is a good idea, but I don't want you all going into this without some backup. What kind of hero would that be?" He kissed Cat and then escorted Shirley out to the vehicle.

"Divide and conquer." Shauna took a pan of brownies out of the oven and set them on the rack to cool. She already had enough food for the afternoon and evening meals set up for the next two days, but she kept adding one more thing.

Cat watched as she made up the trays for the guests. "Did Kevin ever talk about work with you? Was there a problem with any of his developments?"

"There were always problems. He kept having to fly back to Boston at least once a week." Shauna arranged a cookie tray, setting the cookies out in an alternating circle.

Cat watched the design come to life as her friend

made a swirl of treats. Then her words hit her. "Boston. He had partners in Boston."

"Yeah. I guess that's where his silent partner lived. But the guy wasn't very silent. Kevin always grumbled that he was in bed with the devil and didn't know how to get out." Shauna wiped her hands on the tea towel slung over her shoulder. "Why?"

"Because Dante and his family are from Boston. And they have ties here in Aspen Hills. The property I now own is on Michael's list. And Kevin's company manages that property." She paused, looking at her friend. "Do you think it's that easy? That Kevin got sideways with his family connection? Seth asked Brit, but she said it wasn't the family."

"Or it's being kept quiet because it is the family." The kitchen turned still as they considered the connections. Then Shauna took a cookie and broke it in half, offering Cat some. "According to your uncle, someone attacked Kevin in the barn. Maybe they thought the poison was taking too long? That's rage. That's not a clean business hit."

Cat opened her notebook and looked at the prior list she'd made of possible suspects. "If it's not about business, then it's personal."

Their gaze drifted upward as if they could see through the ceiling and into the guest room. "You don't think . . ."

"How angry would you be at a father who brought you to Colorado, then never talked to you?"

The kitchen door flew open, and Uncle Pete came in with a bluster. "I swear, woman, you and your groups are more trouble than the entire fleet of frat boys I have to deal with every semester."

Cat and Shauna watched him as he pulled off his shoes, took off his coat, then poured himself a cup of coffee before he sat down. He leaned in and gave each of them a kiss on the cheek. "Before we get started here, I want to say good morning and it's nice to see each of you."

"Technically, it's good afternoon. Did you come for lunch?" Shauna started to stand, but he put a hand on her arm and she lowered herself back to her seat. "I'm not liking where this discussion is going. Please don't say anyone else is dead."

"No, it's nothing like that. I wanted to see if you'd thought of anything helpful in the Kevin investigation. I've got bubkes and more bubkes. There's a lot of motivation for people wanting him dead, but no one seems to be in the right place at the right time."

"Except me," Shauna added. "I was at the ranch that night."

"I would have seen you leave the house. Quinn did a great job at covering all the entrances and exits with that camera system. Too bad he didn't put up some extras in the barn." He sighed. "You could have made this a lot easier by not buying poison from the hardware store. And what were you thinking, calling Kevin's lawyer and making a fuss?"

"I wanted to know what was happening to the ranch. Well, really, just the horse. I hate to see her just sold off because Paul doesn't like her." Shauna shrugged. "Besides, I should have a say in putting Kevin to rest and what happens to his stuff. We were engaged."

"You were his girlfriend. No legal rights there." Uncle Pete softened his tone. "Look, just let me do my job here. You two are always getting into things that don't concern you." Uncle Pete turned to Cat. "And you. What exactly did you leave me in that envelope?"

"You mean what was on the flash drive? I can't really tell." Cat thought about the charts and figures that Michael had saved. Numbers. The guy lived by numbers.

He shook his head. "No, I meant what was in the envelope. Once you left, a woman came in screaming her husband needed help. Katie jumped up and ran outside, and when she came back in to ask where the husband was, the woman and your envelope were gone."

"How long after I left?" A chill ran down Cat's spine. She'd felt like she'd been followed. Maybe her instincts had been spot-on.

"Katie says ten, fifteen minutes." He took another sip of coffee. "She couldn't be sure as she was reading. But it wasn't longer than it takes her to read a chapter. She was clear on that." He pulled out his notebook and a pen. "So what was on that flash drive that someone wanted it bad enough to steal from a police station?"

Cat opened the tablet and found the three files. She opened them one at a time, giving her uncle time to scan each one before she went to the next. Then she showed him the photos of the pages. "The files look like business graphs and charts. Nothing with a smoking gun, except one of the properties is the one Michael put in my name before he died."

"Michael did these charts?" He closed out the spreadsheets and opened each of the photos of the papers. "And you're sure this is his handwriting on the papers?"

"The papers, yes. It's his handwriting. But it looks like it's in some sort of code. Random names, words that don't mean anything, and more numbers." Cat shrugged. "I think he made up the charts too. I can't really tell. All I know is the flash drive was in the safety deposit box."

Her uncle turned the tablet toward him and clicked a few keys. Then he turned it back to Cat and pointed out a code under PROPERTIES. "It shows the name of the computer if the owner keyed one in, and Michael Latimer did. So at least these were produced by his computer." He waited for both Cat and Shauna to look, then turned back to Cat. "Wait, what safety deposit box?"

Cat filled him in on the visit to the estate lawyer and what she'd found out. When she got to visiting the bank, he groaned. "Angels tread . . ."

"What's that supposed to mean?" Cat picked up his cup and took it to the coffeepot to refill. "I'm not supposed to even visit my bank now? No one knew I was going to check out Michael's safety deposit box."

"And yet, someone did because the flash drive is gone." He opened her email program and sent the files, along with the photos, to his office email. "I don't know what I'm going to be able to make of these, but maybe someone at the college can help me."

The words were out of her mouth before she could stop them. "Don't ask Dean Ngu. He's way too invested in getting Michael's papers. And we know he was the one who gave Michael the lead on the job, according to what Shirley found. I'm thinking he might be working with whoever did this."

"I was already looking at his interest in Michael's papers. Where is Shirley? I wanted to see if I could buy her lunch or dinner tonight." Uncle Pete looked toward the door to the hallway. "I'm probably too late for lunch."

"She's not here." Cat skirted his question.

Uncle Pete narrowed his eyes, somehow hearing the unsaid part of the statement. "So, where is she, and why do I think I'm not going to like the answer to that question?"

"Seth took her into Denver." Cat paused, hoping he would accept that explanation. Instead, he waved his hand in a go-ahead gesture. "She's looking at an apartment in the building I own."

"She's moving here?" Shock rang in his voice.

The look of horror on her uncle's face made her giggle. "No. She's trying to find out if there's a connection between Kevin's company and the building."

"I thought you liked Shirley?" Shauna was watching him now, a twinkle sparkling in her gaze.

"I do like the woman. I'm just not ready for a full-time girlfriend. This week has been a nice trial run, and maybe we'll have a few more of these trials before either of us makes a decision." He stood. "Anyway, I need to get back to the station. Katie's a little antsy about the theft. She's blaming herself." He nodded to the tablet. "Nice move making copies like that."

"I didn't think it wouldn't be safe at the police station. I just didn't want it in the house, just in case."

"You were smart there." He kissed her on the top

of the head, then patted Shauna's shoulder. "Call me if something comes of this wild goose chase in Denver. I'd like to get at least one murder case closed and off my desk this week."

Cat watched her uncle leave, then leaned back into her chair. "Sometimes I think this thing with Michael will never be over. I have to keep locking him and the memories away in this box inside me. And then something, like the flash drive, comes along and pops open the chest."

"We fall for interesting men who die in interesting ways," Shauna noted. "It's our own fault we're miserable. We need to start dating dull, boring men."

"Don't let Seth hear you call him boring."

"Oh, my dear, I think Seth falls into the interesting category. You just need to see it." Shauna walked out of the room.

Chapter 20

When it was time for the afternoon get-together, Cat gathered the group into the living room to talk.

"Where's Shirley?" Pamela stood up. "I'll go get her from her room. I know she'll want to be part of this."

Cat held up a hand. "Shirley took a research trip into Denver today. I'm sure she'll be back before you all go for dinner." Seth and Shirley should be back by five. The showing was scheduled for exactly two. Cat pushed away thoughts of what might be happening and focused on the group. Shauna had brought in a mix of cookies and other desserts and set them up on the coffee table. A pot of hot cocoa, cups, and a bowl of marshmallows sat on a tray nearby.

Melissa took a lemon bar off the plate and curled her legs up underneath her as she settled in for the discussion. "I'm not going to fit into my skinny jeans after this."

One more reason Cat needed to pull the trigger

on building the in-house gym. Or was the fact the Victorian was almost completely remodeled worrying her? Was he only here for the work? Had she seen more of a future in their reunion than really was possible? *Not now, not here*, she chided herself. "It won't do you any good now, but I'm putting in a gym in the basement, for the winter sessions. Maybe you'll come back."

"That's a great idea." Jordon poured a drink, filling the cup with marshmallows, then gently pouring the hot cocoa over them. "I typically run every day at home. But we don't have two feet of snow right now."

"Arizona never has two feet of snow," Pamela reminded him.

Jordon sat in one of the wing chairs next to Collin. "We get snow. Rarely and mostly in the mountains, but we get snow. It's not a foreign concept. Just this much is."

Collin chuckled. "You should see what's up in the mountains. My friend and I went cross-country skiing last month and the snow was at least ten feet deep in places."

"Anyway, we're not here to talk about snow," Melissa interrupted. "You boys can do your story-telling tonight at dinner. Cat, tell us the rest of the story about being an author."

Cat felt everyone's eyes on her. This was the point where they wanted the magic formula. You wrote three books, got an agent, sold to a publisher for big bucks, then became a household name. Easy. Except it wasn't. She hated breaking their fantasy, but a realistic view into publishing would get them farther in this world. She took a deep breath and started. "The one thing you have to realize is the journey is different for everyone."

"You mean where you get published," Jordon clarified.

Melissa added, "Or what genre you write in."

Cat shook her head. "Sorry, no. I mean *everyone's* journey is different. You could write the same exact genre, sub-genre, length, even core story, and one person could be published and the other rejected. It's all about the luck of the draw, who reads you, who gets you, and what the publisher or editor bought last week. You could have an amazing vampire book, but if the publisher just bought a ten-book series, your book may be rejected because they don't want it to compete with the book they just bought."

"Man, you can't control any of this." Jordon set his cup down. "Maybe we should get out now before we get our hearts broken."

"No. You should stay and fight. No one."—she repeated the words—"no one will love your book as much as you do, so you have to keep fighting for it."

Melissa tilted her head. "But when do you give up?"

"When you've done everything you're willing to do. You have to make the decision on when it's time to start a new story rather than keep massaging the one you have. I heard the woman who wrote *The Help* did sixty different drafts or something like that. She would get a rejection, then rewrite. Rinse and repeat. It might be an urban legend, but I heard the last time she rented a hotel room for a weekend because she didn't want her family to see she wasn't giving up."

"So either we're crazy for believing in the book, or crazy for not holding on long enough." Collin shook his head. "At least I'm writing to contract. If I wrote fiction, it would be all on spec until I got a publisher."

"Who made up these rules?" Pamela took another cookie. "Now I'm eating because I'm depressed at the vision of my future."

"You have to ask yourself one question." Cat looked at each guest before she continued. "Do you really love to write and tell stories?"

Each one of them nodded, emphatically.

"Then you hope, and you rewrite, and you write something new, and you keep trying until you get that contract that Collin mentioned." Cat took her own cookie. "Then you try to keep it or get another one. It's a horrible, horrible way to make a living."

"And yet, you love it," Melissa added.

"I do. Which makes me as crazy as the rest of you." Cat ate her cookie. "Now, let's talk a little about the business end of writing. What you need to do before you get that first contract and what you do every day."

"Writing's a craft, not a business," Pamela protested.

Jordon stared at her. "Seriously? What rock have you been living under? Do you expect to get a patron who will support you while you write?"

Cat stepped into the conversation before Pamela could respond as she saw the red staining the young woman's cheeks. "Writing is both, business and craft. But you will only succeed if you treat it like a business. It's kind of like that advice to write drunk but edit sober. You need the creative side to blossom even when you're planning for the more numbers-driven business side."

"Yeah, the IRS isn't going to say, 'Just give us an estimate of what you made and what you spent.'" Jordon nodded. "I talked to a CPA last year about my taxes and when I should be looking at doing an LLC or a corporation status. It's all a numbers game."

The discussion went on way past four, and by the time they finished, Cat felt drained. She wondered if Shauna had dinner plans or if they could order some takeout and have Seth pick it up. She glanced at her watch. When he got home, that was. She heard voices in the lobby and went out to see if Shirley and Seth had returned. Instead, Dante sat on the ornate love seat near the window, with Shauna by his side. He smiled as Cat walked toward them.

"Catherine, I am so glad you were tied up for a few minutes. It gave me time to meet your partner. Shauna is as bright as she is lovely." He stood. "I hate to rush you, but I have a plane to catch. May we use Michael's study for our appointment?"

Cat wasn't going to be played like that. "We had an appointment? I must have forgotten."

"No matter, I'll be in and out before you know it." He took Shauna's hand in both of his and then laid a business card on her palm. "I'm so sorry for your loss. If there's anything I can do, please feel free to reach out."

"Thank you. That's very kind." Shauna looked at Dante like he was a changeling. Definitely not what she'd been expecting if Cat read her expression correctly.

"I'm busy. You can come back tomorrow." She stepped away from the lobby and headed to the back of the house.

"Catherine, please. I won't be here tomorrow and I need to talk to you about something." He glanced at Shauna. "It's important."

She stopped, thinking about the things she wanted to say to him.

"Catherine . . ." His voice had a plea in it she'd never heard before.

"Fine, but I only have a few minutes." Cat pointed toward the study. "I believe you know the way."

Dante chuckled but nodded. "Ladies first."

Cat power walked to the study, held the door open for Dante, then shut and locked it. She turned toward him, her fury barely under control. "What do you want? I believe I was clear the last time you just showed up unannounced."

"Oh, you were clear. And as fun as it was sneaking in here at times, I needed to be seen coming in the front door. By as many people as possible." He sat on her reading chair and pointed to the wingback. "Sit. I need to clear up a few things."

"Like the fact you killed my husband?"

"I didn't kill Michael. He was my friend. We've talked about this." Dante's voice rose and then lowered again.

"Okay, you were friends with my husband." Cat perched on the edge of the chair. "Did he know he was working for you the whole time? Wait, what's going on that you need to be seen by people. Are you setting up an alibi?"

"He wasn't working for me. He was working for Dominic, my brother. And I didn't know he'd gotten in too deep until he called me." Dante ignored her last question, speaking calmly and carefully, like the conversation might be recorded. "When Michael called, it was too late to get him out. We thought if he could get the evidence to me, he'd be safe. Then I could deal with my brother."

"Evidence of what? The only things on that flash drive were charts and property listings." She winced. Not something she really wanted the man sitting next to her to know. Or at least to know that she knew.

Dante's fingers twitched on the edge of the chair. "So you did look at the flash drive. That could have proven deadly. As it was, you put it in an extremely hard place for me to recover."

"*You* stole the flash drive from the station." Cat's eyes narrowed. "Katie said it was a woman."

"My family has people. I didn't steal the flash drive or ask someone else to do it. I told you to be careful. That you were being watched." He held up a hand to stop her next words. "Look, I need to tell you why Michael was killed. You have the right to know."

"We were divorced. I don't have many rights." As she said it, Cat realized the college's human resources department had not called her right back.

"You were divorced to keep you safe." Dante shook his head. "No, let me tell it my way. You have already figured out that Michael and I were college friends. He called me when he realized the job Dean Ngu had set him up with was with the family. But it was Dominic's side business. And Michael quickly realized that my brother was selling off family property at bargain prices to his own holding company. That's the ledgers you saw. Now, I have the evidence to convince the family that Dominic was dirty."

"Your brother had Michael killed before he could give you the evidence." Cat felt sick that Michael had died over money. It was so useless. "Do you know who did it?"

"Not Dominic. He only gave the order. Probably some low-level family assassin." Dante leaned toward Cat. "You have to understand, I tried to save him. And now I have to try to save my brother. When the family finds out what he did, Dominic won't be able to explain his way out of this one."

"Fine. I know. You can go now." Cat didn't want to cry in front of Dante. And somehow, knowing the why behind Michael's death had made the pain sharper. She started to stand, but Dante put his hand on her shoulder, keeping her seated.

He walked around to the other side of the desk, pulled out a drawer. Cat could hear a gear engage. And then the secret compartment she hadn't been able to find popped open. Dante took out an envelope and then closed up the drawer. "Michael sent me a note, telling me about the envelope. We found the desk in a Boston antique store the weekend Michael graduated from Harvard. The owner said it had been owned by one of the generals in the civil war. The guy had hidden his orders there."

Cat had always wondered where the desk had come from. Michael tended to collect pieces that meant something.

"I bought it for him and had it sent over to his

new apartment here in Aspen Hills. It took up most of the living room." Dante smiled at the memory. "No matter what you might think of me, I miss my friend."

Cat didn't respond. She'd had her own mixed feelings about Michael, but Dante's were really messed up. He felt responsible for Michael's death. "He asked for me to give the envelope to you, if any of this ever came out in the light. I should have given this to you months ago."

Dropping it on her lap, he stood and lightly brushed her hair out of her eyes. "Take care, Catherine. I hope I will be able to return someday and we could have another cup of coffee together. I enjoyed that."

Cat watched him shut the door behind him and then opened the envelope. Tears filled her eyes as she read Michael's version of the story Dante had just told her. How Michael had gotten in over his head. How he'd sent her away the only way he'd known how. And how sorry he'd been to cause her any pain. Cat read the last line aloud. "Always remember I loved you more than life itself. It's hard for an economist to be poetic, but I truly, madly, deeply loved you. I hope you have a wonderful life with someone who treats you better than I ever could. Michael."

A knock sounded at the door and Shauna poked her head in. "Just checking to see if you weren't lying in a pool of blood. That man is smooth, like the devil."

Cat waved her in and Shauna took the seat Dante had just left. She brushed away the tears that had dropped on her cheeks as she'd read the note. "His brother killed Michael because he found proof the guy was skimming from the family coffers."

"Well, so it was all about the Mob, just not in the way you thought." Shauna leaned back in her chair, clearly shocked at the news. "What did he say about the building?"

Cat's eyes widened and she tucked the letter back into the envelope. "I didn't even ask. I guess that will be a discussion point for our next conversation, whenever he's back in town."

"He does have a habit of just popping in." Shauna eyed the envelope but didn't ask about it.

"Next time, you're sitting in on the discussion so I don't forget to ask the important stuff." Cat stood and they walked into the hallway. "I'm going up to my office for a minute. What do you say we do Chinese for dinner? Is Seth back?"

"Not yet. I'm beginning to get worried. Should we call his cell?" Shauna followed her out of the room and down the hallway.

As if their words had called him, Seth stepped out of the kitchen. "There you two are. Come in here and let Shirley tell you what she found out."

They gathered around the table where Shirley sat, drinking coffee. "I don't really need the caffeine, but this does taste good."

Cat waited for her to set the cup down before she asked, "What happened?"

"We got there just in time for the appointment. The lofts are beautiful by the way. High ceilings, lots of chrome and glass. And the neighborhood is filled with little restaurants, shops, and even an urgent care clinic." Shirley glanced around the table.

"What? I was supposed to be looking for a new place to live. And if I was considering moving, I'd jump at this place."

"What did you learn about the building itself? The owners?" Cat pressed.

"Not much. Heather—she was the leasing agent who showed up—she works for Shield Holdings. She was upset about the loss of her boss, but not too devastated because his partner, Paul, had already assured the staff that nothing will change due to Kevin's untimely passing."

"That's a pretty big promise." Seth shook his head. "What if the company gets sold or shut down?"

"Paul's making a power play for not only the company but all of Kevin's worldly goods." Shauna shrugged as everyone at the table but Cat turned to look at her. "What? I talked to his attorney again this morning. I think it was his assistant who ratted me out to Paul and your uncle. Which reminds me, I need to hire an attorney of my own. Any suggestions?"

Seth nodded. "Mine is good. He's kind of a bulldog, but he's kept me out of trouble with the building commission since I started my business. I have a card here in my wallet."

"You carry an attorney's card in your wallet, just in case? In case of what? Never mind, I don't want to know." Cat turned back to Shirley. "Okay, so this Heather liked her boss. And she likes the new king. What else did she say? Anything about the building owner?"

"You'll be happy to know you're a pillar of the

community and you have long-term roots in the locally owned Denver area. She told us that conglomerates from out of state were trying to buy up anything that came up for sale. She did say that she couldn't promise the building wouldn't go condo on me, but she was sure that the owner would work with me. Since she's so nice and all." Shirley looked up from her notes. "Have you met this Heather?"

"Never." Cat might have had a Heather in one of her classes, but she didn't remember exactly.

"Well, she talked like you two were best friends."

Seth slipped Shauna the business card, ignoring Cat's glare. "So was she just telling you what you wanted to hear?"

"All good questions, but let me fill you in on what I've discovered since you've been gone." Cat took them through the loss of the flash drive, the visit from Uncle Pete, and finally, the strange visit from Dante. "He wants to take you to dinner, by the way."

"I don't know this Dante. Why would he want to take me to dinner?" Shirley stood and refilled her cup.

"No, not Dante. Uncle Pete." Cat played with the envelope.

"A love letter from Dante?" Seth's voice sounded like he was joking, but there was a slight twist to the words.

"Actually, one from Michael. A few years too late." She looked at the three. "He verified everything Dante told me and then said he staged the inciting incident for the divorce."

"He wanted to keep you safe." Shauna breathed

out the words like a promise or a blessing. "How lovely."

Cat shook her head. "No, not lovely. He didn't trust me enough to share what he'd gotten himself into. He could have figured out a lot of ways to get me to leave Aspen Hills. He could have been honest. Instead, he played a huge charade and broke my heart."

Seth put his hand over hers. "You can never step in the same river."

"What does that mean?" Cat felt surly and didn't want to mess with word puzzles.

Shirley nodded. "He's saying the past is like water in a river. It's gone as soon as you see it pass by."

"I'm sure Michael was doing the best he could at the time," Shauna added.

Cat wanted to be mad. Her hand itched to hit someone. But her friends were right. It was done and over with. "So we solved one murder. Let's say we focus on solving Kevin's?"

Chapter 21

As soon as Cat hit the last stair tread Saturday morning, she heard the voices in the dining room. It sounded as if the entire house was up early and having breakfast together. She paused at the doorway, watching the group talk and laugh together. This group had bonded nicely together. Of course, two were already friends, but even with the mix of ages and experiences, they'd really come together as a group.

She came in and, after grabbing a cup of coffee and a muffin, sat next to Shirley. "How was your dinner last night?"

Shirley flushed as she focused on buttering her own muffin. "Your uncle is very interesting. If I ever wanted to try my hand at fiction, I'm sure I have enough material to write a convincing small-town sheriff now."

"That's the only reason you and he have been hanging out?" Cat sipped her coffee. "I think he'll be disappointed to hear that."

"Don't tell him that." Shirley's head popped up and Cat saw worry in her eyes.

"Shirley has a boyfriend," Jordon teased. "Before you got in the room, she was telling us all how dreamy Pete was."

"I never said dreamy," Shirley corrected. "But yeah, he's interesting and I'm fascinated by him."

"As a sheriff," Cat added.

"Fine, as a man." Shirley stood and refilled her coffee. "And that's all I'm going to say about this. You young ones might kiss and tell, but our generation is a little more discreet about our relationships."

"So he did kiss you." Melissa looked at Pamela. "Pay up. I told you he'd make his move last night."

Pamela pulled a five out of her jeans pocket. "He kind of had to since we're doing a group dinner tonight. You just guessed right."

"I never said he kissed me," Shirley protested.

"So he didn't?" Pamela held the five out of Melissa's reach.

The pink on Shirley's face turned a brighter red and Melissa stood and took the five.

"Told you."

"You guys are terrible." Everyone at the table burst into laughter, except Shirley, who focused on her coffee. Cat loved this part. Friendships molded and grown around a common love of writing. Books ruled. "How was everyone's retreat? Anything you'd like to see changed? Anything that didn't work well this week? You have a formal evaluation in your packet you can drop off at the front desk or send in later, your choice. I'd just like to give you the opportunity to talk now, if you want."

"You should have an in-house gym." Shirley spoke first, apparently happy to have the change of subject.

"Noted and being worked on." Cat opened her notebook and wrote the suggestion down. "Anything else? Food? Drinks? Room issues?"

"My room was way too lovely. I didn't want to leave." Pamela smiled at Cat. "I guess I was expecting more of a hotel atmosphere rather than a real bed-and-breakfast. You guys rock."

"The towels are too soft," Jordon added.

Collin looked at the group. "Seriously? You guys are complaining? I loved everything in my room, and I'd like to just move in and have you two adopt me. "

Shauna came into the room just as Collin was talking. Her face turned pink and Cat knew she was thinking that she'd almost become a real relative to the kid. She dropped off a pan of a breakfast sausage casserole and paused at the door. "We loved having you all here."

"Come sit with us and eat." Cat waved her toward an empty chair. "We're doing a quick review of the retreat. I'd like you to hear this."

Shauna put her hand on Collin's shoulder as she paused at the table. "I've got eggs and bacon cooking for Seth in the kitchen. You all go ahead. I've already eaten."

It had been a strange week, but at least one good thing had come out of the retreat. Collin had gained, if not a relative, at least a friend. Cat glanced around the table. *Two good things*, she corrected herself. Uncle Pete had a new girlfriend. Even if she lived in Alaska.

As the breakfast continued, they talked about books and writing and what happens next. Pamela and Melissa grinned at each other. "You two look like you have something to add." Cat turned the group's attention to the women. "What's going on?"

"We challenged each other to get up the nerve and sent out queries to our top five agents last night." Melissa bounced in her seat. "And we're both determined to keep sending out until we get requests for full manuscripts."

A round of applause met their announcement. Cat nodded. "Great job. Now rinse and repeat. Keep writing, keep sending out, and keep getting better. Determination is just as important in this business as talent. You can have a great story, but if it only stays on your computer's hard drive, you aren't going to ever sell."

"Or if you give up after the first rejection." Jordon stood and went to get more food. "I think I have close to thirty so far. At least that was the count for my first story. I'm hoping this new one will have a better result with the agents."

Cat stayed with the group until people started to leave to get one more writing session in. They were heading to the library for the morning, and then they were going out for one more group lunch. Collin stayed behind and waited for the room to empty.

"I wanted to tell you how much I appreciated everything this week. I am so glad I got to meet Shauna, especially after losing Kevin. It still feels weird, calling him my dad, but at least Shauna can tell me what kind of man he was and if I'm anything like him. I'm sad I never really got to know him."

Collin paused at the door. "My mom tells me things about him, but I can't really trust a lot of things she says. She isn't feeling the best anymore. I try to help, but she's kind of lost in the past."

"I'm sorry to hear that." Cat studied the young man. "But you know, it's not your responsibility to make her happy. She needs to make her own life."

Collin didn't look convinced. "I'm all she has. I guess I'll just have to make it work."

Cat felt bad that Collin's life was being held back by his mother's inability to get past losing Kevin, which had been years ago. She was glad that she finally knew the story behind Michael. If she'd continued to wonder, would she have turned out like Collin's mom? Someone lost in the past?

Seth and Shauna were still in the kitchen. She took her cup and put it into the sink. She grabbed a soda.

"Did you eat? Do you want me to make you a couple of eggs?" Shauna stood and walked toward the stove.

"I'm fine. Collin's a good kid." She sat at the table. "Everyone took off and went to the library. I don't think we'll see them again until we leave for the restaurant."

Seth watched her. "Are you okay?"

"What? Because of Michael?" Cat shook her head. "He made his decision when he didn't trust me enough to deal with the situation he got into."

"He was trying to keep you safe. I respect that." Seth held up a hand. "I know I hated the guy for stealing you away, but honestly, all I ever wanted was for you to be happy. With me would have been a better option, but just happy."

Uncle Pete came through the door. He stood on the entry rug, stamping his feet. When Shauna waved him inside, he shook his head. "I'm on my way over to the college."

"Something wrong?" Chills ran down Cat's neck.

He nodded. "But I think you know what I'm going to say."

"Which one? Dante or Dominic?" One of the brothers hadn't survived the uncovering of the evidence. She liked Dante. Dominic, she didn't know anything about except the man had ordered Michael's death. *Please be Dominic, please.* Her unspoken prayer surprised even her.

Shauna and Seth cast an uneasy glance at her. But they both turned toward Uncle Pete when he cleared his throat. "Dominic. He was Martin's father so I have to go tell the kid that he's dead. Good thing I don't have to say his uncle was the one who killed him. According to the Boston detective who called me this morning, Dominic's death happened during a home robbery. They are holding the two suspects the security team found riffling through his office."

"Convenient." Dante hadn't been in time or able to change the mind of the person in charge of the family. She wanted to think this avenged Michael's death. But Cat knew it was more about Dominic's betrayal of the family. Michael was just collateral damage. Uncle Pete knew it. Everyone in the room knew it.

"The detective said the case was a slam dunk. One of the suspects even confessed to the murder."

"I wonder how high the payment to his family was for taking the fall," Cat murmured, more to herself than her uncle. "Let me pour you a cup of coffee to go. It's cold out there."

"You seem awful calm. Are you all right?" Uncle Pete watched her get one of the traveling mugs down and fill it with the dark roast.

"Why? Just because I went from being divorced from a guy who was cheating to finding out he didn't cheat and he staged the scene so I'd leave? Then he leaves me our house in his will and now I find out he was working for the Mob and trying to help Dante prove his brother was stealing, probably stolen money, from the family?" She handed Uncle Pete the warm cup. "I should have stayed in California."

"And miss all this fun?" Uncle Pete kissed her on the forehead. "None of this changes who you are today. But at least it's over."

A chill came over Cat. She looked over at the doorway, but it seemed to be closed. She pulled her jacket closer. "I hope so. I don't think I could deal with any more of Michael's secrets."

"Well, tomorrow your guests will be heading home and we can go grab some dinner and talk out this whole mess." He took his keys out of his pocket. "You two can come along too. We need to get everything out into the open with this Michael thing."

When he left, Cat rolled her shoulders. "I'm heading upstairs to take a long hot bath, then I'm reading until we have to leave for dinner. I need some downtime to help process all this."

"I could help. If you want company." Seth grinned, his mouth curved into a lazy smile that still made her warm all over.

"Thanks for the offer, but I just want to be alone." Cat laid her head on his shoulder as he pulled her into a hug. "I have to be the charming hostess this evening. I need to get my thoughts together."

"I'm here for you, you know that, right?" He stroked her hair back and she felt protected. A feeling she hadn't had for a long time.

"I know. Thanks Seth." She straightened, brushed the tears away from her eyes, and gave the two a small smile. "One mystery down, one to go."

"We don't need to figure out who killed Kevin," Shauna protested, tears forming in her eyes as well. "Your uncle will do that for us."

"Maybe, but sometimes everyone needs a little help." She headed out the door and took the stairs to her room. The house was quiet. And for the first time since she'd moved back, it felt like her house. A place where she could live, write, and learn to love again.

She shut the door on the past and fell onto her bed. She curled up with a pillow and closed her eyes.

A banging that sounded like a barn door flying open and closed in the wind brought her out of a dream. She'd been on Seth's family farm and they'd been up in the hayloft talking about their future. Cat had just told the seventeen-year-old Seth that it wasn't going to happen that way because somehow in the dream, her teenage self had known about Michael and her marriage. And Seth had taken her hand and kissed it.

"It's okay no matter how it happens, Cat. We're always going to be together. I promise you that. Today, tomorrow, forever."

The barn door banged again, but this time, it was

Shauna knocking on her bedroom door. "Cat, are you asleep? It's almost time to leave for dinner."

She rubbed her face, trying to put the dream back into the nether regions of her mind. She could still smell the straw that had poked at her through her tank top.

"Cat? Are you okay?" Shauna sounded concerned now, and Cat saw her doorknob jittering.

"I'm fine." She stood up and went over to open the door.

Shauna stood in a little black dress she'd bought last year for a dinner party she attended with Kevin. The dress fit her well without being too sexy. It highlighted her red hair, which she'd swept up into an updo and made her green eyes sparkle, even in the dim light of the hallway. Shauna appraised her friend. "You don't look fine."

"Odd dream, that's all." She pushed back her hair. "I'll take a quick shower and get ready. Tell Seth we might be a few minutes late. Maybe we should call the restaurant."

"I'll handle Seth and the restaurant. You go get ready." Shauna paused. "You're taking all this really well."

"Not really, but I'm putting up a great front." Cat smiled at her friend. "I'm holding off on my break-down until the last guest leaves tomorrow. Then I'll be a total mess."

"I'll be joining you in that pity party. The store dropped off two new bottles of my Scottish whiskey with the groceries this afternoon. I adore those guys." Shauna turned back toward her room. "I'm adding some jewelry to this. I have a lovely diamond ring that will look amazing, even if I do have to wear it on my right hand now."

Cat closed the door and headed to her bathroom. Shauna was going to be okay. Maybe not today, but eventually. Her friend had too much spunk to be dragged down, especially over a man who'd been as complicated as Kevin. She looked in the mirror at her drawn face and pointed a finger at the image. "Pot, meet kettle. You need to get this mourning done and over with, now that you know the whole story." Cat wondered if it could be that simple.

She quickly got ready, and as she put on makeup, she realized that was just what she'd been doing. Mourning his loss twice. Once when she'd thought he'd cheated, and now, when she knew he hadn't. She spied the envelope sitting on her nightstand. She opened the drawer and pushed it inside. Cat was done.

Or at least she hoped so.

Chapter 22

"So how long have you known Cat?" Melissa sat in the back passenger seat chatting with Seth. Collin sat beside her. He hadn't said a word during the entire ride, but Cat had seen how he'd looked at Melissa when she'd come down in her red cocktail dress. Adoration was probably the best word to use. The kid had it bad. Too bad Melissa was getting on a plane and leaving tomorrow.

"We were high school sweethearts." Seth didn't look backwards, just kept his eyes on the road. "It's natural I went to work for her when she opened the writers retreat. She was good about giving me orders back then too."

"Give me a break." Cat slapped his arm. She glanced back and saw Shauna looking out the back window. Shauna caught her gaze and pointed behind them. Cat tried to see what she was looking at, but all she saw were headlights. "We dated until he was stationed in Washington and I was accepted to Covington's graduate program. We had a huge fight and broke up."

"Not quite the way I remember it, but that's okay." Seth dropped his voice. "We had a tiny little fight and she dumped me for an older guy."

"That must have hurt." Melissa shot a quick glance at Cat. "Although it makes a perfect backdrop for a reunion trope in a romance."

"I'm always being used as a model for you romance writers. Tell me, it's the rugged jaw line, right?" Seth glanced at Melissa through the rearview mirror as he squeezed Cat's hand.

Cat watched out the side mirror as they turned into the parking lot. A small compact car came up on the turnout and slowed down. She could see the banged-up driver's side. And she bet the back bumper had a Wall Drug bumper sticker. She glanced back at Shauna and nodded.

"I'm not upsetting you, talking about this, am I?" Melissa put her hand on Cat's arm.

"Of course not. Seth and I are comfortable with the past." She winked at the woman sitting behind her. "And now he knows not to argue with me."

"Touché." Seth pulled the SUV next to the door. "Everyone out. I'll park and be in as soon as I've licked my wounds."

"Whatever." Cat climbed out of the front seat, glad she'd worn boots with her dinner dress. The wind was bitterly cold. The rest of the group piled out of the vehicle and they hurried inside the restaurant, where they waited at the hostess section to be seated. When the woman returned, Cat glanced around. "We have a reservation. Latimer for eight?"

Shauna stepped forward. "Sorry, it's not under Latimer. Try Clodagh. Shauna Clodagh."

"Hey, I know you." The hostess grinned at Shauna. "We met over at Aspen Hills Natural Foods last week? I told you about that product I'd been using on my guy?"

"Yes, I remember. Now about our reservation . . ." Shauna's face was pink.

"I told you it would work." The woman dropped her voice, looking around the group. "Or have you tried it out yet?"

"Not yet." Shauna waved a hand toward the dining room. "Our table?"

"Sorry, I'm such a chatterbox." The woman nodded at Shauna knowingly, then frowned looking at the list. "Oh, yes, here it is. They put it under Clark. She must have misunderstood when you called. I tell them to ask for a spelling, but you know how people can be. They think they know more than they do."

As the woman walked them to the table, Shauna fell in step with Cat. "So you saw the car?"

"I did. I think we should tell Uncle Pete about this." When Shauna nodded, Cat felt relieved that she wasn't going to have to argue the point. Whoever was following her friend had spooked her enough that she was willing to call in for help. "What was that about?"

Shauna pulled her aside. "I need to tell you something."

Cat waved the rest of the group away and stepped into an alcove with Shauna. "What do you need to tell me?"

"I put something in Kevin's stew that night." She glanced around, making sure they weren't being overheard. "I know Seth told you that I was being weird around the stew that night."

"You poisoned Kevin?" Cat couldn't believe what she was hearing.

"God, no." Shauna pressed her hand against her chest. "Why would you say that?"

Cat took a deep breath. "Okay, let's start over. What did you put in Kevin's stew?"

The red flushed over Shauna's face as Cat watched her friend formulate her answer. "Ginseng. I got it at the health food store. Our hostess said she used it to cure her husband's ED."

"ED?" Awareness took over. "You put something in his stew to make him perform better?"

"Well, yes. He was so worried all the time, he had, well, problems sometimes. I thought if we were going to celebrate our engagement anyway, I'd prepare the stage." Shauna shook her head. "You don't think that helped kill him, do you?"

"I don't think so, but you might have some explaining to do to Uncle Pete if it shows up on the tox screen." She took Shauna's arm. "We'll talk about this later. Right now we have guests to entertain."

Seth joined them before everyone settled in. He looked at Cat and Shauna. "From the looks on your faces, I take it you've seen them?"

"Seen who?" Cat twisted in her chair and followed his gaze. Paul, Jade, and two young boys were seated across the room. Paul nodded his head in their direction, but Jade was too busy talking to the children to notice. "I hope this doesn't turn into a shouting match."

Shauna glanced over, then returned her attention to her menu. "I'll be good if she will."

Seth ordered two pitchers of margaritas, and the waitress brought baskets of chips and bowls of salsa for the group. After their guests got talking and eating, he turned toward Cat. "So if Paul hadn't caught your attention, what were you and Shauna upset about?"

"Did you see the small car following us?" Cat kept her voice low. "I think it was blue?"

Seth nodded. "After I dropped you off, it made a circle in the parking lot, then took off back toward town. I figured someone thought the restaurant was too busy and didn't want to deal with the wait."

"Shauna says it's been following her since Kevin died." She glanced over her shoulder toward Paul's table. "She thinks Paul's keeping tabs on her."

This time, Seth let his gaze linger on the table across the dining room. "I don't understand what would be his reason though. Do you?"

"I don't have a clue." Cat poured a glass from the pitcher and passed the frosty drink to Seth, who passed it on to Collin, who also filled his glass. "Any guesses?"

"No. But you need to tell Pete about this. If it's true, maybe Paul isn't the warm family man he's portraying himself to be lately." Seth leaned back and took a long sip of his Coke.

The waitress came for their order and ended any more talk about the car or Paul. When she'd left, Jordon stood and held up his glass. "Here's to the Warm Springs Retreat. Thanks to Cat and Shauna for their gracious hosting and thanks to my new best friends. May we keep in touch."

The group drank to Jordon's toast, and as he sat down, Shirley stood. "You have something really special here. Thank you for sharing it."

The group took another drink from their glasses. Melissa and Pamela also stood with toasts. Cat wondered if they were going to have to roll everyone out to the car when it was time to go.

Finally, Collin stood. "I came to the retreat looking for answers to more than just my writing questions. Thank you both for giving me hope for the future. We may not be family, but I'll always have your back as if you were."

The rest of the group clinked glasses, but shared a few puzzled looks.

"Thanks, Collin. That's lovely." Shauna smiled at the young man.

"You look so much like my mother did when she was young. I can see Kevin had a type." He sat back down in his chair and ducked his head. Cat thought he felt like he'd said too much and wondered how to get the uncomfortable silence that surrounded the table to go away.

Luckily the moment passed and the food started coming to the table. The group talked and laughed while they ate and Cat relaxed. Everything was going to be all right. The mystery behind Michael's death had finally been solved. The retreat business was doing well. And she'd had an email from her agent saying the publisher was talking about extending her contract on the Tori books.

She excused herself and went to the bathroom. When she came out of the stall, Jade leaned against the sink counter, waiting for her.

"Leave me alone, Jade." Cat went to the end sink and washed her hands.

"You think you're so smart. You probably were in on Kevin's murder with that witch and the boy." Jade's words were slurred and Cat knew she'd drunk too much. "She's going to pay for what she did to Kevin."

Cat turned and fired back. She was tired of the woman's accusations. "Shauna didn't do anything to Kevin except love him. They were getting married. Something neither I nor your brother approved of, but there's no accounting for taste. Kevin was a jerk. Now he's a dead jerk who has broken my friend's heart. So leave her alone."

Jade's eyes went wide and Cat left. When she reached the hallway, Paul stood by the doorway. He glanced behind Cat, looking for his sister. "Is she okay?"

"She's rude and mean, just like you. And she's drunk. So you probably should get her out of here before she does something stupider than just yell at me in the bathroom." Cat looked toward the table where Shauna and the group sat. They hadn't seen her and Paul talking, and she wanted to keep it that way. "And call off your spy. If we see that car following Shauna again, we're telling my uncle and filing a restraining order."

"What are you talking about? I don't have a . . ." Paul's eyes widened and he stepped around her. "Never mind, I'll talk to you next week."

Cat looked back and saw Jade fall out of the bathroom onto the hallway floor, and she moved quickly out of sight so she wouldn't get yelled at again. When she got back to the table, Seth leaned close.

"You okay?" His gaze drifted behind her and she realized he'd seen the discussion with Paul. "Do I have to kick his butt?"

Cat smiled and leaned into his shoulder. "The offer is well meaning, but honestly, I just want them to leave us alone."

"It would be nice to have an evening free of stress for once." He nodded toward Shirley, who was chatting with Melissa. "She's got an appointment with your uncle at Bernie's after this."

"An appointment?" Cat giggled. If she relaxed, she might be able to feel the tequila trying to make her feel warm and happy. She hoped it wouldn't make her head pound in the morning.

Seth shrugged, seemingly as amused at the word choice as she was. "That's what she called it, an appointment."

As they drove to the bar, she thought about what Collin had said. Shauna looked like a younger version of his mother. It was a long shot, but maybe Uncle Pete should check into where Collin's mother had been when Kevin died? She thought about pulling him aside when they dropped off Shirley, but then pushed it aside. Let him have one evening where he was just a guy with a girl.

They were dropping Shirley off at Bernie's when Uncle Pete came outside to walk with her from the parking lot into the bar. Cat rolled down her window. "Shirley's plane leaves at four tomorrow. Make sure you get her home at a reasonable time. And call me later. I need to talk about something."

"Yes, mother," her uncle called back causing her to break out in giggles again. They were almost home when Shauna slapped the back of the seat in front of her.

"The car is following us again." She took her cell phone out and started snapping pictures of the headlights behind them.

"Are you sure it's the same one?" Cat tried to focus on the side mirror, but she could see only the lights.

"What car?" Jordon moved to Shauna's bench and peered out the back window. "How do you know it's following us?"

"Duh." Melissa giggled, a little tipsy from the margaritas. "It's behind us. So it has to be following us."

Pamela rolled her eyes at her friend. "I don't think that's what they meant."

Cat watched as Collin went to the back to look out the window. "That looks like Terry's car. My roommate? Maybe he's coming to see me for some reason."

"Your roommate's been following me for the last week. Does he work for Paul?" Shauna turned on Collin, and even from a distance, Cat could see her eyes dance in anger.

"Wait, it can't be Terry. He's out of town until next week." Collin sank back into his seat, ignoring the car behind them.

"Calm down, everyone. We'll deal with it when we get to the house." Seth turned the vehicle onto Warm Springs, but the car that had been following went straight.

Collin sank into his seat. "I guess it wasn't Terry."

"I'm sorry. I've been a little on edge." Shauna put a hand on Collin's shoulder. "I shouldn't have snapped at you."

"No worries." But even Cat could see the kid felt beat down.

When they parked, Jordon helped Pamela walk Melissa into the house and right up the stairs. Seth watched as they followed. "She's not going to have a fun trip tomorrow. Not with that hangover."

Collin, Shauna, Seth, and Cat were in the lobby when the door blew open, snow flying. When it slammed shut, a small woman in a man's coat and beanie stood in the entryway. Her eyes were wide as she took in the scene.

All Cat saw was the gun she held out in front of her. Her hands shook as she pointed it at the four of them.

"Collin, you come over here," the woman ordered. Her red hair flowed wild and tangled around her shoulders.

"Mom. What are you doing? Why are you here in Colorado?" Collin stepped in between the gun and the woman. "Put Uncle Jess's gun down."

"I gave you an order. Listen to your mother," the woman barked, but Collin didn't move.

Cat reached into her pocket to get her phone, but she'd put it in her purse and that was on the table behind her. She looked at Shauna and Seth. Neither of them had cells within reach either. She focused on Collin. "What's going on? Why is your mother pointing a gun at us?"

"Stop talking. I know you're just trying to get

into his head." The woman's hand shook harder. "Just like all those teachers, telling him that I wasn't fit to take care of him. Who else would? His father?"

"You're Kevin's first love." Shauna's voice came out soft, like she was caressing the words. "The mother of his child."

"And where did that get me?" Collin's mother looked around the large lobby area. "Definitely not a grand house like this one. He even stopped paying child support when Collin got older, like I could live on that anyway."

"Kevin didn't give Shauna this house." Cat peeked around Collin. "I own the house."

"Sure you do." The woman cackled. "You must have been sleeping with him too. You should have left when I dropped off the rat. But no. No one ever listens to me."

"Mom. Stop." The worry in Collin's voice was palpable. "Let's go outside. We'll go get some coffee and figure this out."

"There's no going back. Not now. Your father tried to trick me too. Said he'd take care of me again. Of us. He was lying. I knew he was lying. He always lied." She held the gun up higher. "Move now so I can deal with this. I have to go back to the ranch and clean out that place too."

Cat wasn't sure what exactly happened next, but all she heard was her uncle's voice telling her to get down. Then the front door swung open and Collin's mother was on the floor. Quinn kicked the gun away from her hand, and Shirley picked it up and aimed it at the woman until Quinn had the cuffs on her.

Seth helped her up from the floor. "Are you okay?"

"You keep asking me that." Cat brushed dust off her dress. "What the heck was that? And where did you guys come from?"

Quinn handed the woman over to another officer, who took her out to one of the four police cars out in front of the house. Now, they had lights flashing, but she hadn't seen them approach. "I told you that you needed a security system."

Cat sank onto the small couch next to Shauna, who seemed to be taking this way too well. She felt her leg starting to shake. Was she in shock? "What happened?"

"I saw you guys come home. I was waiting because Ms. Clodagh had called and asked me to come by after your dinner. I saw you pull up so I was waiting to let you go in and get settled. Then someone approached from the back of the house. The perp had a gun." He turned toward Seth. "Then I called 911 and the night dispatch contacted the chief."

Seth pulled up a chair next to the sofa and took one of Cat's hands in his.

The contact calmed her. "Okay, so you called Uncle Pete because you saw Collin's mother come in with a gun."

Collin stepped closer, interrupting the story. "I am so sorry. I didn't know she was even in town. She's supposed to be staying with my aunt while I'm in school. She's not well."

"That's an understatement," Seth said.

"What's your mom's name?" Shirley stepped closer

to Collin, putting her hand on the young man's shoulder.

"Alice. Alice Adams." Collin sank down into a crouching position. "She's going to go away for this, isn't she?"

"Maybe. But Collin"—Uncle Pete put his hand on Collin's shoulder—"we'll get her some help. Do you think she could have killed Kevin Shield?"

Collin started to cry, but everyone saw the nod before Seth pulled him to standing and put an arm around his shoulder. "Let's go get some coffee."

Shauna and Shirley went with the men into the kitchen, leaving Cat alone with Quinn and Uncle Pete. Quinn opened a laptop and searched for a file. "I found this when I was waiting for you to arrive tonight. Shauna—I mean, Ms. Clodagh—gave me the clue of where to look."

They watched the screen outside the horse barn and saw Alice Adams standing there, a long knife twinkling in her hand. When Kevin approached, she put it behind her back. The man never even noticed the movement. Kevin waved his hand, indicating the horse barn, and then they both disappeared.

Quinn hit a button on the keyboard that fast-forwarded the video. "They were in there twenty minutes. Then this . . ."

The group watched as a dazed Alice stepped out of the barn, glanced around, then took off into the woods.

"She must have had a car parked on the forest access road." Quinn closed up the laptop.

Uncle Pete spoke first. "Send me that file. Although a good defense attorney's going to play hell with you not turning over everything at the start of the investigation. What were you thinking?"

"I didn't have permission of the land owner to be taping. I thought he might expand his system once I showed him the additional coverage he could have." Quinn squirmed a little. "And the company is having a sale in March. I thought I'd present it then."

Cat sighed. "I guess it was a good thing you were watching the house tonight."

Quinn perked up, his eyes going bright. "Does that mean you're buying a system?"

"Come back in March when it's on sale. We'll talk." Cat stood. "I'm going to get me some cocoa. Then, if you don't need me, I'm beat."

"We can get statements in the morning." Uncle Pete walked to the kitchen with her. "I need to say good-night to my date and go into the station to book the suspect. Although I believe we'll get a mental health check before we go too far."

Collin sat at the table, holding on to his cup like he was keeping it safe. He looked up at Uncle Pete as the group entered. "She killed my dad, didn't she?"

"We think so, son." Uncle Pete put his hand on Collins shoulder. "Can you come down to the station tomorrow morning? If your mom isn't able to talk yet, I'll need to ask you some questions about her."

"I didn't know. I mean, I knew she was fixated on him. She always has been. But I thought she was getting better when I went to college. She was in treatment and seemed better when I'd visit."

Collin shook his head. "I should never have left Philadelphia."

"No. You did what you needed to do." Shauna handed Pete a mug. "I figured you might want some to go."

"Thank you. You're a blessing." Uncle Pete looked around the room. "I'll see you all in the morning for statements. Quinn, let's go. Shirley, will you walk me out?"

After they'd left the kitchen, Collin stood as well. "I'm heading upstairs. I need to call my aunt and tell her what happened."

The kitchen was quiet with Cat, Seth, and Shauna all sipping their cocoa. Cat was the first one to break the silence. "That was interesting."

"I'd really, really like a peaceful retreat one of these days. You have your guests, they do their writing thing, you all talk about books, then they go home. It's a simple wish." Seth finished off his cocoa and stood. "I'll walk around and lock up. I feel like I need to check all the entrances, including the cellar, before I turn in or I'll be tossing and turning all night."

"Uncle Pete has her in custody," Cat reminded him as he leaned down to kiss her.

He tapped her nose after the long, soft kiss. "I still want to make sure. Call me paranoid."

They waited for him to leave the room. Then Cat turned to her friend. "Are you all right?"

"Collin was the key all along. He said his mom had warned him not to come to Colorado. That bad things happened when people were near Kevin. I guess she was trying to protect her son in a weird way." Shauna stood and refilled her cup. "Do you want some more?"

Cat yawned and took her cup to the sink. "I'm heading to bed, unless you want to talk."

"I'm talked out. I think tomorrow's going to be a lot of talking. I just want to sit here and think about all the good times I had with the man." Shauna smiled sadly. "I think I'm ready to say good-bye."

Chapter 23

By the time Cat got downstairs the next morning, the place was humming with excitement. Melissa, Pamela, and Jordon had been filled in by Shirley on the ruckus that had occurred after they'd retired for the night.

"We heard noises, but we thought you all were just talking. I always miss out on the fun." Melissa took a big bite of the biscuits and gravy that Shauna must have prepared earlier. Typically, full breakfast didn't occur until after seven, but it was only six-fifteen and everyone was downstairs and chatting.

Everyone except Collin. His face was pale and he pushed the food around his plate with his fork rather than actually eating. Cat sat next to him after pouring herself a glass of orange juice. "You need to eat. The next few days are going to be hard."

"I know. I just can't believe she did this. Even last night, I couldn't see my mother in the woman that held the gun. She looked like a stranger." Collin set his fork down. "If they send her away, I'm alone in the world now."

Cat thought the wording should be *when* they sent Alice away, but she didn't correct him. "You're not alone. You have your aunt and uncle. And besides, what you said last night at the restaurant is still true. You have Shauna and me."

"That was before she found out my mother killed Kevin. I don't think she's going to want to see me again." Collin's words hung in the air as Shauna entered the room.

"Now, don't you be going playing the pity card on me, Collin Adams. I told you I considered you family, whether or not your father was alive, and I stand by my word." Shauna set the platter of bacon down on the sideboard, but no one moved. "You are welcome here any time and for any reason, even if it is just to talk."

Collin blinked back tears and swallowed hard before he answered. "Yes, ma'am."

"You just got told." Jordon slapped him on the back. "You want some bacon?"

The men got up and walked around the table to where Shauna stood, her hands on her hips surveying the crowd. She patted Collin on the back as he walked past. "Anything else you all need before I let Aspen Hills's finest know that you're ready for your exit interviews? I've held them off until we finished our meal."

When they all shook their heads, Shauna nodded. "Good. I'm letting them talk to you in order of your travel plans. Melissa and Pamela? You two are up first as Seth will be driving you to the airport and leaving exactly at eight. You are packed, I hope?"

The women looked at each other, their eyes wide.

"Not quite," Pamela squeaked. Then she finished her juice. "I will be in a few minutes."

"Bring your suitcases down when you're ready. I'll have cookies and cocoa for the drive if you're still hungry." Shauna then recited from memory the rest of the group's departures. Collin would be the last to leave since he lived in the Covington's dorms. His aunt and uncle were flying in later that day, and Seth would bring them into town when he dropped off Shirley.

When Shauna finished, Cat followed her into the kitchen. "You could muster an army. I can't believe you're so organized, even after all that happened this week."

"It's because of everything that happened, I think." Shauna went to the fridge and pulled out a carton of eggs. "Scrambled?"

"Sure, but really, I could eat with the gang today. You don't have to cook more food." Cat went to the coffeepot for coffee. When she turned around, she found Shauna staring at her. "What?"

"You still don't get it. I like cooking for people. It makes me feel connected and useful." She went to the table and sat down, waving Cat over. "That's why I never took Kevin or anyone else up on their offer to run their kitchen. What we're doing here is important. I know it. I want to see the person I'm feeding. I want to be part of their lives, if only in this small way."

Cat thought she understood. The writers' retreat had given her something unexpected too. She felt connected to the writing community in a way she never had teaching. She felt like part of their journey to become authors and release their stories into the world. And with that connection, she felt stronger herself as a writer. She didn't know how to put all that feeling into words so she just kept it simple. "The retreat is good for both of us."

The rest of the morning was hectic with Uncle Pete running his interviews out of Michael's office. Cat paused at the door when Jordon came out. She thought she needed to call the room something else, but she thought she might just keep the name and the memories of her first husband in the room. It fit.

"Come on in. I've got one more person to talk to, then I'll be out of here." Uncle Pete sat at the desk, his notebook in front of him and a pen on the desktop.

"I wanted to see if you needed more coffee." Cat came in and perched on the arm of the wingback chair.

"I'm about coffee'd out. But don't tell Shauna that. She's been keeping my cup filled all morning." He leaned back in his chair. "How is she? I can't tell from the short conversations we've had this morning."

"She's good. Solid, I think, now that the killer has been caught. She really likes Collin." Cat smiled at the mention of the kid.

"He's going to need some help getting over this. He's losing the only parent he ever had." Uncle Pete shook his head. "She's not talking, by the way. I've got a consult coming in from Denver this afternoon to see if she needs to be hospitalized."

"It's so sad." Cat thought about Kevin and the women in his life. "Kevin's caused some pretty big ripples in people's lives."

"Every action has a reaction." Uncle Pete looked up and smiled. "Come on in, son. I'm ready for you."

Cat turned and saw Collin in the doorway. She headed out of the room, pausing at the door to ask, "You want something to drink?"

He shook his head and then she was dismissed. She gently closed the door and left Collin and his demons to talk to Uncle Pete.

Frank stood at the reception desk, a vase filled with white carnations sitting in front of him. "Hey, I was just about to leave. You are a popular girl this week."

The roses from Linda Cook sat on a table near the stairwell, only slightly showing the wear of the few days.

"Where did these come from?" She smiled as she took the card. "Let me guess—Seth. It's been a crazy week."

"I didn't see Seth's name on the order, but you know I don't read the cards. Mrs. Ashley handles all that. I just drive around." Frank handed her a clipboard and she signed quickly, the card still unopened in her hand. "Anything you want me to tell Mrs. Rice when she orders in her gossip flowers?"

"No, not really." Cat hadn't even had to go over to her neighbor's to pump out information about Kevin's death. The murderer had come right to the house. Cat opened the card and frowned. The note wasn't from Seth. She handed Frank his tip and then waited for him to go outside before she read the card aloud. "I am deeply sorry for your loss. He was my friend and I hope someday I can call you by the same endearment. D."

White carnations. Cat's eyes stung with tears.

Dante had known her favorite flower. He'd probably been the one to leave one at her office door.

She could finally finish grieving the loss of her marriage. Now, a friendship with Dante? That was a whole 'nother conversation. She looked up when the door opened, expecting Frank. "What did you forget?"

Her question died on her lips as she watched Paul and Jade come in the lobby.

"I'm sorry to bother you, but can we speak to Shauna?" Paul took his leather gloves off, but left his wool coat on. Jade didn't raise her gaze.

Cat shook her head. "I don't think so."

A noise behind her made her turn. Shauna stood in the doorway between the hall and the kitchen. She stepped forward, her back ramrod straight. In a cool voice, she asked, "What do you want?"

"Kevin's funeral service will be at ten o'clock Tuesday at St. Paul's Church. I would like you to attend." Jade finally raised her gaze, but she didn't look at anyone but Shauna. "And the will reading will be next week. His attorney will call you."

Paul shifted, but Jade put a hand on his arm. "We are not contesting the new will. Whatever last requests Kevin made, we'll honor."

Shauna stopped walking when she reached Cat. "I'll be there. I'd like to bring Collin as well. He's been through a lot."

Jade nodded. "A son should honor his father." She looked up at her brother. "And a father should honor his son. We'll see you at the service."

The two turned around and left through the front door. Cat turned toward Shauna. "Wow. That was unexpected. I'll come with you, if you want."

Shauna smiled. "Of course you'll be there. You and Seth. You all are my family." A frown creased her brows, and she stepped around Cat to the reception desk. "Where did the flowers come from?"

Cat picked a white carnation out of the vase and held it up to her nose. There were a lot of unanswered questions still in her world, especially around Michael and his business, but one thing was clear: Their marriage had been good. At least once upon a time. With that door finally closed behind her, she could go on with her life.

A good life with friends, family, and the most important part: hope. Instead of answering Shauna's question, she grabbed the booking book for the retreat. Leading Shauna into the kitchen, she said, "Seth had some great ideas about future sessions. Do you have some time to help me plan?"

Love Cat's adventures?
Don't miss the first two books in the series

A STORY TO KILL

and

FATALITY BY FIRELIGHT

Available now
Wherever books are sold

And keep an eye out
for the Farm-to-Fork Mysteries,
a brand new series by Lynn Cahoon.
Coming soon from Lyrical Books!